An Empty House

by the

River

by

Robert Hays

An Empty House by the River
Copyright 2022 by Robert Hays

Published by Thomas-Jacob Publishing, LLC
TJPub@thomas-jacobpublishing.com

All rights reserved. No part of this book may be reproduced or transmitted in any form or by any means without written permission from the publisher, with the exception of brief quotations within a review.

This book is a work of fiction. While some of the places referenced may be real, characters and incidents are the product of the author's imagination and are used fictitiously. Any resemblance to events or persons living or dead is purely coincidental.

Library of Congress Control Number: 2022942901
1. Contemporary fiction 2. Literary fiction
ISBN-13: 978-1-950750-48-1
ISBN-10: 1-950750-48-5
Thomas-Jacob Publishing, LLC, Deltona, Florida

First hardcover printing Thomas-Jacob Publishing, LLC
Printed in the United States of America

To my friend and mentor, Smoky Zeidel

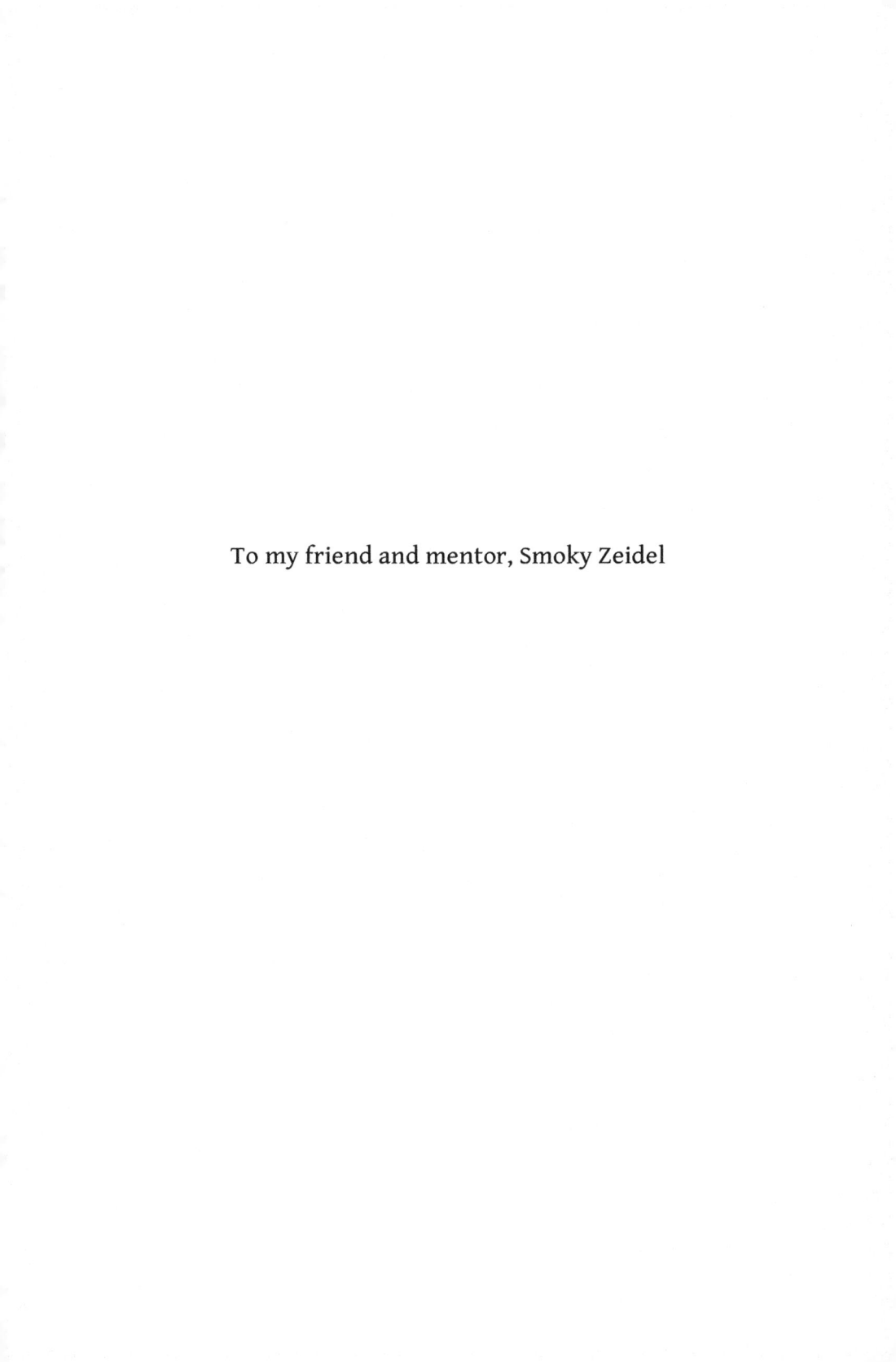

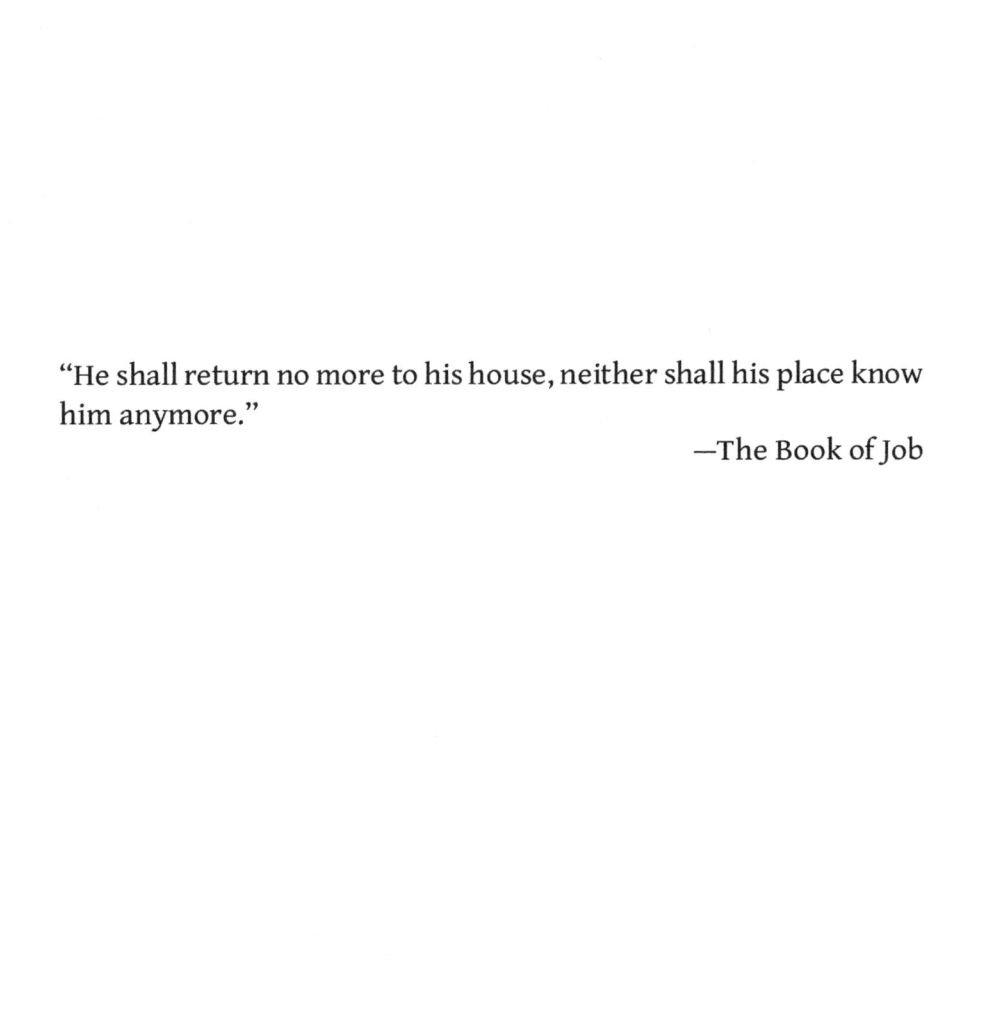

"He shall return no more to his house, neither shall his place know him anymore."

—The Book of Job

1

Singleton's Branch is not the Mississippi, and even among locals it hardly registers as an important landmark except in times of flood. But to us it was "the river." It affected our lives in ways I'm only now coming to fully understand. The river gave us place and sometimes gave us purpose, and brought us together in common cause. In the end, though, it took more than it gave.

Lacy and I grew up in a stately old Victorian style house that sat atop a wooded bluff on the river's west bank, sheltered at the back by a magnificent white oak and tall sycamore and cottonwood trees underlain by redbuds and dogwoods. The river curved gently around the base of the bluff, leaving a shoal on our side that offered endless hours of fun in the shallow water on hot summer days. A well-worn path with randomly placed flat sandstone steps angled down the steep slope and gave us an easy route to the water's edge.

I suppose in most ways our life might have been considered idyllic. We were accustomed to having our mother always there and our father home every night. Sammy, our little brother, came along a few years behind Lacy and me and was so much our mother's favorite we never felt guilty about our efforts to ignore his presence. We are well into our later years now, but I never outgrew a deeply felt need to look after my little sister. Unfortunately, my worry that one day I might not be there when she needed me proved to be prophetic.

The story I'm going to tell is rooted in a prolonged period of high water the summer I turned 15. This is a summer I'll never forget. It still burns in my memory as hot as if it all happened only yesterday.

We suffered little of the damage the flood wrought on the true river people—those who lived close to the water's edge along the east bank. Much of what they had was lost, even including a dozen or more houses, and after the water went down it took several weeks to clean up things and get them dried out. It was only the combination of courage and desperation we often see in those who never have had it easy that got the river people back on their feet. Most of them, anyway.

I suppose they had ample reason to be left feeling bitter over nothing more than the unkind hand nature had dealt them. They did nothing wrong and were victims only of time and circumstance.

If they needed extra incentive, though, they surely were taunted by the proclamation that this was the second of those "once in a hundred years" floods in just over a ten-year span. Especially for those who'd been there for the first one, a decade hardly constituted the promised century. None wanted to be there if it happened again.

In my mind's eye, I still can see the floodwaters, sparkling in the low-angled late afternoon sunshine as if studded by diamonds, spread out before us as we looked down from atop the bluff. Our high vantage point offered a dismal view. The flood covered the open countryside for miles up and down the river and well into the distance to the east. Roofs and chimneys barely peeking out of the water marked the homes of long-time friends and neighbors.

The spring rains started early. Heavier than usual, they had seemed endless, bringing muddy headwaters that turned Singleton's Branch into a swollen sea of raging currents. These would be stilled in time by silent backwaters after the mighty Ohio River filled to capacity with runoff from its vast drainage area and refused further offerings. The new threat, which might have been seen as impotent next to the powerful currents, was in its own way even more insidious as it inched back onto lands as yet not nearly recovered from the devastation of an earlier passing. Night after night, exasperated river watchers measured its coming with small stakes stuck at the water's edge and hoped for a sign of recession in the morning. And morning after morning they found yesterday's marker submerged, until spirits that had been weakened before but not yet broken were splintered into near hopelessness.

My mother was among those who said their resolve was overcome. She vowed that one way or another she'd move away from the river and plant herself someplace miles from any stream. I believe this was mostly from guilt, the true anguish of having observed the incalculable misfortune that befell so many others while suffering none herself.

My father said no, life on the river was the life he wanted. My father was the one who made such decisions.

I was glad. I liked the river, too, and couldn't imagine living somewhere else. But of course for me this was the only home I'd ever known, and it was here that I had felt the comfort and security of family. It was here, too, that Lacy and I had relished the companionship of older brother and little sister who guarded our closeness as if afraid it might slip away during the dark of night.

And although I didn't realize it at the time, it also mattered immensely that this was the place where Victor and Bobbi had come much more deeply into my life. Theirs would be a lasting presence.

Singleton's Branch is a lesser tributary flowing north into the Ohio, combining waters with the latter some fifty miles upstream from the confluence of the Ohio and the Mississippi at Cairo, Illinois. Unless you are an astute scholar in the geography of Middle America, you should not be expected to know this means western Kentucky. This is not important to my story. I mention it only to make you aware that our culture tends to draw rather heavily on Southern roots. We are neither proud nor ashamed of this, but accept it as our lot and only on rare occasion find it to make any difference as we struggle through life much like most other inhabitants of God's green earth.

My family was not prominent. My father's name was Graden Prather. He was the only Graden I ever heard of. He and my mother—her name was Evelyn Childs—were married when he was 22 and she was 18.

Graden Prather was a good man, and hard-working. He had an air of competence and being in control and the rugged good looks of a movie star like Gary Cooper. He had thick black hair and piercing brown eyes, wore a carefully trimmed moustache, and never went more than three weeks without visiting Harvey Bowman's barber shop. And although he never wore expensive clothes, he always dressed neatly and appropriate to the occasion and made sure his shoes were shined.

He was a good father, although at the time we thought he was much too strict. His rules were meant to be obeyed and there was a penalty to be paid if you broke one. I suppose, looking back, we were somewhat intimidated by him. We never called him "Daddy" or even "Dad." It was always "Father." I can't say whether this was his choice or ours.

I loved my Grandpa and Grandma Childs and they were an important part of our lives. My Grandmother Prather passed away before I was born and my Grandfather Prather lived in St. Louis and we never saw him. I remember Father going on a train to visit him a couple of times, but I don't remember him ever coming to visit us.

Lacy and I assumed he was rich. He sent each of us a ten-dollar bill with Father, who seemed proud to be the bearer of such gifts.

"Your Grandfather Prather loves you very much," he told us. "He wants you to know he misses his grandchildren and hopes one day you can come with me when I visit."

This gave us false hope, of course. For the next year or so we talked often of the train trip we were going to take to St. Louis. We'd never ridden on a train or been to a city and fanaticized what it would be like. Surely there was an exciting world beyond the one we knew. Our hopes eroded as the months rolled past and Father never mentioned it again. I'm not sure Father went back, either, until he got word that Grandfather Prather had passed away.

Six days a week Father drove an old Dodge pickup truck the three miles of pot-holed county blacktop highway into town for his job at Ficklin's Hardware. Ficklin's most notable distinction was that it happened to be the only real hardware store in Erinville, the population of which has held steady at about thirty thousand souls unto the present day. Citizens gave the store credit both for stocking what they needed and offering outstanding service.

I doubt Father ever realized how truly indispensable he was to Seth Ficklin, who would have been lost without his daily presence and remarkable ability to answer customers' questions about tools or paint or plumbing and electrical fixtures or building supplies, or anything else one might expect to find in a hardware store. I can think of very few new houses built in Erinville during my entire life, and Ficklin's customers often sought Father's advice on how to fix the small things that went wrong in the aging homes most of them occupied.

He always had an answer. When a customer expressed gratitude for his help, he shrugged it off with a modest, "That's what I'm here for."

Father didn't play golf or go hunting or fishing like most of the Erinville men did, or spend his time in bars or taverns. His recreation was reading. Ranelle Bishop, director of the Erinville Public Library, looked on him as one of her primary patrons and urged him to run for the library board. He told her he was honored, but declined.

"That's a commendable public service," he told her, "but nobody ought to do it unless they can devote all their spare time and effort to it and I don't believe I'm up to that."

Hardly a night went by that he didn't spend an hour or two sitting in his ratty old wingback chair under a perfectly positioned swing-arm floor lamp with a book in his hands. His taste was eclectic. He favored non-fiction, but he claimed to have read most of the classics and loved a good novel. It wasn't uncommon for him to go back to something he really liked for a second reading.

We weren't supposed to know, but there were times Mama got up in the middle of the night and came looking, only to find him fast asleep in his chair, a book still in his hand or dropped on the floor. She would gently remove the reading glasses and lead him to bed and knew he would not remember this come morning.

Our mother was a quiet woman, shy in the presence of strangers but warm and friendly once she became acquainted. She had a kind but expressive face, with soft grey eyes that gave outlet to her feelings, usually contented and at peace with her world but occasionally flashing the deep resentment of a woman and mother wronged.

I don't think I ever heard Mama raise her voice. A frown was her way of letting us know she disapproved of something, and for Lacy and me that was enough. It was different with Sammy, who demanded a firmer hand, but then she rarely if ever disapproved of anything our little brother did.

Mama spent most of her time in the kitchen. She was a wonderful cook. She took this as a mother's principal responsibility and was her own most severe critic. She insisted on doing all the grocery shopping, made careful lists of what she needed, and planned most of the coming week's meals before Father took her to the store on Sunday afternoon. She complained sometimes that Sundays weren't meant for shopping, but that was Father's only day off and so the only day she had a ride to the grocery store.

She once decided she needed a bicycle, and said if she had one with a large enough basket she could ride into Erinville any time she needed to shop and leave Sunday free for church. This idea never came to fruition. Father said there was not a large enough bicycle basket on planet Earth to hold her groceries, let alone all the "extras" she usually loaded into the pickup.

I remember a few occasions on which Mama went down to the shoal with us and waded in the water. She liked to stand in one spot and feel the gentle current wash pebbles around her feet. She showed us where the elderberries grew, and the blackberries, hazel nuts, and wild strawberries. We easily found on our own the hickory nuts, walnuts, and pecans when they fell from the trees in the fall.

Neither Lacy nor I really liked elderberries, yet we went to great effort to keep tabs on the bushes and know when the berries were ripe. They represented nature's bounty, plentiful and free for the taking, and we felt obligated to accept what was given. Anyway, it was fun to try to cast our images onto the water when the juicy clusters had painted our faces purple. Lacy mastered the art of making funny faces and I came to admire her talent.

Because Victor Kenton is such an important part of this story, I also need to tell you about him. He and I had been friends since first grade. He was my age, but looked older because of his husky physical stature. When he was 12 years old he probably could have passed for one of the high school football players, only a little short. Both he and his older brother had their father's rugged build.

I remember Victor running up and hugging me at school one day when we were little. I was embarrassed and looked about to see if anyone was watching.

"I wish you were my brother," he told me. "Sometimes I pretend you are."

The Kentons were among those driven out of their homes that summer by the flood. Beginning then, it was almost as if Victor were part of our family. He would be, in time, and much of what I'm about to tell would not have happened had this not been so. Sometimes I lie awake at night thinking about him—trying to sort out my feelings after all that's gone on. If there really is a love/hate relationship, this is what developed between Victor and me. I'm sorry for this. Much of the fault surely is mine. My conscience tells me he deserved better.

As we got older I happily accepted Victor for what he was: a decent boy who wanted to do the right thing, but often was unsure of himself. This would have been the end of it except for Lacy, and from the summer of the flood forward it was my efforts to shelter her that led to such difficulties as I had with Victor. Some might question my application of this to the later years, but they don't know the whole story.

Lacy is only two years younger than I. She was named after some distant relative, maybe a great-grandmother. I used to know, but have long since forgotten. She would have been proud of this had she been aware of it. Such trivia often escaped Lacy's thinking, though, something I saw from the time she was little. She had problems in school and her teachers considered her a slow learner. I knew she was smart. I think it likely she had some variety of attention deficit disorder or something of that sort that wasn't caught by any of those trained to recognize the symptoms.

· I doubt that Father would have accepted such a diagnosis and allowed her to be treated, even if someone had grasped the situation. While Lacy would have rolled with the punches easily and without complaint, Father didn't like anything he thought might tarnish the Prather name. No daughter of his could be stigmatized by some label that set her apart as different.

Lacy always was the prettiest girl in the room before Bobbi came along. She had her mother's honey-colored hair and soft grey eyes. As she got older she became a virtual magnet for the boys' attention. They wasted their time, because Lacy already considered herself bound to Victor. Close as I was to my little sister, even I was slow to recognize that what may have begun as quite ordinary "puppy love" plainly had grown deeper over time.

I believe Victor already had strong feelings for her, too, although sometimes it seemed as if he was embarrassed by her presence. Apparently there were instances when he deliberately avoided her when classmates were around. I don't think she ever noticed, but the other girls tried to tell her.

"They act like they think Victor is weird or something," she told me one day on our walk home from Hemingway Terrace School. "I just told them it takes weird to know weird."

I didn't know how to answer.

Lacy's ready acceptance of any personality quirks Victor might have was not limited to him. For her, "different" only meant more interesting. She always said the world would be a monotonous place if people were all the same. She thought it appropriate the human race should parallel the rest of nature, given that we all inhabited the same planet.

"What if all the flowers were alike?" she said. "Or the birds? Or the furry little things that dig into the river bank? I'm happy they're all so different and I love them all."

And she did. She would have made pets of the groundhogs and chipmunks that burrowed into the bluff below our house, and she could sit all day just counting the different kinds of birds she saw and admiring their varied colors. She noted all the small things, such as how some hopped and others ran with their legs moving much like those of humans. She separated "ground" birds from those who never left the trees and was fascinated by how they all became diligent nest-builders in the spring.

But I think it was the wildflowers she liked best. She adored the pink and purple carpet of spring beauties and wood violets that spread beneath the trees along the bluff and the ubiquitous bugleweed that started to flower in April and May and waited eagerly for the daisies that followed. In the fall, when the black-eyed Susans and wild sunflower and goldenrod and ironweed and Spanish needle all bloomed at once she would wade through the waves of purple and yellow and express her gratitude to the "god of everything" for such splendid gifts. Mama liked for her to pick wildflowers for the kitchen, but Lacy decided flowers were living things and she had no right to kill them.

I suppose it was inevitable that at some point she would learn of the violence that routinely occurs among wild animals. She witnessed it with her own eyes one winter morning, right outside a kitchen window, and was terribly upset.

Once cold weather came, Lacy habitually went to the window almost every morning to look for a flock of mourning doves that sat and warmed themselves in the sun beneath the big pine tree on the south side of the house. Their color blended well into that of pine straw on the ground, so they were nearly invisible—except to sharp-eyed predators overhead. She was standing at the window watching when a red-tailed hawk swooped down and carried off one of the doves in its claws, the rest of the flock fleeing in terror.

Lacy cried all day.

Beginning the next morning and for days to come she stood watch, looking in vain for the doves to return. I could tell it was hard for her to accept what she had seen. The pain was visible in her eyes, but I had learned she wouldn't talk about it until she was ready. For better or worse, Lacy was remarkably consistent.

I knew, too, that she would work at this until she had convinced herself it was the way things should be. When the time came, she was eager to explain.

"I understand it now," she told me. "Birds are not like us. They have small brains, our teacher said, and live pretty much by instinct. That means they probably don't feel pain like we do. They don't have funerals and mourn when one of them dies, and birds work like crazy to feed their babies, then kick them out of the nest and pretend they don't even know their own children after they're gone."

I agreed. I told her this made a lot of sense to me, and I commended her for coming up with such a comprehensive theory.

"The hawk probably had babies to feed," she went on. There was an element of excitement in her voice. "Birds can't go to the store like us and buy food. The god of everything provided for the mother hawk so her babies wouldn't starve. And I think birds probably know they're not going to live very long and don't worry about dying. Maybe they even feel honored if they are chosen to feed another bird's babies. And people eat chickens and turkeys. Don't you think all this makes their lives easier and it's why birds are happy all the time?"

"You're probably right. I guess that's why they sing."

"Why can't we be more like the birds? They don't attack each other because they're different colors and stuff. A red daddy cardinal bird will feed other birds' blue babies when they get out of the nest and run around on the ground just like they were his own. Didn't you ever see that?"

I told her yes, I had, and was rewarded by her sweet smile and an expression of smug satisfaction.

Lacy was the kindest and gentlest person I ever knew. There was no apparent change in her personality as she got older. I developed something of a sense of dread just knowing she would face challenges as she journeyed farther into the cruel world. It wasn't physical danger that worried me; it was my concern that this loving, innocent girl who expected others to be as good as she was, who saw beauty wherever she looked, faced endless disappointment. She wanted the whole world to be perfect and the world was going to come up far short of her expectations.

Still, as we came of age in the imposing old Prather house on the bluff overlooking Singleton's Branch, there was nothing that could have prepared me for what lay ahead. I remember that time as a time of beginning. A time of ending was of far greater consequence and was not so long ago.

At no point along the way could I have envisioned the terrible day that would take Victor from us, leave Lacy shattered almost beyond repair, and cause Bobbi to be abandoned. I can barely force myself to contemplate it now, even though I was there and was drawn into the heartrending affair to a degree that left me, too, with no way to save myself. My life story, if it ever were to be told, would be divided into two parts. Part I would cover the years before that day and Part II the years since.

I won't pretend not to be bitter. I was blindsided by events over which I had no control. But Father taught us that cursing the darkness doesn't bring light, and no words of mine now can possibly soften the painful images engraved deeply in my memory after what happened that day. I can only hope you will understand.

Like the river, life gives and life takes away.

2

The old Prather house had three wood-burning fireplaces, which I think of now because this led indirectly to a game Lacy and I played simply to spite Father. The only fireplace still used was the big one in the first-floor sitting room. Father loved to keep it burning during cold weather. It had an immense capacity which allowed him to stack it with good-sized logs.

Firewood was easy to come by, but Father set strict requirements and trusted only one source: a man named Vincent Shield. He lived up river from us a mile or so past Amos and Blanche Bromwell and delivered two wagon loads of wood every fall. He cut small hickory and sycamore logs into the exact lengths Father wanted and let them dry at least a year before delivery so they were sure to burn well.

Mr. Shield hauled his logs on an old farm wagon which he pulled with an ancient Farmall tractor, and sang as he drove the back roads between his place and our house. We sometimes heard him coming even before he came into sight from behind the trees. He always acted like he was very happy to see Lacy and me and teased us good-naturedly.

"Well, here it is," he'd say. "I 'spect your daddy would like you to get it unloaded right away now."

Then he would sit on the tractor seat without moving for a few minutes, as if actually thinking we would unload the logs.

When we didn't move, he might taunt us for being lazy, and then pretend he was put out that he had to do our job. We knew the routine well and would have been sorely disappointed if he hadn't begun it.

It wasn't Vincent Shield himself who led to our game. It was his name.

"Vin Shield is one of the most reliable men I know," Father told Mama one night at supper, after having just received the second load of fireplace logs of the season.

Lacy looked at me and burst out laughing. "Windshield. Old Windshield and his load of wood and he wants us to unload it."

I laughed too. Lacy always was clever with names.

"None of that, now!" Father demanded. "Shakespeare said if you filch a man's good name you make him poor. You can't make fun of a name without making fun of the person."

We were duly chastened, but during the rest of the meal we kept slipping glances and sly smiles at each other knowing Father wouldn't notice. It became a game for us to try to think of people whose names we could make fun of. Father, of course, never knew.

Looking back now, even I am surprised when I recall how much our lives revolved around the house in which we lived.

Every year, as warm days and longer hours of sunshine signaled the coming of spring, Father would begin occasional walks down to the lower part of the long and gently sloping front yard where he'd stand and gaze at our old house as if viewing it for the first time. He said he wanted to see it as it looked to those who passed by on the county blacktop at the foot of the hill on their way to or from Erinville.

Sometimes Lacy and I would run down the slope to join him. He would barely acknowledge our presence, concentrating on the house as if searching for some change that might make it even more appealing.

His willingness to carry out such a project if one had occurred to him probably would have come as a surprise to most of his friends and neighbors. They all knew Father was conservative in handling his money. As Grandma Childs put it, "Graden's as tight as a hangman's knot." I still waver when trying to decide how much of his tendency toward careful spending grew out of actual stinginess and how much came from his inordinate self-consciousness. He always worried about having something others might see as ostentatious.

Seth Ficklin paid him well and kicked in occasional bonuses when business had been especially good, and our living costs were modest—no mortgage or car payments and a simple life style—so Father readily could have afforded something better than the old Dodge truck. But he said it was good for another fifty thousand miles. He looked down on those men who bought new cars every few years "just to show off."

"His old car was as good as his new one," he'd say. "The new one may be fancier, but there are better ways to waste your money than buying more chrome."

The simple life style I referred to meant, among other things, we never wore fancy clothes. Sammy, Lacy, and I got new shoes when our old ones wore out. Mama got new dresses so seldom it was an occasion of note when she did. This was unfortunate; she looked very pretty when she got dressed up to go into town shopping on Sunday afternoons and on those rare occasions when she was able to go to church. She hardly ever asked for anything, though, and except for Christmas and birthdays Father was not one to spend money on gifts.

The lone exception to both his concern about having something pretentious and his inclination not to spend money on non-essentials was the house and anything related to it. He said it already was very old when Grandfather Prather bought it and deserved to be maintained as a monument to the Prather lifestyle and good taste. His pride in the old Prather house on the bluff overlooking Singleton's Branch paralleled his pride in the family name.

I didn't understand his feelings then, but I do now. Our house, seen from a distance, stood out like one of those in some famous artist's landscape painting. It would have had a commanding presence in any setting. Even the stately oaks and maples in front and single big pine tree at one side couldn't hide its inherent grandeur.

Father was fascinated by the old house's history. He told us when he was little both staircases still were unchanged from when the house was built. This meant they had an odd-measure step the builders put in as a security precaution. One step would be a couple of inches higher than all the others.

We asked why. He said people who lived in the house knew which step it was and so didn't trip, but if an intruder was trying to slip up the stairs in the dark he was likely to trip and fall and make noise.

"It was kind of primitive," he said, "but it probably worked. They didn't have electronic alarms in those days."

We didn't have electronic alarms, either. Father said they were an unnecessary expense. He said we had good locks on our doors and, besides, people in our part of the country didn't break into a house and sneak up somebody's stairs in the dark. Lacy and I never had considered this possibility before, but for the next few nights we slept uneasily and listened for someone sneaking up the stairs.

Maintaining the house to his high standard meant it must get a fresh coat of paint every four years. Father adamantly refused to hire painters. He said there was no need to pay someone else to do something he could do. Mama said this went beyond his reluctance to spend money. He worried someone else wouldn't do the quality job he demanded and was sure he could do it better.

One year Mama asked if the house could be painted white for a change, but he insisted on keeping the original pastel yellow. He had read about the Victorian style going back to its long-past origins in England and felt that white was not traditional and therefore not appropriate.

"It's Victorian," he told her. "You have to keep a Victorian a nice traditional color."

You probably know, Victorian style houses are not plain and simple structures. The Prather House had three stained-glass bay windows across the front on the ground level and pairs of arched and round windows on the second story. There were bay windows with multi-paned clear glass on the upstairs back side. Even without these, the steep gabled roof would have given it distinctive character. The roofline gave the impression of having been angled precisely to anchor a six-sided mini-tower at the center. The tower served no function, but undoubtedly was seen by the architect as an added touch of elegance and I suppose it was.

Unlike the tower, the wide porch that extended the length of the house in front and wrapped part way around the south end was one of the most functional elements any home could have. It hosted family gatherings and offered a place of comfortable respite when it caught the cool breezes on a warm summer evening. Lacy and I spent countless rainy days there, taking advantage of ample outdoor space still under roof.

The interior was equally grand. The rooms had high ceilings with crown molding and ornate trim around doors and windows. There was a large formal dining room and two parlors or sitting rooms and private little nooks tucked in here and there that Lacy and I adored but Mama complained did nothing but add to her housekeeping chores.

On winter days we weren't in school, Lacy and I often slipped up to the attic. This was where Mama stored old clothes and other things she no longer used. Mama never threw anything away. It was always warm there, and even though it was for the most part a large open area, it had a kind of cozy feeling we hadn't found anywhere else. There were two large dormers on each side that let in streams of sunlight. When we couldn't think of anything else to do, we could spend our time just running around to stir up dust particles and watch them dance in the light of the sun.

Among other castoff pieces of furniture, the attic held an old mattress and a pair of rickety old upholstered chairs. One day I lay down on the mattress and went to sleep. The next thing I knew, Lacy was shaking me and reporting excitedly that she had found something I must see. This turned out to be a small hinged panel on the wall above the front porch, barely visible underneath built-in shelving designed as orderly storage space.

"It opens!" she told me. "And I looked in. You've got to see!"

I was still half asleep, but the promise of new adventure jarred me awake.

We always had speculated there must be something more above the attic, given the high peaked roof on the old house. And then there was the tower. The tower had windows. Windows meant an inhabitable space, and yet the only way to it we could see was to climb a ladder from the top of the porch. It would be far more than we could manage to get the long ladder from the garage and get it onto the roof. And anyway, though we hated to admit it, both of us were afraid of heights.

Lacy lifted the panel, hinged on top. This created an opening that looked just big enough for an adult to crawl through.

"You want to go in, or do you want me to?" she asked. There wasn't a hint of hesitation, as there might be if she questioned whether or not we ought to enter at all.

I crawled through the opening without bothering to answer. Once I was a foot or two beyond the open panel, Lacy followed. There was just enough light to let us see where we were going as we crawled forward.

We saw it in an instant: A built-in wooden ladder attached to the outside wall. The only place it could lead to was the tower. A herd of elephants couldn't have stopped us from starting up that ladder. It was only a short climb. The ladder ended at an opening in the tower floor and, scrambling through it, we were there.

The tower was bright inside. There was a window in each side, three holding stained glass in bright-colored panels and three with clear glass. The space was unfinished. But there was a low, slender table in the center of the room and on it sat a small figurine. It looked to be cast in bronze and was a fat little man with a pointed head, wearing a wide smile. He had small, pointed ears and a single knot of hair in the middle of his head.

"I think that's Buddha," Lacy said, speaking in a low voice as if she feared she might violate the solemn quiet of a sacred place.

"Yes, I think it is."

"But why would it be here?"

I had no answer. We decided the architect might have been a Buddhist, or maybe the builders. But we shared a somewhat weird feeling recognizing the little god had always been there, right over our heads, its presence entirely secret.

We spent a half hour in the tower, marveling over the little statue and speculating about Father's reaction if he knew. We knew nothing about Buddha. Was his presence over our home good or bad? Lacy was certain he symbolized some sinister religion, and wished he wasn't there. I vowed to have nothing to do with the figurine and even pretend it didn't exist, hoping this would help minimize her worry.

Aside from the Buddha, though, we had discovered a marvelous lookout post from which we could see far into the distance in all directions. We knew we would be back.

It was a winter later when I found the true identity of the little statue in our tower. I was in the school library working on a paper when I happened onto a picture of Buddha. The figurine we had come to know was not Buddha. It was a Billiken, the god of the way things ought to be.

Lacy was surprised when I told her.

"I'm glad," she said, her face suddenly lit by her pretty smile. "I was afraid Buddha might not work good with my god of everything."

3

Rachel McNary was one of my high school teachers I never liked very much at the time. Now, I believe she was a good teacher. Her intensity led us to understand that she believed what she had to say was important and genuinely wanted us to learn it. She taught a sociology class, which I never had, and a course in anthropology.

I took her anthropology course during my senior year. I can't say I remember much of what I learned, but there's one thing I do recall: Mrs. McNary drilled into us an ironclad dictum that life happens one day at a time. She said we will have memories of "little things" that pop up now and then and, even if they were long ago, are as familiar as if they happened only yesterday. I came to appreciate this as I grew older, and it's funny what we happen to recall.

An example for me, as I think back on life in the old Prather house in general, is a time Sammy had been acting up all day, having nothing to do with Lacy or me and talking back to his mother at a level even she found intolerable. Lacy and I were down by the river when Father got home from work so I don't know exactly what happened, but I know Sammy got a whipping and Mama and Father had a big argument and weren't speaking when we came up to the house for supper.

As Grandma Childs would have said, "There was so much tension in the air you could cut it with a knife."

It was not all that unusual for our parents to quarrel, but it was unusual for the bad feelings to linger for several days as they did in this case. For at least the next week they hardly spoke to one another and when they did their tones were cold and indifferent. Mama slept on a couch in the living room.

Sammy didn't seem to notice, but Lacy and I worried the obvious gulf between them might be a lasting one. We knew other kids whose parents had divorced. The mere notion that it could happen to us was unbearable.

I tried to think of examples of kids who didn't seem to mind their moms and dads not being together. I thought this might help ease Lacy's anxiety a bit. I couldn't come up with any, though, and decided there wasn't anything I could say to make her feel better. We stopped talking about it.

This may have been Mama's and Father's only disagreement ever to end with Father taking the first steps to smooth things over. Saturday was a beautiful day, warm and sunny, and when he got home from Ficklin's Hardware Saturday evening he suggested that if Sunday turned out the same way we should all go visit Grandma and Grandpa Childs.

I knew this was solely to placate Mama. She didn't get to visit her parents nearly as often as she wanted, and Father always gave her a hard time when she brought it up. Weather was a factor, too. There was room for only three inside the pickup and this meant Lacy and I had to ride in the open bed of the old Dodge. We thought it was fun, as long as the weather was good.

Once I was past ten or 12 years old they made the trip on occasion when it was cold or rainy and we stayed home. Father always left me with a stern lecture about how I was responsible for everything under the sun while they were gone. I took that role very seriously, at times laying down new rules Lacy found repressive but reluctantly agreed to.

I never let Father down. I assumed he noticed, but he never said anything.

Grandma and Grandpa Childs lived in Golconda, Illinois, not far from us but on the other side of the Ohio River. Grandpa was a retired railroad worker and I think Grandma worked at their church, probably for nothing. Mama was their only child. I loved to visit them because getting there meant a ride across the Ohio on the ferry boat at Cave-in-Rock. Compared to Singleton's Branch, the Ohio seemed as wide as the Pacific Ocean.

There wasn't much to Golconda. Its claim to fame—or claim to *shame* as Grandma Childs liked to say—was its reputation as the starting point of the Trail of Tears across southern Illinois. I heard my grandparents bickering about it and asked Father what it meant and he said it was where the Cherokee and other tribes of Native Americans walked across the area on their forced march from the East to the Indian Territory many years ago. They all crossed the Ohio River at Golconda. He didn't know exactly when it was, but said it was President Andrew Jackson's fault.

I heard Grandpa say the Indians got too much sympathy. He said some of them were slave-holders, "and even had their black slaves with them when they come through here."

Grandma Childs said that didn't make any difference; they still were forced out of their homes and made to move way across the country just because they weren't lily-white people. She said they didn't deserve that, even if they were the Devil's angels. Grandpa didn't say anything more.

This was the only time I ever heard my grandparents disagree on anything. Compared to Mama and Father, they seemed to be very well matched. Sometimes they even acted almost like newlyweds. I always worried this might happen, because their shows of affection embarrassed me and often caused Lacy to giggle.

Sammy enjoyed all the extra attention he got when we went to Golconda, and Lacy and I looked forward to going down to the river with Grandpa and getting inside the levee. The Ohio was awesome compared to our river. We played along the bank and threw rocks in the water and watched for strings of barges heading up or down stream. Grandpa taught us how to tell if the barges were loaded or empty, as marked by their depth in the water.

Lacy noticed that most of the barges going upstream carried unidentifiable cargo such as manufactured goods packed for shipping, while those going downstream were more likely to be loaded with bulk raw materials or agricultural products—such things as corn, soybeans, coal, and gravel. Grandpa Childs commended her for being this observant, which made her very proud.

The day we went there after Mama and Father's quarrel was one of the best visits I remember. This was a given after we saw how it closed the gap between them. By the time we arrived, they were smiling at one another and even held hands after they got out of the truck and started walking toward the house. Lacy whispered to me that everything was going to be all right; our parents would not be divorced, after all.

"Come on Lacy," I told her. "They weren't going to be divorced. How come you saw the worst possible outcome in this when you usually see the best?"

She looked to be a bit unsure of herself.

"You don't know what could have happened," she said. "Sometimes the god of everything is too busy with little kids or animals to look after stubborn grownups. You were a little bit worried, too. You just won't admit it."

As usual, she was right.

It also was during this visit that I spent a rare period alone with Grandpa and had a serious conversation. I was surprised he understood me so well. Maybe he simply knew the typical uncertainties faced by teenaged boys, but I had a feeling he had watched me closely as I was growing up and knew me better than Father or Mama did—or maybe cared more.

We sat out on the front porch while the others talked inside and recovered from Grandma's usual heavy noon meal. Lacy had gone upstairs to take a nap.

"You're just about grown up, boy," Grandpa said. This struck me as so abrupt I thought later he might have planned it to lead into a discussion of my future.

I wanted to say something mature sounding, but couldn't think fast enough. "Yeah, I'm fourteen now," I said.

"That's not to be taken lightly. You're about to start high school and before you know it you'll be old enough to have a job and even to vote. Pretty soon you will begin to worry about responsibilities you probably haven't even thought of yet."

"I know," I said. "We talk about that stuff at school."

Grandpa chuckled. "That's kind of what school's for, I guess. Here's what I want you to think about, though. You've got the rest of your life to be an adult. Coming of age should be fun. You know, getting around a bit, going out with girls and all that. Learn what you enjoy doing before it's too late."

"Yeah, I guess that's what I want to do."

"You've got to do more than *want* to do it, boy. You have to work at it. Get out there and do it!"

I didn't know what to say. When I didn't speak, he went right on.

"Life's full of choices. There's plenty of times when you find yourself forced to choose between two things that don't appeal to you one way or the other, and there are times when the possibilities are all good. You won't always make the right choice, but the more experience you've had the more likely you will."

"Was working on the railroad your first choice?" I asked.

Grandpa hesitated before saying anything, unusual for him. When he spoke he seemed to be choosing his words carefully.

"Well, I can't rightly say it was my first choice. But I guess it was my *best* choice. Your mama was a baby and your grandmamma had some problems after having her—physical problems, I mean—and I didn't make enough money working part-time for a barge line to take care of them properly. The railroad paid a lot better."

"You worked on the railroad a lot of years."

"Yeah, the railroad was pretty much my life. I got good at my job, too. They hated to lose me when I retired."

"You don't seem old, Grandpa. I'll bet you could have kept on working for a long time yet."

Grandpa turned and looked me square in the eyes. His tone was firm when he spoke. "That kind of gets to the point I was trying to make. Everybody deserves time off when they get older. You don't have that much time left and you ought to be able to spend your days doing something besides making a living. Thanks to the union I've got pretty good retirement income."

I wanted to say I was happy for this, but he kept on talking.

"But everybody doesn't have that, boy. I'm lucky. And it *was* luck. That's what I'm talking about. When I was a young man I should have got around more and seen more of the world, you know what I mean? I think I was smart enough to have figured out a way to make a good living and have a good retirement without just depending on good luck."

"I know you were. I've always thought you are very smart."

"Well, I thank you for that. But there's more to what I want to say. I also ought to have traveled, seen different places. I've never seen an ocean or been to a big city. We have the time now, and I guess even the money, but Grandma and I are too old to start traveling now. This is a good place, but I wish I knew more about the rest of our great land. America's a big country."

Grandpa was almost misty-eyed, and I knew he was feeling really sorry that he had not been able to do all the things he wanted to do. I was about to say something sympathetic, but Lacy ran up at this point and interrupted our conversation.

I was irritated with her, because I was enjoying my talk with Grandpa. He was happy to see her, though, and swooped her up in his arms and whirled her around two or three times and had her laughing like crazy. Remembering her worry about Mama and Father, I felt good to hear her laugh.

I had other serious discussions with Grandpa Childs over the next few years and they always left me feeling good. My grandfather really was interested in me, in my wellbeing. He wanted to know how things were going in my life. He cared. It wasn't until much later in life that I came even close to getting the same sense of feeling about my father.

I can honestly say I've remembered and tried to live up to the last bit of advice I recall Grandpa Childs giving me. It's simple, and of course could apply to anyone.

"Boy," he said, "no matter what life brings, try to leave the world a better place because you were here."

It is painful for me to say, but once I was older and no longer lived with Mama and Father in the old Prather house on the bluff I seldom made an effort to see my grandparents again. And then it was too late. Mama called from a Paducah hospital to tell me Grandpa had passed away. I tried to remember how long it had been since I'd last seen him, but whenever it was I knew it had been too long.

If I had forgotten Grandpa Childs, though, he had not forgotten me. In his will he left me five thousand dollars, with the stipulation it be used as "travel money." I broke down and cried when I saw this.

Mama tried to get Grandma Childs to move into the old Prather house with her and Father. There was plenty of room. Grandma said no, she still had a life in Golconda and friends she didn't want to leave. She lived another year, then passed away suddenly one day at work, seated at her desk in the church office.

Mama said that was the way Grandma would have wanted it. "Most of us aren't as fortunate as she was. We don't get to choose how we go."

4

Whether from foresight or just dumb luck I don't know, but our school also was on the west side of the river. The school building was a long and low structure offering a silhouette that from the road was barely visible through the white oak and hard maple trees around it, now grown to full height. Parents, especially, and taxpayers in general were pleased it squatted on high ground. It was safe there from Singleton's Branch floods.

Hemingway Terrace School was an outlier in the Erinville Community Consolidated District and relatively new as school buildings go. It had been planned originally as a junior high and high school, but with a shifting population and a more creative school board it had gained an added section that housed middle school students, too.

I'm not sure what the total attendance was, but I believe it was something on the order of three hundred girls and boys. Most of them were, as Grandma Childs would say, "lily-white." I can't cite numbers but I know there had been a growing influx of black students into the older schools and this no doubt was one reason for the growth of Hemingway Terrace. Erinville was no worse than the rest of Kentucky when it came to race relations, but certainly no better.

We didn't appreciate it at the time, but having been planned and built more recently on a reasonably large tract of land, our school had something most others in the area lacked: It was well landscaped. Different varieties of crepe myrtle had been used as plantings to separate sections of the parking lot and evergreen hedges of boxwood formed attractive barriers wherever these were needed. There were pink and purple butterfly bushes, and the oaks and maples usually gained their most brilliant color not long after the start of school in the fall.

For us, the most important thing about Hemingway Terrace was that it was a mere half-mile walk from home for Sammy, Lacy, and me. Father might drop us off on his way to work during bad weather but we were on our own at the end of the school day. A good-sized group of other students shared part of the trek with us, some of them facing as much as another mile to go. The narrow blacktop road was ours for the taking; there was little automobile traffic at this time of day to force us to make way. This gave us an attitude of invincibility that probably was dangerous.

If a day at school was tiring, the afterschool walk was rejuvenating. Especially on Fridays in the spring, with winter past and summer soon to be in view. We accepted it as a time to celebrate. We might hurry when it rained or on those rare occasions when we faced unseasonably cold winds, but we relished the freedom to set own pace, unencumbered by someone else's rules. This was *our* time.

The older boys and girls often paired off and sometimes even dared, self-consciously, to hold hands as we walked. Victor and Lacy were the first to always walk side-by-side. Bobbi and I paired off, too, but not so early. She made the first move. I heard her running behind me, and once she was alongside she slowed to my pace. Neither of us acknowledged the other directly and we only began talking several minutes later.

Under ordinary circumstances, Victor probably would not have been walking with us. His family had to move out of their house during the flood and find temporary living space on our side of the river. I think they were staying in somebody's barn. Victor made it a habit to stop at our house for an hour or so on most afternoons, which we—especially Lacy—encouraged. Mama always asked him to stay for supper and usually he did.

Mama liked Victor. He was the youngest of six children in the Kenton family, and there was a wide gap in age between him and his brother and four sisters. Mama said he was a "surprise" baby to a mother who was more than forty years old, shaking her head sadly as if this was somehow a tragic event. This struck me as somewhat ironic, given that the story of Sammy's arrival in our family was much the same.

Mama worried that no one else among the Kentons would be at home in the barn for some time after Victor got out of school. He said it didn't matter, but I knew it did. He had told me he hated being alone in the big barn.

His sisters lived in town and his brother worked at a used car dealer where his father was sales manager. Because of the hard times brought on by the flood, his mother had taken a job as an evening shift checkout clerk at the Erinville Northside Kroger store. Makeshift cooking facilities in the barn seriously limited her ability to prepare meals for the family, and Victor said she took out most of her earnings in ready-to-eat food brought home from the Kroger deli.

You will understand Victor better if I tell you about Larry Eliot. Larry was a bully, maybe not qualified to be called *the* school bully because there were others, but usually a nasty character to deal with. I think he envied Victor's physical strength and, knowing Victor was not one to fight back, challenged him constantly. I don't know how Victor took it as long as he did.

I was walking across the schoolyard with him the day his patience finally ran out. Larry Eliot taunted him about his girlfriend, Lacy, mocking him as a "ladies' man" too sissy to play football because his pretty nose might get flattened. Victor turned and tried to walk away, but Larry followed us and kept on trying to provoke him.

"Why don't you just go over yonder and play with the girls?" Larry called after him, deliberately raising his voice to attract attention. "Don't make your little Lacy have to come looking for you!"

Victor suddenly wheeled about and ran toward Larry, his fist cocked and ready to strike. Larry barely had time to duck. Victor body-slammed him to the ground and sat astride him, forcing his face into the schoolyard dust. As other students hurried close to get a better view of what was going on, Victor slapped Larry on both sides of his head. The onlookers cheered.

The fight was over as quickly as it had begun. Just as I got there, Victor got up and walked away, saying nothing. Larry pulled himself up on his knees, wiping the dust from his face, and started to cry. He got no sympathy from most in the crowd, but I honestly felt a little sorry for him.

Not surprisingly, word of the incident soon reached the principal's office. Both Larry and Victor were suspended for three days. Victor's father apparently punished him for this, but I tried to persuade him the outcome was worth it. He had become a schoolyard hero.

Larry Eliot's behavior changed after that. He no longer tried to intimidate other students and over time was a more likeable person. He avoided Victor as much as possible.

Mama soon came to look on Victor almost as one of her own. Lacy actually complained one afternoon that he was Mama's favorite, after Sammy. I thought she was joking, but realized later she really believed this. Even if she may have been jealous at that instant, though, I know it made her happy. Having Victor treated as family suited Lacy very well. She wouldn't have had it any other way.

For my part, I did not spend all my time worrying about Lacy or looking for things to do with Victor. I was 15, had no interest in sports, and could take or leave my studies. My teenage hormones had kicked in and the first thing on my mind was girls. It was funny that I'd never noticed before how many pretty girls there were at Hemingway Terrace.

And then there was Bobbi Hoard.

Bobbi was in my grade, but we had not gone to school together before. Her family had moved to Erinville from Pennsylvania during the summer. I saw her the first day of classes, wandering in the hall looking somewhat lost, but was too shy—Mama would have said backward—to stop and talk with her and help her find her way.

I almost came to believe in Lacy's god of everything when I got to my civics class the first thing after lunch and saw her sitting in the front row. I slipped into a seat behind her, so close I imagined I could smell her beautiful auburn hair. I wondered why I'd never noticed a girl's hair before.

After a few class sessions I found the courage to move to the front row. Bobbi Hoard and I now sat side-by-side. It was hard for me to concentrate during my morning classes because my mind already was on my civics class in the afternoon. I couldn't wait to see Bobbi and once in the room wished the class would go on forever.

Bobbi was the youngest of three sisters. Her oldest sister, Gayle, was in college somewhere in New York and the middle one, Carly, worked in her father's business in Erinville and lived in her own apartment in town. She admired them both but didn't talk about them much.

Spring semester always had seemed endless before. But this one flew by, and almost before I knew it the time had come for the annual school open house. At Hemingway Terrace this was a popular community event. Most of the parents came, and lots of graduates showed up even if they had no children enrolled there.

The principal and teachers and a six-member parents committee named several weeks in advance put together an array of fun things to do. There had to be games that offered prizes and face painting regularly ranked as one of the most popular activities for the younger ones. A popcorn wagon and snow cone booth were brought in and kept busy. Many of the students, especially those doing well in their classes, were proud to have parents meet their teachers and relished the praise the teachers generously ladled out.

With the exception of the school janitors, it virtually was assured that at the end of the evening almost everyone would go home happy. The janitors were left with far more than the usual amount of trash to sweep up and dispose of.

The open house this year fell at a time when Singleton's Branch was at a record high flood level. Not only did the floodwaters visible from our bluff cover a wide swath of low-lying farmland, but the backwaters of the river also had forced the closing of one of the two main highways leading into town. The flood was about the only thing people talked about.

The school board, following a well-established tradition, scheduled a meeting the night of the open house and encouraged the visitors to stay around and see their public servants in action. The connection seemed to work. Board meetings usually attracted no one except maybe a couple of soreheads with complaints to voice, but the one after open house was held in the auditorium to accommodate the expected crowd.

Mama was tired and ready to go home by the time the meeting was scheduled to begin. She complained the session always dragged on forever because board members liked having an audience.

"They all want to talk, even if they have nothing to say," she said. "I guess they think that impresses people, but if they could hear how dumb they sound sometimes they'd know better."

Father was determined to attend. He said it was important to see democracy at work and, since members of the board were elected, voters should witness them on the job. Mama said he could go to a meeting some other time but he just glared and went on to the auditorium and took a seat. She had no choice but to join him there, along with Sammy and Lacy.

I was at the meeting, too. My civics class had been assigned a late-semester project requiring us to attend and write a report on the event. Our teacher, Sarah Jennings, directed us to pay particular attention to the public comment period. She said it was a way to witness peoples' views not often expressed openly.

"It's safe to assume that what one person says also represents the thinking of a good many others who don't speak," Miss Jennings said. "Especially in times of crisis, like our floods, open discussions like this can be a good measure of public opinion—what people are worried about."

Then she backstopped herself a bit by adding there also were lots of times when no one wanted to speak, or one or two people who might or might not be representative of the group would dominate the session. She said the meat of the assignment simply was to have the experience of sitting through a school board meeting and write a report on it.

"Don't go in with any particular expectations," she told us. "Pretend you're going to a movie or a play. Let the actors take the stage and see how it all turns out."

We liked Miss Jennings a lot. She was younger than most of our teachers and very pretty. The girls admired her and some of the boys had crushes on her. She had a way of being overly dramatic, and at times she tried too hard and we almost wanted to laugh. Bobbi told me later Miss Jennings wouldn't have lasted long in the school she went to in Philadelphia. Students there didn't have our small-town manners and patience, she said, and there were rowdies who liked to make fun of teachers and would have picked on her without mercy.

Students from our civics class were scattered around the auditorium when the meeting started. Bobbi and I sat close to the front.

The meeting was chaired by the board president, an aging farmer named John Meriwether. I'd never seen or heard of him before, as far as I can remember. He made a good impression on us—meaning the students. Bobbi said he apparently was very competent and ran a smooth meeting, paying careful attention to even the smallest detail.

When he announced the period for public comment, Seth Ficklin stood up and said he'd like to speak.

"Go ahead, Seth," Mr. Meriwether said. "Speakin's what I just called for."

Seth was a powerful speaker. Mama said he should have been an evangelist, while others charged him with being too fond of the sound of his own voice. He rambled a while about how all the people of Erinville had come together during hard times caused by the floods and lavished praise on everyone who had anything to do with the school's location on high ground. Several members of the audience murmured approval.

"It doesn't always work out this good," Seth lamented. "You may know, over in Missouri they built a school right on top of the New Madrid Fault. There's likely to be another earthquake over there one of these days and it could just swallow up that school and all the kids in it."

Father had told us often that Seth Ficklin usually knew what he was talking about. Listeners in the school auditorium apparently found him convincing. Some uttered expressions of alarm. But there was at least one doubter.

"Are you sure that's true, Seth?" Jack Loveland called out from the back row of folding chairs set up for the occasion, standing so he could be heard. "Sometimes stories like that get around and people believe them whether they're true or not. I've got relatives that live over in that area and I never heard anything about this before. You'd think they'd know."

"Yeah, Jack, it's true," Seth told him. "I wouldn't blame locals for not wanting to spread it around, though. Makes 'em look kind of dumb, I'd say."

Harvey Bowman stood and waited for attention.

"You have the floor, Harvey," Mr. Meriwether said, after Seth Ficklin had taken a seat.

Except for the mayor and possibly a minister or two, Harvey Bowman probably was the best known man in town. Half the people patronized his barber shop. He also was a notary public who always was there to notarize official things for a small fee, and a justice of the peace. Father claimed he made a lot of money performing weddings for underage couples who showed up with their parents from other counties with licenses issued in Erinville.

"I don't have anything to add," Harvey Bowman said. "I only want to say loud and clear that if Seth Ficklin says something's true, it's true."

With that, he sat down.

We couldn't tell whether or not Jack Loveland was persuaded, and of course we really didn't care. We simply were busy writing things down so we could have something to report back to Miss Jennings.

I convinced myself that I was unsure of a given matter and needed confirmation. No doubt Bobbi would know. We were seated side-by-side and it was easy to compare notes.

Over the course of the semester, I had become pretty creative with excuses to ask Bobbi Hoard for help. I was afraid I'd given her ample reason to think I must be dumb as a stick. She told me later she knew right from the outset what was going on, though, and was good with it. She wanted a reason for us to get together, too.

There was something between us even then that we knew might well be permanent. We didn't talk about it, but we felt it when we were together. First love is best when it grows into the great and lasting love of one's life.

5

Nature is remarkably talented at repairing her own damage. The flood left the river bank, high up the front of the bluff, muddy with sediment. We would look down the path and wonder if our shoal ever would be clean again. We had to pick up and dispose of some trash, but a few summer thunderstorms washed away the mud in no time and the stream below ran clear and inviting again.

The summer heat drove Lacy, Victor, and me back to this site where we knew our days would be enjoyable. We sat on the flat rocks along the river's edge, dangling our feet in the cool water. I supposed it was only a matter of time before Lacy and Victor set off on their own, but given the heat any activity that required physical exertion was not inviting.

Lacy turned sideways so that her feet touched Victor's, wiggled her toes, and giggled. He cupped his hand, scooped up a handful of water, and splashed it in her face.

"You're mean, Victor!" she yelled, laughing.

His response was to repeat the act, this time with a double handful of clear Singleton's Branch water. She stood and leaned toward him, as if about to attack, then suddenly froze in this position. She was looking past us, farther down the bank of the river.

"Oh, such a poor thing. Look!"

We both turned in the direction of her gaze. A few yards away, cautiously slinking toward us was no doubt the most filthy and bedraggled dog I've ever seen. It was skin-and-bone thin, with matted fur and a clump of cockleburs clinging to its tail. All four legs and its belly half way up its sides were smeared with mud. It hesitated when Lacy spoke.

Victor clapped his hands together and yelled, "Get! Get out of here!"

"No! Don't chase it away, Victor. The poor thing's hungry," Lacy urged. "I'll get it something to eat."

I said the dog might be sick, and maybe not safe to go near. Victor reacted to my words as if I'd issued a dire warning. He ran to the trembling animal, grabbed it up in his arms, and threw it into the river.

"Try to make the other side," he yelled. "Somebody over there might want you."

Lacy screamed and began to cry. "It could drown, Victor!"

"Oh, yeah? What a loss that would be!" He laughed and clapped his hands. "Swim for it, cur!"

I told Lacy dogs are good swimmers. Then I saw the gentle current was washing this one slowly downstream and it had turned back toward the bank from which it had just been thrown.

"See," I told her. "It's going to be okay."

Lacy didn't respond. She turned and ran. "I hate you, Victor!" she yelled over her shoulder as she reached the foot of the path up the bluff. She climbed the steep incline on the run and quickly disappeared over the top.

The dog, meanwhile, had reached the river bank and was struggling its way ashore some twenty yards downstream. It managed to clear the water and dragged itself up onto dry ground and disappeared under the flowering umbrella of a pink marsh mallow bush. Victor watched it intently.

I wanted to run after Lacy and turned toward the bluff. I needed to catch and comfort her, to let her know the dog had made it safely out of the river onto dry land. But if I left Victor, what would he do? I couldn't take a chance he might decide to do the dog further harm. I stood, silent, and waited for him to speak.

"That's the sorriest looking mutt I've even seen," he said. "Wouldn't have been much of a loss if it had drowned."

"You are wrong about that, Victor. It's somebody's pet—or at least it was. It probably has been lost a while, and sure looked hungry. But you don't know anything about that dog. It may be the best dog in the world."

I could see he was a little taken aback, and pressed my point. "And even if it is a poor specimen, I have to say, what you did was cruel."

I was hoping for some expression of remorse. There was none.

"It's not like it's human," he said sarcastically. "It's a dog."

He started walking toward the bluff and I followed.

Neither of us spoke as we climbed the incline. Victor hesitated when we got to the top and looked at me, as if waiting for me to say something. I walked with him around to the front of the house, and when I still didn't speak he shuffled off and headed down the lane toward the county blacktop.

I ran into the kitchen looking for Lacy. Mama said she had been there, but just left.

"She was all bent out of shape about something," Mama said. "Crying like a baby. I asked her what was the matter but she wouldn't talk. Don't know how she could be hungry this time of day, but she took a couple of biscuits out of the tin and took off. That child can be so strange sometimes."

I didn't wait to tell Mama what had happened. Lacy would be back on the river bank, looking for the hungry dog. I needed to find her.

Weeds and grass under the marsh mallow bush were trampled and still wet. The dog had spent some time here. And there was more: a faint image of a shoe heel print. Lacy had found the dog here and probably fed it the biscuits. I was relieved to some small extent, assuming the dog had accepted her and not done her any harm. Father had told us a scared or injured dog may feel endangered and bite anyone who comes within reach.

Now that she had the dog, Lacy would do whatever it took to protect it.

I called for her, as loud as I could yell. After a few minutes of complete quiet, I called again. And then a third time. All I heard in return was some chatter among the crows in trees lining the bank across the river.

"Don't panic," I demanded of myself. *They couldn't have got very far.* But it was false confidence. Lacy could not be counted on to act rationally when it came to protecting an animal. She was afraid Victor might find the dog again and didn't trust him not to hurt it. She would be hiding somewhere, even from me.

There was no way to know which way she may have gone. If I went upstream and she and the dog had gone downstream, I would only be getting farther from her. And the opposite was true also, of course. With nothing to go on, I'd just have to take a chance and hope to guess right. Maybe just once Lacy's god of everything would be on my side. And hers.

I was still in a swimsuit, most of my body bare. The thick grass scraped at the skin on my ankles and legs as I pushed my way forward. Away from our shoal, there had been little human traffic along the river. The narrow plateau between the base of the bluff and the water's edge was a jungle of tall grass, weeds of all kinds, and briars and coarse shrubs.

I struggled to fight off the panic I knew couldn't be held back forever. I would find her. She would be all right. With the dog apparently being no danger, there was nothing to hurt her. But still— Whether it was panic I don't really know, but suddenly I found it hard to get my breath.

I couldn't make it any farther without stopping to rest. I dropped to my knees, then turned with my back to a tree and sat. If it hadn't been panic before, it was now—full blown. There never had been a time in my entire life when I felt more helpless. Lacy was out there somewhere in what to me looked like a complete wilderness. She had a sickly dog she would make any sacrifice to protect. And it was getting dark.

I began to cry. Silent sobs, but tears blurring my vision.

Get hold of yourself! You'll be of no help to Lacy if you let yourself fall apart like this!

This was true. Lacy was out there somewhere and needed me. It was essential I concentrate on this. Think about her, and not worry about myself. I had always been there when Lacy needed me. I wouldn't fail her now.

I stood and yelled her name again and was greeted with nothing but silence. Even the crows apparently had gone to sleep. She probably would respond now if she heard me, I reasoned, and I surely had made my way upstream as far as she and the dog could have before having to stop and rest. I had gambled on the wrong direction.

By the time I made my way back to the shoal it was too dark to risk trying to go farther. I knew every inch of the path up the bluff, so I hurried to the house with no problem, slipped quietly in the back door and crept to my room upstairs. It wasn't that I was afraid to run into Mama or Father, exactly, but I did not want to waste time explaining what was going on. I needed a small flashlight that was in a drawer of a small chest backed against the north wall.

I got the flashlight without making a sound. But I bumped a wall as I made my way back to the stairs and held my breath until I was sure I hadn't been heard. The house still was silent so I slipped back down the stairs and out the back door, rushing but staying quiet.

Back at the river bank, I felt a surge of confidence. I'd managed to get to my room without being confronted by either of our parents. And now, with the flashlight, I could find Lacy. I was sure it wouldn't take long.

This, again, was a mistake. I spent the next two hours fighting my way through the brush, looking under trees, calling her name softly. I'd made my way far enough downstream that I wasn't sure whether there were homes atop the bluff over my head, or even on the east side of Singleton's Branch. Yelling, as I had before, could bring problems of a different kind.

Now it came to feel like a foolish mission. Did I really expect to find Lacy and the dog somewhere out here along the river bank, with no place to sleep? She would have climbed the bluff by now, maybe even have gone home. I was about to turn and go the other way when the beam of my flashlight reflected back from the eyes of the dog, alert and watching me, but curled up next to Lacy. She lay sleeping on a bed of needles scraped together at the base of a tall loblolly pine.

The dog stood as I walked nearer, wagging its tail in greeting. His movement woke Lacy. She looked at me, rubbed her eyes, and said, "Well, hey there. Good to see you, big brother. Oh, meet my dog, Oscar."

I took her hands and helped her up. The dog stretched and yawned but stood still, as if waiting for her to set something in motion. Lacy stooped and stroked its head.

"We need to get you home," I said. "Father and Mama will be worried to death. Besides, it's getting cool out here in the woods."

"Oh, yeah, like they ever bothered with me. Do you think Father will let me keep my dog?"

I pretended confidence I really didn't have. "Sure. I think he used to have a dog. I remember hearing him talk about it."

"Maybe. But if Oscar pees on the floor or something he'll get mad at us. And you know he's gonna bitch about having to buy dog food and all that. Mama will take my side and Sammy won't care one way or the other. So how about you?"

I pulled her to me in a tight hug.

"I'm always on your side. You know that. I'll go to bat for you if Father gives you a hard time. I'll tell him the Prather house needs a good watch dog." I stroked the dog's head, too. "How 'bout that, Oscar? You a good watch dog? Don't let me promise more than you can deliver."

When we got home, I helped her slip the dog into the house as quietly as possible. In truth, I had no idea how Father was going to react. But for now I was contented simply to get all three of us upstairs to our rooms without waking him or Mama. It must be getting close to his getting-up time and after that he'd soon be off to work. We would have all day to plan the introduction of Oscar.

When I consider this wild night now, I'm truly amazed we pulled it off. I am glad we did. Oscar became a part of the Prather family and offered Lacy valued companionship. He wouldn't have made much of a watch dog, however, because he was friendly toward all comers.

And I surprised myself the next evening when Father got home from work. Lacy promised to keep Oscar quiet upstairs in her room until I'd told him about our new dog and got some indication he would accept it. I had rehearsed several different wordings in my head, hopeful but not overly optimistic. A lot depended on Father's mood when he faced a surprise of any sort. I felt as ready as I could be as I waited at a front window for the old Dodge pickup to pull up in front of the house.

I didn't expect his greeting.

"You and Lacy were out pretty late last night," he declared as soon as he saw me. "What were you up to?"

For the first time ever with Father, I was fast on my feet with a clever reply. "We didn't want to disturb your reading by coming inside," I lied. "We were down by the old hawthorn hedge studying the moon. I'm teaching Lacy about its phases."

"Well ..." He seemed at a loss for words. "That's good, then. She can learn these things. Someone just has to have the patience to teach her."

I felt a surge of anger, quickly compromised by gratitude that Lacy wasn't there to hear what he said. I wanted to tell him he didn't know Lacy, his own daughter. I wanted to scream at him that my little sister was smart. But I knew the best thing for me to do was stay quiet.

I waited nervously as he turned and walked toward the kitchen, afraid he'd ask more pressing questions and knowing I would very quickly run out of answers. He and Mama soon were talking and laughing, and then I heard the sound of a spoon stirring his coffee. I couldn't ask for more.

Lacy probably was holding her breath, too, waiting with Oscar up in her room. I rushed to join them.

"So?" That's all she said.

"So I think he's in a good mood. I thought we ought to wait till after supper, but now may be as good a time as any."

She had tied a string around Oscar's neck in lieu of a leash. She tugged gently on the string and urged him to come with her toward the door. He responded as if this were all routine, trotting beside her to and down the stairs and straight to the kitchen. We could hear our parents laughing. Now was as good a time as we were going to get.

"Father," Lacy said as we entered the room, "this is my new dog, Oscar."

If I have made it sound as if Father was predictable, I've misled you. He was a creature of habit when it came to his routine—breakfast, work, home, supper, reading chair, bedtime—but we never knew how he might react when faced with anything new and surprising, or even when getting unexpected questions he didn't have a ready answer for.

Lacy and I had talked about this any number of times. We rarely started a conversation with him until he spoke first. But now Lacy found it necessary to take the initiative and announce Oscar's presence even before Father might have noticed. We waited nervously for him to react.

He put down his coffee cup and stood studying Oscar, saying nothing. Oscar apparently sensed Lacy's tension, slunk behind her and lay down on the floor with his nose resting on his front paws. She had bathed him during the afternoon and he was well fed and satisfied and, to my surprise, he was a very handsome dog.

Father walked over and leaned down to get a closer look.

"He's a nice dog, but a bit skinny," he said. "Where did you get him?"

Lacy hesitated, and looked at me as if waiting for me to answer. I don't know if she expected me to respond to Father, or merely hoped I would. It didn't matter. I had to fill the gap.

"Victor brought him. I think he belonged to one of the Kentons' neighbors and they wanted to find him a new home. He knew Oscar would be welcome here."

Lacy stared at me, her mouth open like she wanted to speak but didn't know what to say. She must have been surprised by my performance. I know I was. And I had no remorse for having lied. I did it for Lacy and Oscar, not myself, and I was rather proud of my creativity. We held our breaths in trepidation as to how Father might respond.

Father straightened up and walked back to the table to pick up his cup. We waited what seemed an eternity for him to sip his coffee before he said anything. There was no discernable clue as to how he was going to react. When he finally spoke it was to Mama.

"Do we have anything to feed a dog, or do I need to go back and bring some from the store?"

6

Once Father had accepted Oscar, I began to worry about the rift between Lacy and Victor. He would be back one of these days and they would have to face one another. I wanted us to talk about it. Would she be receptive toward him or would the hate she'd expressed prove to be real and lasting?

This seemed important to me only because their relationship had become a critical element of Lacy's life. If suddenly there was no Victor, I thought Lacy probably would go into a deep funk and I didn't want this to happen. If she wanted his presence, so did I.

I hadn't found the courage to bring up the subject until it was too late. Lacy and I were down at the shoal the next morning, half-heartedly enjoying a rock-throwing competition, when Victor showed up. He seemed not even to notice me, but walked straight to Lacy.

"I'm sorry," he said.

Lacy took a long time to answer. "What you did was cruel, Victor. I don't have any respect for anybody who would hurt an animal. Any animal. I like you, but I don't ever want to see you do something like you did to Oscar again. I'll teach you to love animals the way I do."

Victor had a blank look on his face, but smiled. He stepped to her and they hugged for a minute, then waded out into the gently flowing waters of Singleton's Branch and joined Oscar in his search for something of interest.

Lacy's reaction should not have surprised me. She always was ready to forgive, if not forget. Her generosity never faltered.

Although my major concern was taken care of, I still wondered whether she might not have second thoughts about Oscar. I remembered her saying she didn't want a pet and didn't think anybody should have one.

Making a pet of an animal took away its "individual being," she insisted. She said the god of everything intended for animals to be as free as humans, and equal. And if they were equal, humans had no right to take control the way they did when they took animals as pets. Now that she had Oscar, I wondered whether she would reconsider her position on this.

And, as usual, I underestimated Lacy. She worked things out in her mind to her own satisfaction. No matter what anybody else thought, she declared, Oscar was *not* her pet.

They were good friends who wanted to be together, she explained, and the god of everything expected them to take care of each other. This meant it was all right for her to make sure Oscar was well fed and had a warm bed to sleep in as long as wanted to. And the warm bed, of course, was hers.

Oscar, who displayed himself proudly as if recognizing he was a handsome fellow now that he was all cleaned up, apparently found no problem with this arrangement. If he worried his "individual being" might somehow be compromised, it didn't show. The two of them were an instant pair, one hardly ever to be seen without the other.

Oscar was a good dog. He was as mutt as a mutt could be, with small likenesses to every breed I've ever seen. He was friendly with everyone in the family and usually unobtrusive, but could make his presence known in powerful ways. This was likely to happen if he thought Lacy was somehow endangered. I have no doubt he would have given his life in an instant to protect her.

Father said if he had searched the whole Commonwealth of Kentucky for a dog he never could have found one he liked better. Not only did this signal his acceptance, but it went even farther. It was high praise. All the fragments now fit together; being liked by Father was the essential corner piece of any puzzle faced by the Prather family.

Having said the dog was friendly to everyone in the family, though, I should make clear this did not necessarily include Victor. There was no doubt he remembered Victor from their first meeting on the bank of the river and in addition to this he was jealous. He wanted Lacy to himself and Victor was competition. There were times when I saw Victor deliberately teasing him by grabbing Lacy when she and Oscar were together and running off with her. Oscar would chase after them in vain, sometimes to return later with his head down and looking for all the world like he had been totally rejected.

Victor got a job working three days a week at the used car dealership with his father and older brother. He only talked about his work a time or two, but I think he was just a flunky they could call on when they needed an extra hand. It sounded like he spent most of his time cleaning and washing cars they took in or those that had been on the lot for a long time.

I was looking for work that summer, too, but so far hadn't found anything. The days Victor worked were like the old days for Lacy and me. We spent hours in the shoal, but even in the summer heat took time to climb up into the tower and enjoy the view of the lush countryside.

"Mother Nature never lets us down," Lacy liked to say. And she was right. We were surrounded by a beautiful scene, there for anyone who would take the time to see it.

Although the area was heavily wooded, there were wide patches of open fields under cultivation by the farmers and planted in corn and soybeans and, in a few instances, cotton and tobacco. Father said there was no local tobacco market anymore and the closest cotton gin was too far away to be convenient. He predicted that neither of these would be grown as cash crops in the region much longer. We assumed he knew what he was talking about. And even if we had had doubts, we didn't question Father.

We could watch the combines in the fields of winter wheat, now golden and ready for harvest. A couple of small farms produced tomatoes, okra, and other vegetables to be sold in the Erinville farmers' market and one had fields of watermelon and cantaloupe. It seemed as if there always were men working in these, often loading trucks to haul their melons off to be sold in Paducah or Evansville, or maybe Nashville.

Lacy always pointed out the melon patches. One day she said she would go help them if she could.

"Do you know why?" she asked.

"No. Why?"

"Because then if somebody tried to pull something over on poor, dumb little Lacy I could say, 'I didn't just fall off the watermelon truck!'"

I laughed, but found her joke more touching than funny.

"I wish you wouldn't call yourself dumb," I told her, more concern in my voice than I intended. "Nobody thinks you're dumb, Lacy."

She simply looked away without comment. I turned back to a window and marveled anew at the vast area we could see from the tower.

Much of the land to the southwest was too hilly for regular cultivation. Some of this was devoted to the production of hay, mostly alfalfa and oats, but most was fenced off as pasture land. Lacy tried several times to count the Black Angus cattle on one farm without success. I didn't know then but do now that this was the farm of John Meriwether, the school board president.

We would not have admitted it to ourselves, but the marvelous view was no longer our primary reason for climbing up to the tower. We went to curry favor from the Billiken, the god of the way things ought to be.

Lacy actually took to stroking the little statue's head and pretending to kneel in prayer before it. Once, she even took a small offering of flowers.

I never made fun of Lacy. She most often was serious, counted every living thing as precious, and clearly had a sense of reverence toward her own chosen deity, her god of everything. She would explain her feelings toward the Billiken in due time.

When she did, I understood her motives very well.

"The god of everything is awful busy," she told me. "As soon as he looks after one thing there's always something else. I know he must get tired of all the bad things that happen, but he still has to check them out. Don't you think he must be happy to have the Billiken looking after all the good things, so he doesn't have to?"

I told her I did.

She said it was time for us to go back to the real world. She wanted to see Oscar. She knew he was lonely without her, and no man or beast ever should have to be lonely.

Oscar usually waited patiently on the porch when we were inside the house. He greeted Lacy with enthusiasm when we came out, eager to race down the bluff to the shoal and play in the water. He couldn't hide his disappointment if we did something else, but as long as he could be with Lacy he was happy. All he really wanted was to be with her.

I had come to dread the days we were joined by Victor. When he was there, it almost was as if I didn't exist. Victor and Lacy were off in their own space, and even Oscar ignored me to stay close to her as long as he could. Lacy seemed to have forgotten her self-proclaimed view on loneliness. On some days I went to the tower alone, sat on the floor and looked out over the low window sills to survey the surrounding countryside for something new or different.

One day I began to talk to the little Billiken. I asked if he missed Lacy's visits and almost could have believed he answered. I told him about Bobbi. I felt better just saying her name.

"It's like a boy's name, except it is spelled different," I explained, and then felt foolish.

But I climbed to the tower again the next day and described her, told the miniature deity she was the most beautiful girl I knew, and complained I had gone too long without seeing her. I fancied the response I wanted, the Billiken declaring I should not let this happen. I pretended he was telling me my fate was in my own hands.

I knew at this moment I would manage to see Bobbi again soon. I needed no excuse except that I missed her and I was encouraged by my confidence she missed me, too.

Bobbi's house was in easy walking distance. I went there the next afternoon, and found her working among the flowers in a large bed alongside the driveway. She was cutting marigolds, seeking out those with the longest stems and putting them in a vase of water sitting on the ground beside her. She didn't hear me coming.

I slipped up behind her and put my hands over her eyes.

"Guess who?" I said.

Bobbi knew my voice, of course. She turned as she stood. She started to speak, then threw her arms around me and pulled me close without saying anything. We stood this way for some time. I never had felt her body against mine before, and I knew I would be content to stand like this forever.

"Why did you wait so long?" she said softly. "I've missed seeing you."

"Me, too. I don't know, I thought you might be busy or something."

Neither of us had done anything important to tell about. It didn't matter. I told her the flowers were pretty. She placed one in a button hole on my shirt. She asked if I was tired from the walk. I told her it was not far. She took my hand and led me around the house to a bench in the shade of a large silver maple tree. We sat, holding hands, making idle conversation until her mother called from the back door to let Bobbi know she was home from work.

This was my cue to leave. I had been there at least two hours but the time had flown by and it might have been almost no time at all. I squeezed Bobbi's hand and stood, and without looking back I walked around the house and down the driveway to the county blacktop road. The walk I'd thought was surprisingly short when I came seemed terribly long before I got home to the old Prather house on the bluff.

7

Samuel Louis Prather was without doubt a very smart little boy. Lacy and I knew it, but didn't pay much attention. Father scolded us for this, and said someday Sammy would make us all proud. I think he may have been disappointed in Lacy and me. Neither of us ever had impressed him with our brilliant intellect.

Looking back on those early years, I think it was pretty simply a case of Father knowing Sammy better. Lacy and I never put ourselves out to spend time with Father, or even with Mama. Sammy almost always was in the house whenever Father was there. And Sammy's interests were more like Father's. Even before he turned five years old he began asking questions that made Father realize this. The immediate effect was that Father often asked him questions in turn and this no doubt encouraged our little brother.

From the youngest times I remember, Sammy was fascinated by things Lacy and I didn't care about. Anything mechanical or related to how things were built. While we merely looked on the flooded river with awe and accepted it as nature at work, Sammy thought about ways flooding might be controlled. When he first saw locks and dams on the Ohio, he actually jumped up and down in his excitement.

"I thought stuff like this could be done," he said, his voice high-pitched almost to a squeal. "They could do this on our river, too."

"Our river" meant Singleton's Branch, of course. Until the Ohio it was the only river he'd ever seen.

One night when Lacy and I were late for supper, Father demanded an accounting of our day's activities. We didn't have much to tell. Playing along the river bank, looking for wild strawberries, trying to mimic the noisy crows on the other side that had been having some kind of squabble for much of the afternoon. We may have added the strawberries to pad out our thin list.

"What did you learn today?"

We had no answer.

"It's a wasted day you don't learn something," Father declared. "Sammy learned to use a compass."

Sammy offered a proud smirk.

"Father showed me," he said.

Father went on to tell us how Albert Einstein received a compass for his birthday when he turned five and quickly recognized it reacted to some force he could not see, feel, or sense. And yet he had to be surrounded by it. He went from room to room and the instrument reacted to this force the same way wherever he took it.

"This is how Einstein recognized the magnetic force," Father said. "And a lot of his later theories grew out of this experience. If he hadn't been an inquisitive child he never would have become the famous physicist he did and you never would have heard of him."

I suppose if our interests had been broader or if we'd been more open to new ones, we might have appreciated the knowledge Father gained from his reading. This is easy to see now, but we didn't see it then.

We found out later in life that Father wanted to go to college and study to be an engineer, but tight-fisted old Grandfather

Prather gave him no support. The old man thought college was a waste of time. He, himself, had never gone, and he felt he had done quite well. Entirely missing from his equation was the fact his wealth was inherited and he went through it all so there was little left for Father except the old Prather house on the bluff.

I think it was his disappointment at not getting to go to college that led Father to marry young, seeing marriage and a family as his best route to independence. Maybe I understand this now because I took a similar path. The big difference is I had no desire to go beyond high school and no notion what I wanted to do with my life. There's nothing commendable in this, but I never felt bad about not reaching a goal I didn't have.

Sammy was more outgoing than either Lacy or I. From the time he started first grade he always was popular in school. He especially liked the little girls and the little girls liked him. He told us he had a girlfriend, and not long after that told us he had a new girlfriend, and soon enough there was yet another.

Lacy said he was fickle—a word she had learned only recently—and she considered this a terrible thing.

"You've got to learn what loyalty means," she told Sammy. "You can't be a good person if you're not loyal."

He had no idea what she was talking about. I tried to persuade her he was too immature to understand, and pointed out he had not made a commitment to any one of the girls.

"He's only now getting to know girls," I said. "Maybe it's good he has found so many he likes."

Lacy stood her ground. "If he keeps it up he won't have many friends when he gets older," she insisted. Seeing I was not going to carry the debate any farther, she hit me with one of her favorites: "Don't treat me like I was dumb. I'm so smart I can tie my shoes in the dark."

I'd heard this many times. Lacy often said it to someone she thought looked down on her, and then secretly enjoyed their inevitable uncertainty as to how they should respond. While they wondered whether she realized this proved her to be slow, she explained, she laughed all the way home about having bested them with her clever mental game.

Sammy, meanwhile, had turned his back on us and went on to other things. I believe he may have sensed Father didn't have much respect for our views on things so why should he?

It was not only girls that were gaining Sammy's attention. Now that he was out of Mama's kitchen, he began to notice airplanes. One of the Paducah airport flight paths brought much of the air traffic to and from the east directly over our heads. Sammy was fascinated by the planes and told Mama matter-of-factly he would be a pilot someday. She told him that was good.

"And you'll be the first one to ride in my plane," he said.

Mama seemed just to laugh him off, but I knew Sammy was serious. And determined. I was beginning to pay more attention to the little guy. To this day I remember clearly the look in his eyes that day in Mama's kitchen, the anguish he felt when she didn't respond to his earnest appeal. He was making her a special promise and expected her to share his excitement.

I think Sammy was about ten years old when we made a family jaunt up into the rolling hills of the Illinois Ozarks to visit the Garden of the Gods wilderness area in the Shawnee National Forest. Father often had promised we would go there one day, but it is not far from Golconda and visits to Grandpa and Grandma Childs was as near as we ever got. Lacy had heard about it from friends in school and wanted to see it, but told Victor she had given up ever getting there.

"Father says we will," she said, "but it's a big deal to him even to get up to see Grandma and Grandpa. He acts like he's taken us on a grand trip or something and it's like he can't believe we could expect anything more."

Victor took pride in helping Lacy get what she wanted. Although I could barely get Father's attention, Victor had a knack for pulling his string and making things happen. He asked Lacy to give him a day or so to come up with an idea and then, "Just watch me." He was good to his word. He'd studied up on the region and asked Father if it was true there was an "almost" volcano in southern Illinois, not far from us.

Father responded exactly as Victor expected. He went into a long discourse on ancient geology, which none of us understood. Millions of years ago, he explained, there was a massive underground implosion that left a shallow crater on the earth's surface now called Hicks Dome. He said it is ten miles wide and visible from the air and, yes, it was pretty close—except on the other side of the Ohio River.

Sammy was listening intently to Father's recitation. I could see he was bursting with questions.

"Is that how come there's fluorspar mines up there?" he asked.

"I'm not sure there are any there anymore," Father told him. "But, yes, there used to be. And I suppose that's why. But how did you know about fluorspar mines?"

Sammy hesitated. "I don't remember," he said. "I guess I just read about it somewhere. And I read there's an old silver mine, too, but nobody knows where it is."

"Well, you and me like our reading. That's how we learn most of the things we know."

Sammy agreed. He enjoyed nothing more than having Father put the two of them in the same boat.

Victor's plan worked perfectly. Before we knew it, he was able to slip the Garden of the Gods into the conversation and Father declared with some enthusiasm we must go there one day soon. Victor offered a sly smile to Lacy, who was grinning from ear to ear. I was impressed by his cleverness.

We made the trip two weeks later. There were a number of vehicles in the parking lot at the recreation area visitors' site maintained by the U.S. Forest Service. Lacy, Victor, and I scrambled out of the back of the old Dodge while Sammy climbed over Mama, who already had the door open. We couldn't wait to see what spectacular natural wonders lay before us.

"Yeah, just what I expected," Father announced, once we all were out and standing beside the truck. "Going to be crowded."

"But I don't see hardly any people," Sammy said.

The area was far from crowded. There were trails in all directions, granting easy access to the monumental sandstone rock formations and high cliffs with stunning overlooks. Wherever all the other people were, they were widely scattered. Father ignored Sammy's remark and started walking toward one of the trails.

Mama had been here before, but it had been years ago.

"I'd forgot how beautiful this place is," she said to Father. "Why don't we come more? It's not that far."

"Well, we're here now," he answered.

I was irritated by his sarcastic tone. The rest of us were excited to be here, so why couldn't he relax and enjoy himself? Mama didn't seem to notice.

Sammy was virtually entranced. How could such a place have come about? He read every mounted sign or plaque with descriptive information and a couple of times went back and read one again. He urged me to read them, too, and I was somewhat awed to learn the cliffs and rock formations were formed over millions of years on land once covered by vast oceans.

Lacy was taken in by the miles of natural beauty. The high cliffs offered striking views of the vast tract of old growth hardwood forest surrounding us, and she and Victor surely visited every lookout point there was. Mama had a hard time walking some of the rugged up-and-down trails and finally said she wanted just to sit on a bench in the shade and rest. There were a number of benches along the trails that offered comfortable resting places with open views of the valleys below.

I knew Father was tired, too, but wouldn't admit it. He would sit with Mama, though, and I couldn't help but think she would suffer through some long and boring explanations of things she actually didn't care to know.

But for Sammy, the outing made an impression that affected the direction of his life. He apparently talked about it endlessly at school and one of his teachers, Gerald Fenton, encouraged his interest. Sammy wanted material not available in the school library and Mr. Fenton suggested he contact the Kentucky State Library in Frankfort. Sammy may have had as many as a dozen books delivered by mail and received each one like a boy dying of thirst getting a jug of cool water.

I'm nowhere near knowledgeable enough in geology to do justice to what I know Sammy learned. He wanted to talk about things from the books to Lacy, Victor, and me and I'm ashamed to say, we seldom gave him any time. I remember he said the underground volcano that created Hicks Dome pushed up rocks from four thousand feel below, but mostly he talked about geologic periods like the Jurassic and Devonian and, his favorite, the Cambrian. All I understood was that these lasted for millions of years.

Sammy's captivation with the Illinois Garden of the Gods led him not only to a new interest, geology, but also to a new vision of his own future. What he saw there told him the earth had existed for many millions of years, while parallel accounts of human history in the area went back only a few centuries. He was intrigued by this paradox.

"So there could have been people here a million years ago," he reasoned. "And maybe in other places, too. That means there could be intelligent life somewhere that is a million years ahead of us."

He said if this is true, he hoped we will make contact during his lifetime. Given his fascination with flight, he slid easily into an intense interest in all things related to space travel. Expecting to be a pilot someday was no longer enough; he wanted to go into space.

The outing seemed to bring Lacy and Victor even closer. In the weeks that followed, they managed to get away by themselves anytime they could. We might be playing in the cool and clear water of Singleton's Branch in the shoal below the bluff, and all at once the two of them would go walking off and I might not see them again until hours later.

    I came to accept this as normal. I would have liked to have company, but I knew Sammy wasn't likely to join me and there was no one else. I whiled away my time alone, reasonably content with the hand I'd been dealt. It never occurred to me I should be worried about Lacy.

8

Lacy had just turned 15 when I first noticed the swelling of her breasts. I didn't realize what it meant at first, but after a week or so I recognized it for what it was. This was not merely a sign of puberty. It was an unmistakable marker of pregnancy. I lay awake all night hoping for some magic inspiration, some sudden awareness that could help me know what to do. There was none.

Fatherhood was never a question. She and Victor had been too close for there to be any doubt. And I realized almost at once that we should have seen this coming.

How could I have ignored all the times the two of them left me at the shoal and went off on their own? And there were those afternoon walks home from school, when Victor and Lacy often broke away from the rest of us and went their own direction, showing up at home long after Sammy and I got there. I had been blind to the danger, probably because I still saw Lacy as an innocent child.

It was not my overwhelming concern for Lacy's welfare that kept me awake. It was my fear of how Father would react. How much time did we have before he noticed what I had, saw the obvious changes in Lacy's body? How far along was she? Should I tell, or simply let things be? Did I even have the courage to face her and Victor and let them know I knew? Or, how likely was it they, themselves, didn't yet know?

There hadn't been much religion in my upbringing, but I prayed to God for help. Would He not be merciful and make things well? What I needed was far beyond my power to accomplish but I doubted there was a deity who would come to my aid.

Lacy, it turned out, was way ahead of me. She had known for a couple of weeks but was uncertain whether she should tell. I think she was relieved when I confronted her with the question.

"Yes! I'm going to have a baby!" she told me, clearly indicating excitement but without a hint of whether she considered this positive or negative news.

"Does Father know?"

"Of course not. He never pays any attention to me."

"It's Victor's, isn't it." I said this as a statement of fact, not a question. "Does he know?"

"We haven't talked about it."

At the moment, I felt so helpless it was like I was paralyzed, unable to think or act, knowing this was the start of the most trying struggle I could imagine and having no clue what to do. I wanted Lacy not to be hurt. I wanted to hide the truth from Father, though I knew this was impossible. Her condition could not be concealed for long. How would Mama react? But I had to consider Lacy first.

"You have to see a doctor," I said.

"I don't think I've ever been to a doctor before."

"You have. When you were little."

"Do you think Father will be mad?"

"Yes, I'm afraid so."

Less than 24 hours later, as we sat at the breakfast table in Mama's kitchen, our secret was discovered. Mama fixed her gaze on Lacy and asked her to stand. Then she came over and examined her more closely, her eyes scanning every portion of Lacy's young body. We could tell she knew, but had to wait for her to speak.

"About the last thing I expected was for you to make me a grandmamma, child," Mama said, showing no particular emotion.

"You can't be very far along, but we gotta get you taken care of. You want to tell Father when he comes, or want me to?"

I've been wrong many times in my life, but never more wrong than when I predicted Father's anger. Even now I'm still dumbfounded by his reaction once he knew. He was not angry, even at Victor, but openly receptive and in fact proud that he was about to become a grandfather. The shame and guilt I expected him to project on Lacy never materialized.

Mama was the one upset about it, but in her usual manner kept her true feelings to herself. And Mama never failed. No matter how much she might disapprove, she would accept it and do what she could to make the best of things. This was the Mama we loved and leaned on, the only Mama we knew.

She took Lacy to see Dr. Dan Emmett, who had been our family doctor forever. Not that we did much doctoring. You didn't go to the doctor unless you were sick and there was not a lot of sickness among the Prathers. Dr. Emmett recognized immediately that the pregnancy was farther along than we had assumed. Lacy would be a mother in no more than five months.

Mama went to work. Lacy had to have maternity clothes and there had to be things for the baby. The following Sunday Father drove her into town and she shopped for three hours, mostly at Dunlevy's Department Store but also at the Baby Nook and a resale shop known for having a large stock of good used baby clothes. They came home with so many bags and packages that, once they got the old Dodge unloaded, it took two trips to bring them all inside.

Lacy's reaction was exactly what I expected.

She plunged into the stack of merchandise like it was fields of autumn flowers. She hurriedly opened every box and bag, tried on every bit of clothing that was hers, and laid all the baby things out on the floor in two rows, neatly arranged. She checked each item as she went, making sure what it was and expressing her gratitude multiple times over. Her excitement was wonderful to see.

As I look back on all this now, it seems strange that Victor and I did not talk more about what was going on. I didn't know until months later his father was outraged by what he'd done, threatened to beat him, and made clear that Victor, Lacy, and the baby would get no support from the Kentons. It was almost like they disowned him or thought he had disgraced the family name.

Victor never had talked much about his family and I hadn't known what to expect from them. I felt sorry for him. He needed family support, too, and he would have it. It would not come from his family, but from ours, especially from Father.

Victor expressed his undying love for Lacy and the baby and vowed to be the best father a man could be. He wished he and Lacy were old enough to get married. Father said he thought this might be possible and set out to make it so. He went to the barber shop to see Harvey Bowman, and as he expected Harvey knew exactly what to do.

Harvey told Father Kentucky law allowed for a marriage license to be issued, even at Lacy's tender age, if she was pregnant and a district court judge would order it. He knew a judge who always was sympathetic. Two days later Victor and Lacy had a license in hand. Harvey performed the ceremony, taking a break from cutting hair and shaving chins. Both his last customer and the next one in line stood by and looked on almost reverently, as if honored to have been invited.

The old Prather house, with six bedrooms, had plenty of space for adding Victor and the baby as new residents. Father and Mama began to redecorate Lacy's room as a nursery and the newlyweds moved into one of the larger upstairs bedrooms that had two bay windows looking out over the bluff and Singleton's Branch. Our family was larger, and we readily accepted the fact life had become more complicated. We could not foresee what those complications might be, though, and were yet to learn just how much our lives might change.

Father's usual conservative response to anything that called for spending money evaporated when it came to the new nursery. Whatever Mama or Lacy suggested, he was happy to go along with. New curtains? Of course. Carpeting? Yes, and be sure to get good quality. New paint? Sure. The baby's room must be the brightest room in the house.

As Lacy watched the progression of changes, she was even more surprised by Father's new attitude than I was. She asked if I'd been watching.

"He always says 'no' to everything," she whispered to me. "Now it's like we could ask for an elevator or something and he'd be good with it. Maybe even gold plate on the window sills."

She laughed about her own creative exaggeration.

"Yeah, I guess thinking about being a grandfather makes him feel good," I told her, hoping to sound as if I found it nothing unusual. This was needless effort, of course. She knew better.

Father barely got the nursery finished in time. The baby came two weeks or so early. A tiny girl. The delivery was easy on Lacy, which brought tears to Mama's eyes after her weeks of worry. She went from wringing her hands as Lacy went into labor to clapping when the baby was delivered.

Victor seemed numb to the news. He didn't show up at the hospital until three hours after he'd been told Lacy was in labor, but then he kissed her passionately and clung to her in the delivery room until deciding he surely must be in the way. He paced the hallway nervously until he was invited to come see his new daughter. I think he wanted to show his pride in being a new father but wasn't sure what was expected of him. He'd never seen how a new father behaved.

They said everything went well, and on Sunday mother and baby came home. Father looked to be as excited as if he were driving the Queen of England in the old Dodge. Victor made sure the special passengers were safely stowed between Father and Mama, then joined me in the back of the truck. All he said during the ride was, "Boy, oh boy. Ain't she something!"

I agreed.

For me, the biggest change brought by the new baby was in my relationship with Lacy. With Victor at hand and the baby to care for, she no longer had much time for me. I wanted to talk to her about going back to school but she wasn't interested. She had forgotten the tower, and maybe the Billiken. Even the shoal—our special place in Singleton's Branch, the river that had been the center of our lives—held no attraction. She was a mother now, was married to the man she loved, and this was all she cared about.

It worried me that this seemed to leave her with nothing to look forward to, but she said this didn't matter. Her life was complete.

They named the baby Violet. This was Lacy's choice, and Victor said whatever she wanted was good with him. I couldn't tell if he genuinely wanted Lacy's preference to prevail or just really didn't care. He was content to leave everything related to the baby in the hands of Lacy and Mama. He never told his parents about the birth and said it didn't matter whether they knew because they had no interest in their new granddaughter, anyway. But he did tell his brother.

I loved little Violet from the first time I saw her. Even in this tiny little girl I could see something of Lacy. I guessed that as she got older she would be a virtual copy of her mother. The resemblance grew even stronger as her eye color steadied and her hair began to grow. I could picture us having to distinguish between "big Lacy" and "little Lacy" someday.

Bobbi was fascinated by the baby, loved holding her, and would have been happy to spend hours with her every day. I almost had to drag her out of the nursery or Lacy's and Victor's room, wherever little Violet was, to get time with her. One day I got even more irritated than usual about Bobbi's behavior and went and sat by myself among the ferns at the top of the bluff and took comfort in the closeness of the river below.

I could always count on Singleton's Branch.

Bobbi eventually came looking for me. She was not happy with my behavior, and said my pouting was "not becoming." Nonetheless, she was more careful after that not to let the baby take so much of her time.

I'm not sure I can accurately say I was possessive of Bobbi. It was more a feeling of being alone without her presence. I wanted to be as close with her as Lacy was with Victor and the baby. And I had no one else. Lacy was no longer my companion and Sammy walked a different path. Bobbi was my center of attention.

Since the afternoon I walked to her house and until little Violet was born, we had managed to spend some part of almost every day together. I would be at her house one day and she would be at our house the next. The two of us had settled into a comfort zone probably unusual at our age, almost taking each other's presence for granted. We were passionate without physical demonstrations of our passion. To say we were compatible would be an understatement. We were like two peas in a pod.

We were in love, but we didn't make a big deal of it.

9

Their new parenthood meant the end of school for both Lacy and Victor. She had no interest in going back and Victor, feeling he had a family to support, said he needed a full-time paying job. He went to work at a large Erinville printing and publishing company with the unambiguous business name, The Print Shop.

He complained to Father that his salary was almost too low to make the job worthwhile. Father told him he was lucky to find work so quickly, and if he concentrated on learning his job and doing it well pay raises were sure to come. Victor considered this encouragement. This was something he had not had a great deal of before and I think it gave him a much more positive attitude about his job.

Victor's brother told him he needed transportation, both to get to and from work and to have available when he needed to take Lacy and the baby somewhere. Victor came home the next day in a five-year-old, mechanically sound black Ford Taurus. His brother had selected it for him and arranged easy financing and his father had let him drive it off the lot even before all the paperwork was finished. I couldn't tell if Victor realized his father had backed off a bit on his rancor.

The big Ford looked luxurious to me. I had dreamed for years about having my own car some day, and thought this would be the greatest excitement of my life. Victor showed no particular pride in it and didn't seem to consider it anything out of the ordinary. It was functional and that's all that mattered.

Although the daily routine in the old Prather house didn't change much, I paid a small price for the new family environment. My room was next to Lacy's and Victor's and hardly a night passed that I didn't lie awake and listen to them make love next door. I decided they were sex fiends or something. They kept me aroused and frustrated, but I had fun recalling the discussions Lacy and I had had about Father and Mama in bed together. We could not see them having sex. Mama was too modest and we weren't sure Father considered it proper.

Mama helped Lacy take care of baby Violet and Lacy helped Mama in the kitchen. The newlyweds kept on eating their meals with us. Lacy said she felt guilty not helping with groceries, but Father waved off her concern.

"You live under my roof, you eat my food," he declared.

Victor, though, was more independent. He came and went freely. Most times he didn't tell anyone where he was going or when he would be back, not even Lacy. Lacy trusted him to make his own decisions. She told Mama her husband was a grown-up man and father and didn't need a wife who tried to tell him what to do.

Father was less sanguine about all this. It irritated him when he heard Victor's Ford come and go at night, and particularly when Victor came in late and interrupted his reading or, even worse, woke him from his sleep. I know he complained to Mama but I don't think he said anything to Victor or Lacy in the beginning.

This changed dramatically one night when the car he heard in the driveway turned out not to be Victor's. It was Landon Cloyd, the county sheriff.

Sheriff Cloyd and Father had been friends for many years, going back to well before Cloyd was elected. Father had worked diligently to get out the vote in his campaign and sometimes referred back to that experience as if it made him an expert at politics. It was the only time he ever got involved in any election, as far as I know, but to hear him tell it he might have been responsible for electing Abraham Lincoln.

Had it not been for this personal friendship, Victor would have been in serious trouble. He had been in a minor accident, the sheriff said, and it was clear he had been drinking. Fortunately, no one was hurt. The sheriff said he would not file charges because of Victor's relationship to Father, but wanted Father to know.

"And here's the big thing, Graden," Sheriff Cloyd said. "As you know, Victor is underage to be drinking. I don't know where he got the alcohol, but I intend to find out. That means I'll likely be talking to him again. If it gets out, well, there's only so much I can do to protect him."

The incident seriously strained things between Father and Victor. I think Father tended to look upon Victor almost like a son—he lived there in the old Prather house, after all—and felt free or perhaps even obligated to make demands on his behavior. And of course Victor resented this.

Lacy said little Violet was her best protection. Father would back off if he thought he might provoke Victor to the point she and Victor and the baby might move out. I doubted he worried about this very much, but didn't say so to Lacy. Father knew Victor didn't earn enough for them to live on.

For me, it was depressing to realize the old summer days playing in the shoal below the bluff were gone forever. My life had changed dramatically in the few months since Violet had come along. I looked forward to the start of school. And it was more than seeing Bobbi every day; school would bring some structure to my days.

Once school began, we missed Lacy on our walks home from Hemingway Terrace but Sammy filled the sibling role she had abandoned. He was eager to tell what he had learned every day and quickly included Bobbi as audience for his reports. Our conversations usually commenced with his standard opening line: "Did you know that ...?"

Bobbi often did know. I usually did not. She remembered what she had learned in school on whatever the subject was but most of the time I didn't. Sammy soon wrote me off as a starting point and began his conversations directly with her. She asked if this bothered me. It didn't, and I told her it actually was something of a relief. Sometimes I was embarrassed by what I didn't know.

I was paying more attention to Sammy. It made me proud to have a brother who was so smart. I could see he was happy just to *know* things, regardless of whether they were things in which he was especially interested or expected to study further. I've no doubt we all are exposed to bits of trivia in our normal activities, but unlike Sammy, we tend to forget them almost immediately. They seemed to stick with him so that he became a virtual walking encyclopedia.

We had barely left the schoolyard on the fourth day of school when Sammy ran up behind us and demanded, "Did you know that George the Third was only 22 years old when they made him the king of England?"

Bobbi said she didn't know. He didn't wait for me to say I didn't know, either.

"Well, he was. And he was king for 59 years and then he went crazy or something."

It turned out he already was well into the subject matter of his Early American History class and had read the first five chapters of the text book.

Sammy seemed to think he was entertaining Bobbi and me with his recitations, and to some extent he was. But we didn't need or want to be entertained. We wanted to hold hands and walk slowly and talk to each other. It didn't matter what we talked about. Sammy never caught on, but eventually decided we were boring and started to walk with others.

Bobbi often asked about Violet. She missed her, and said it seemed ages since she'd last seen her little sweetheart.

"Well, she's still just a baby," I said. "I don't think she's changed much. I don't see her every day, myself. Most of the time when I'm home she is asleep up in the nursery or in Lacy's room."

"She'll grow up fast, though. I have a little cousin who is three years old. Those three years went very fast."

I said yes, and people said as we got older time goes even faster. Before we knew it, Violet would be following in our footsteps, walking this very road on her way home from Hemingway Terrace.

"Unless your mama gets her wish and gets to move to town, away from the river."

I was surprised. I had heard Mama say she wanted to move, but I didn't think she would have told anyone else. It was a firm rule with Mama never to complain about anything in life to anyone who wasn't family.

"Did she tell you that?" I asked Bobbi.

"Yes. Three or four times."

I said it was because of the flood, and there wouldn't be another one for years. Bobbi shook her head.

"No, it's not just the flood," she said. "Your mama's afraid somebody is going to drown. She says it's a miracle it hasn't happened before now, with the Prather family living on the bluff and kids playing in the water ever since your father was a little boy."

I didn't know how Mama could be afraid of the river, except for the flood. She had waded in the shoal where we played and said the water was so shallow somebody would have to hold your face down in it before you could drown. But I trusted Bobbi's word.

Bobbi had no desire to carry this discussion any further. I didn't think any more about what she had told me. Probably, in the back of my mind, I persisted in thinking Mama's only discomfort from living on Singleton's Branch related to the flood.

Sammy apparently found other students even less receptive to his discussions than we were. He was back in a few days, running up behind us and blurting out a typical opening question even before we knew he was there.

"Bobbi," he said, "did you know they had airplanes in the First World War?"

We both told him this was news to us—even though we knew—and he went into a long discourse on how fast flying developed after the Wright Brothers invented the first airplane and look where we were now, with craft that had taken men to the moon and could fly into deep space. If I ever had doubted his devotion to flying, I could see now it was not going away.

It was only a few years later that Sammy had a high school teacher who owned his own plane, and frequently took him flying. He let Sammy take control from time to time and said he had the makings of a good pilot. Sammy thought he already was one.

About the third week of school I began stopping at Bobbi's house on our walks home. There was no problem in letting Sammy go on without me. He didn't have that far to go and there were other students walking with him. I knew Father might be angry when he found out but, well—it was Bobbi. I would do whatever I could to get more time with her.

"I don't want you to get in trouble at home because of me," Bobbi said.

I assured her I wouldn't.

"You think your father's okay with you leaving Sammy to walk without you?"

"Sure. Sammy's old enough. Besides, Father thinks Sammy is a lot smarter than I am. Knows he won't get lost or anything like that. Probably thinks I'd be more likely to have a problem than Sammy would."

Bobbi laughed. And to hear her laugh was enough reward for me to risk being in trouble at home. There was more than just the pleasure I found in her company. She raised my spirits at a time I couldn't see that I had a lot going for me. School was a drag, and all I wanted was to get through this final year and graduate. I had no interest in college. Mama said that was just as well; with my grades I'd have a hard time getting in, anyway.

The single thing in my life that mattered now was Bobbi Hoard. I had come to take it as a given we would be married one day and spend the rest of our lives together. My life would be incomplete without her. We hadn't talked about it then, but now I know she felt the same way.

Sometimes I thought about the advice Grandpa Childs had given, that I get around more, see more of the world before I settled down. It seemed like meeting girls was a good part of that. Yes, his had been good advice. I had followed it, in a way. And I had met the girl that mattered. I didn't need to meet any others.

"Oh, my mother said I should ask you to come to dinner Sunday," Bobbi said, sounding as if she'd just remembered. "I'd like that. Will you?"

"Sure. Do I need to get dressed up or anything?"

Bobbi laughed again. "No," she said, "just dress like you do every day for school. My parents want to get to know you better."

"Sometimes I wear dirty jeans to school."

"No problem. You can wear dirty jeans to my house."

"And I guess you expect me to wear shoes?"

She probably knew I was trying to make light of the situation because I was nervous. Being Bobbi, she played along and let me drag on with my silly questions as long as I wanted. Or as long as I needed.

My day, my future, my life had just brightened. I wanted to run and jump and dance like a small child, throwing off the inhibitions of self-consciousness and fear of ridicule. And I did, in a limited way. I grasped Bobbi's hands and we swirled like a merry-go-round, circling from one side of the road to the other but still moving forward.

Looking back on that day now, I still can feel the thrill of knowing my connection with Bobbi was unbreakable. It was by any measure one of the best days of my life. If only all the rest of our days could have been as happy as that one!

10

I suppose it was inevitable that the visit from Sheriff Landon Cloyd led to continuing tension between Victor and Father. After the sheriff left that night, Father stayed up and waited for Victor all night long, determined to confront him as soon as he showed up.

Victor's car was slightly damaged in the accident, just enough that he couldn't drive it until it had been repaired. He had to call his brother to pick him up and drive him to the Prather house and didn't get there until nearly four o'clock in the morning. Father met him at the front door.

Lacy told me later the two men had a terrible quarrel. She said Victor was furious when he got to their room.

"He told me to pack up and get ready to move out," she said. "He said there was no way he would live under the same roof with that man—meaning Father."

I told her not to be in any rush. They couldn't move until they had someplace to move to and she'd be the first to know if Victor got one. Even if he was out looking right now it wasn't going to happen overnight. Lacy was somewhat relieved, but I knew she still was going to worry Victor might stick to his guns.

Even Victor had to acknowledge the emptiness of his threat in the end. He and Lacy might sleep in the car but the baby had to have a safe and comfortable place to live. In his initial rage, though, Victor had gone on to say he never wanted a baby to begin with and blamed Lacy for not knowing how to avoid getting pregnant.

"He said he was sorry after a bit, and said he didn't mean those things," she told me. "But he did. I don't even know if he loves the baby. I know he doesn't really love me."

All I could do was pretend I knew better. I told her Victor had said to me many times that he loved her, and I thought he was the happiest man I'd ever seen when he found out about the baby. I was lying. Lacy knew me too well to be taken in.

"Who do you think you're talking to?" she demanded. "If I can't get the truth from you, what am I supposed to do?"

I couldn't admit I'd lied, stealing from her the last bit of hope she might cling to. I insisted what I had said was true. I reminded her how the three of us played in the shoal and how Victor's attention always was on her. I asked couldn't she see that even Oscar was jealous of the way they stuck together? I told her Victor had sacrificed his place with his own family for her.

"Come on, Lacy," I begged. "You know we all say things we don't mean when we're mad. A big blowout with Father is enough to leave anybody half-crazy. Victor hadn't—"

"You don't have to say any more. He's stuck with us, whether he likes it or not."

With that she turned and walked away, in Lacy Prather style.

Victor didn't come to meals for the next few days. Mama encouraged him to slip into the kitchen whenever he could and always had something ready for him. But given his work schedule and his determination not to run into Father, this was not an easy way out. He had bought lunch in town ever since he started his job at The Print Shop and I'd guess he started buying supper, too. This also meant less time with Lacy and little Violet.

Sheriff Cloyd came by again a few nights later to let Father know he'd found the source of Victor's alcohol. It was less threatening than he'd feared. Victor's brother had given him half a bottle of vodka. He told the sheriff that with Victor having a family and making it on his own, it seemed like he was an adult and he didn't even think about his age when he gave him the bottle.

"He promised to be more careful," the sheriff said. "He doesn't want to get in any trouble and I don't think he wants any trouble for Victor, so I expect he will."

Father had vowed that if Victor ever came home drunk he would throw him out, Lacy and the baby or not. This seemed extreme to me. I'd never seen Father drunk, but he often had a beer or two at night while he was reading. He may have feared an intoxicated Victor could harm Lacy or Violet. But it didn't matter; when Father warned us of something we didn't ask questions.

I didn't hear the new parents making love in their room next to mine any more. More important, I didn't hear any quarrels. Whatever went on there was very quiet. The only exception was an occasional outburst of crying by baby Violet.

I was used to hearing Lacy comfort the baby and try to stop the crying, but now it was Victor. He ended up carrying her up and down the hall, trying to sooth her with his low voice and rocking her gently in his arms. Violet was not impressed. After ten minutes of this she still was wailing at the top of her lungs and Victor was ready to give up.

Lacy joined the two of them in the hall. I often slept with my door open because of poor air circulation in the old house. This was one of those nights. I could hear everything that went on in the hallway.

"I'm tired of this," Lacy said. "It's like she sleeps all day and cries all night. You can't stay up with her. You have to go to work in the morning."

"Babies cry," Victor said. "She'll get over this soon. And don't worry about me. I get plenty of sleep."

It struck me that it was Victor who demonstrated patience and caring instead of Lacy. After what she had told me, this was surprising. Was it possible my response to her was not a lie, after all? I still had strong doubts, but concentrating on this let me drift off to sleep so I didn't hear anything more from the hallway or the next room.

There was nothing unusual for the rest of the week, except a big change in the weather. Highlights of my days were lunch hour and the walk home from school. Bobbi and I didn't have a class together that semester, but we met in the cafeteria at noon and treasured our time together at the end of the school day. Sammy looked to have discovered yet another new girlfriend. He walked ahead of or behind us with a pretty little blonde girl. We could tell he wanted to keep enough distance there was no chance we might overhear anything they said.

As to the weather, Mama once said there'd never been a September in her whole life that didn't end up scorching hot at the end, soon after school started. Her words certainly held up this year.

On Saturday morning, I slept late and Mama was cross with me when I went to breakfast. She said everyone else already was down at the shoal trying to keep cool.

"Everybody? You mean even Sammy?"

Mama laughed, which I was happy to hear. She had got over being irritated with me.

"It's little Violet," she said. "He's so taken with that baby he wants to be wherever she is."

"They took the baby down to get in the water?"

"Yes. Lacy's had her down there almost every day this week. Victor finally got a Saturday off, and he couldn't wait to get down there with them and watch the baby play in the water. Don't worry. She's big enough now."

It seemed a long time since I'd been to the shoal. Like Victor, I couldn't wait. I hurried through breakfast and ran up to my room and got into a swimsuit, ran to the bluff and scrambled down the path to the river. Oscar heard me coming and ran to meet me, wagging his tail and jumping up and down in greeting.

Lacy sat on a rock at the water's edge, holding Violet on her lap. Sammy was nearby. Victor was swimming in the deeper water toward the middle of the river and popped to the surface just as I got to Lacy. He saw me and waved, and began swimming toward us. A few strokes brought him to the shallow water of the shoal.

"You can come here and take the baby now," Lacy called to him. "I want to get out there some."

Victor splashed his way to her, lifted Violet from her lap, and took a seat on another rock at the water's edge. Lacy jumped up and ran toward the deeper water. As soon as she got close to the edge of the shoal she dove in and quickly disappeared beneath the rippling surface of the river.

"Hey, boy!" Victor said, turning to me. "You're late!"

"There was no schedule. How can I be late?"

I moved close and he reached over and punched me on the shoulder with a barely formed fist. Little Violet, awakened by the change in holders, looked in my direction but was not focused on me. She was alert and responding to her surroundings. Sammy noticed this and asked Victor if he could hold her and Victor handed his baby over.

"I guess you got here in time for the main event, anyway," Victor said.

"Main event? What's that?"

"You'll see, soon enough."

Violet was gurgling and smiling at Sammy, who obviously was thrilled to get this response. He looked like a boy who just had found the pot of gold at the end of a rainbow. Victor nudged me with his elbow and nodded toward Sammy. We both tried hard not to laugh. We didn't want to embarrass him and make him timid about asking to hold Violet next time.

Lacy swam up to the edge of the shoal and stood. She shook the water out of her hair and wiped her face with her fingers before walking toward us.

"Oh, oh, I think this is it," Victor whispered, nudging me again.

Lacy walked straight to Sammy. Without speaking, she reached down and took Violet from him. She walked a few steps away, then turned and faced Victor and me.

"You are witnesses," she said. She held the baby girl in front of her, dangling from her hands, and lowered her gently until her feet were in the water. "I baptize you, my daughter Violet Prather Kenton, in the name of the god of everything," she said solemnly. "I trust you to his care."

She started to lift Violet up, but hesitated.

"Your god of everything will be busy sometimes," she said, her head lowered again to face the baby. "For extra safekeeping, I place you in the hands of the Billiken, the god of things as they ought to be."

She straightened and pulled Violet against her breast, laughing happily. Victor stood and applauded and Sammy and I followed his lead. Lacy came and gave the baby back to Sammy and hugged both Victor and me tightly.

"That was sweet," Victor told her.

I said, "You did a good thing."

Lacy repaid us with her sweetest smile. We had had an almost glorious morning in the cooling shoal waters of Singleton's Branch and there still were hours left in the day. We made the best of these, too, taking advantage of the fun we had playing together like children again. When it came time to get back to the house for supper, we were so tired we almost had to drag ourselves up the bluff. Mama had the refrigerator stuffed with the lunch we hadn't even thought of.

I woke early Sunday morning. A series of bizarre dreams had made my sleep restless and caused me to wake with a foggy brain. I felt a sense of excitement and recalled the ceremony in the shoal yesterday, but knew there was something more. Yes, it was eager anticipation. I would see Bobbi today.

Mama asked a lot of questions while I was eating breakfast. She wanted to know how things were going at school, whether I saw Sammy during the day, if Bobbi and I were still spending time together, whether the school cafeteria food was good, and if I thought Lacy and Victor were getting along well. I knew something bothered her.

"I just worry so about that baby," she said, after I'd told her I thought Lacy and Victor were doing just fine. "What would become of her if her mama and daddy split up?"

"You don't have to worry about that, Mama. You should have seen them yesterday in the river. They still play together like kids."

Whether or not I had eased her concern, she changed the subject. Father would be driving her to the grocery store in the afternoon. She was making up next week's menus in her head. Was there anything in particular I'd like? She was always open to suggestion but nobody ever said anything.

"Unless I make something someone doesn't like," she added. "Then I hear plenty of complaints."

I told her I liked everything she fixed. I was happy to let her decide what that would be. I said she was good at saving money by leaving space on her lists for things the store might have on sale, and she had world-class talent for picking things to serve with these.

"You'd make a marvelous manager for some big restaurant, Mama, but I won't tell anyone because I don't want to lose you as the Prather chef."

She gave me a big smile and was about to reply, but Sammy walked in and she turned her attention to him. We'd all promised at one time or another to come to breakfast at the same time, if she told us what time she wanted to have it ready. She said that wasn't necessary; she was happy to feed us at any time. I didn't understand this then, but believe now she enjoyed having us there individually.

Dinner—we called it supper—was at a set time and it often felt like we were an impersonal crowd of hungry people who had come to eat but had no interest in conversation. Mama liked to know what was going on in her family and we tended not to tell unless she asked.

I had not told her about my invitation to have dinner with Bobbi's family. Once Sammy was there I didn't want to bring it up. Sammy would ask a lot of irrelevant questions. He wasn't nosey and never tried to poke into my affairs, but he always was curious. He would ask questions I wouldn't want to answer. Or, more likely, didn't know the answers to. I finished breakfast without saying anything more.

So no one knew I was going to the Hoards for dinner, and I assumed no one cared. No one in the Prather house. Bobbi cared, and apparently her mother, who had told Bobbi to invite me. And now I was beginning to get nervous.

It was another very hot day. The old Prather house was not air conditioned, but had a huge attic fan and system of vents that created a constant breeze. It also was well shaded by trees on all sides. But it still was uncomfortable on days like this and I had no desire to sit around in the heat and deal with Sammy's questions. I went half way down the bluff and crawled into a sweet-smelling cave of honeysuckle vine and went to sleep.

Unlike the first time earlier in the day, I woke with a clear head. It still was not yet noon. I had a few more hours to kill before I got ready to go to the Hoard house.

A large shortnose gar fish was swimming upstream near the surface of the river when I got to the shoal. We seldom saw fish in Singleton's Branch. Father said there were lots of them there, but they stayed in the deep water out of sight. Gars were the exception. We knew they were harmless, despite their vicious appearance, and always hoped one would swim close to the shallow water where we could see it up close. None had, and this one wasn't going to, either.

Sighting it reminded me of when Lacy was still little and saw one for the first time. She was several feet from the bank in the shallow water of the shoal when it came swimming close. It terrified her. She screamed and tried to run back to me at the bank but fell face-down in the water.

The gar fish had disappeared by the time I got her on her feet, but she still was afraid and insisted on getting onto dry land. I think this was the first time I realized how much she trusted me. I told her the gar was harmless and couldn't bite even if it wanted to because its jaws didn't open wide enough. She stood looking me in the face with something of a sense of wonder in her eyes while I talked.

"So it's not gonna hurt me, then?" she said.

"It's not. It probably was only curious and came to check you out. After all, it's not in your territory—you are in its territory."

"So maybe it likes having company."

I agreed that it might.

The next day when we played in the shoal she waded out and stood, watching for the gar fish. She said she wanted them to be friends.

This was not so long ago, but how my world had changed. Lacy was a mother now. And I was an *uncle*. This hadn't occurred to me before, and just the thought of it made me proud. I made a conscious decision to play my uncle's role like that of the stereotypical grandmother Mama had joked about. She said she was free to enjoy her granddaughter but had no responsibility to help take care of her.

As I walked the blacktop highway toward Bobbi's house later, I still had pleasant thoughts of Lacy as a mother and me as little Violet's uncle. The Prather family ties were stronger now than they ever had been before in my lifetime.

Bobbi waited for me on the porch.

"Oh, I'm so glad to see you," she greeted me. "My mama and daddy can't wait to meet you."

"I hope they don't expect too much."

"Don't be silly. Come on in."

She held open the door and waited for me to go in first. Her house was much different from the old Prather house. Unlike my home, Bobbi's was a modest, one-story structure similar to probably half those in Erinville. It was modern by Father's definition, anything built after World War II.

Bobbi's father sat on a sofa just inside the door reading a newspaper. He stood as I came in and extended a hand. He was a big man, I guessed to be more than six feet tall and weighing more than two hundred pounds.

"Jackson Hoard," he said, with a smile I took to be genuine.

"I'm happy to meet you, sir."

"No need to be formal, lad. Call me Jack. And here's Bobbi's mother."

Bobbi had led her mother from the kitchen. They looked more alike than any mother and daughter I'd ever seen before. Her mother didn't look that much older, even. She too extended her hand and had a pleasant smile. She asked us to sit; dinner would be ready in ten minutes.

It didn't take long for me to feel at home. Jackson and Jen Hoard were down-to-earth, welcoming people. They reminded me of a younger version of Grandpa and Grandma Childs. I had expected at least a hint of animosity—I was pursuing their daughter, after all—but there was none. I got an impression of just the opposite. If I was good enough for Bobbi, I was good enough for them.

I learned pretty much all there was to know about Bobbi's parents. They originally were from Marshalltown, Iowa, where both had grown up, and had gone to school together all the way from first grade through high school. Jackson Hoard enjoyed telling their story.

"I couldn't get her to pay any attention to me until we were done with school and I had a job and got a new car," he said, clearly not intending to be taken too seriously.

Bobbi's mother shook her head. "Your memory must be failing, Jack," she teased. "That car was five years old."

They asked just enough questions to get to know me, but I didn't feel like I was being grilled. For each thing they learned about me, I may have learned two things about them. Mr. Hoard liked to talk. He spoke little of himself, but mostly about Mrs. Hoard and their three daughters. Bobbi got embarrassed a couple of times and asked him to change the subject.

I wanted him to ignore her pleas; she was the one I wanted to hear about. He was sympathetic, though. He commenced a new topic and told me how he'd struggled to start his own business in Marshalltown.

"I didn't know what I was doing," he confessed. "I knew I had a head for business, but I had no experience—no background to grow from. I might have made it anyway, but I got a good offer from this little auto parts company that was opening new stores all over the country and we packed up and moved to Philadelphia."

"You can't begin to believe the change." Bobbi's mother said. "Neither of us had ever been anywhere bigger than Des Moines. Philadelphia was scary."

But they grew accustomed to it quickly, she said, and came to love it. It was home for a good many years and the place where their three daughters were born. The company became a national chain and his success in Philadelphia ultimately led to Mr. Hoard's big opportunity with his appointment as a regional manager in Erinville.

I had sat and listened quietly, enjoying the roast beef and mashed potatoes and gravy and occasionally slipping my hand down to touch Bobbi's. Jen Hoard paused, as if waiting for me to comment.

"So here you are," I said, and immediately felt foolish. "I mean, how do you like Erinville?"

I knew I had missed the opportunity to give them credit for handling these tough moves well. I should have complimented them on their flexibility and Mr. Hoard on his business competence. As usual, my mouth was ahead of my brain. They were too generous to let it show if they noticed.

Both she and Mr. Hoard agreed Erinville was a good place to live. The people had been welcoming and friendly and the city administration supported its businesses well. And most important, they were happy with Bobbi's school. She had had good teachers at Hemingway Terrace.

The possibility that Bobbi's family might move away from Erinville had not occurred to me. Now it did, but it came with the parallel reassurance that this was very unlikely. Even though I knew now it could happen, I felt it was one thing I wouldn't have to worry about. An extremely important thing!

All the conversation slowed dinner, so that it was eight o'clock when we finished. Bobbi wanted to go for a walk. She led me to a farm road that ran behind their property, parallel to the county road in front. It passed in back of two more houses and then led into semi-wooded pastureland. She had not walked it often, but knew it as a pleasant path favored by neighbors' children for happy bicycle jaunts.

The night air still was warm.

We walked slowly toward the east, away from the houses, holding hands and breathing in the aroma of honeysuckle and sweet fennel. A thin slice of moon lit our surroundings and the way ahead. Then arms encircled waists. We stopped, turned face-to-face.

It was my first kiss, and hers. Bobbi Hoard's kisses were even sweeter in the flesh than they had been in my dreams. I wanted to hold her like this forever, body against body, passion surging as comes most powerfully in young love. If there really was a heaven I had found it.

11

Just as certain as Mama's forecast of hot weather at the end of September was the prospect of this being followed by a cold spell. We woke Monday to a frosty morning with chilly winds from the northwest, so the choice of light-weight clothing was no longer adequate. Those who insisted on coming to school coatless or even wearing summer shorts found themselves huddling behind a corner of the building and seeking the sun when they went outdoors.

Bobbi and I finished lunch in the cafeteria and left by way of the schoolhouse's main East entranceway, planning to sit on the coping of a parking lot divider and enjoy the secluded privacy. I still was buoyed by the memory of the night before. I wanted to hold her and kiss her again—would have run from the schoolyard and found a hiding place had she been willing. But I knew Bobbi was a good student who played by the rules. She no doubt would think less of me if I so much as mentioned this.

We had walked only a few yards from the doors when a gust of cold wind struck. Bobbi threw up her hands and yelled.

"No, no! Let's get back in."

I was ready to go back inside, too, but took time to tease her for being a sissy. She said she'd rather be a sissy than to be turned into a frozen statue that might not thaw out until July. I tried to pretend I wasn't cold but she knew better. Once inside we went back to the commons area next to the cafeteria and, although it was more crowded than usual, promptly found an empty table.

"Victor would say it's like there is nothing between us and the North Pole but a barbed wire fence," I said.

"Victor has an interesting way with words sometimes. By the way, how are the newlyweds doing these days?"

She cupped her hands over her cold ears and shivered. The school building was warm, but it was taking a long time for us to soak up enough heat to be comfortable. She pulled her arms tight against her sides for extra warmth as she waited for me to answer.

"I guess they're doing okay," I told her. "You know they had some rough spots, but they have the sweetest baby in the world. Lacy claims to be the happiest person on the planet and I hope she is. Victor is so moody sometimes it's hard to tell about him."

"You have to wonder about both of them. He's only 18 years old. Not many boys would want to be tied down with family responsibilities at that age. And Lacy—"

"Lacy's tougher than people know."

"But she's still just a child, herself," Bobbi said. "Don't you feel like that?"

The bell rang and we had to go to our respective classes. I wondered how Bobbi would stand the cold on the walk home when school was out later in the day. This turned out not to be an issue; one of her friends offered her a ride and she had only an instant to yell and tell me before climbing into the backseat of a rattly old Chevrolet coupe and riding away.

Without her, I welcomed Sammy's company for the walk home. He didn't disappoint, plunging immediately into a typical opening question as soon as we began to walk.

"Did you know the Aztecs had a calendar?" he asked.

"No. But I'll bet you can tell me about it."

"Sure. I guess most people don't know. They had a year the same length as ours, and they had a sophisticated system of counting cycles of fifty-two years as measures of advancement."

He went on to tell me a great deal more than I would have thought I really cared to know about the Aztecs. But he soon had me listening with interest. He was confident his information was sound, and he was able to explain some pretty complex elements of Aztec science and religion in ways I could understand. My little brother was a walking book of facts, complete with answers to my questions.

Our coats weren't heavy enough to keep us warm in face of the cold winds and we needed caps and gloves we didn't have. The only way we could compensate was to walk fast. Sammy was sure we made it to the old Prather house on the bluff in record time and scribbled this on Mama's big kitchen calendar.

One immediate result of the sudden cold weather that would have an indirect but significant effect on me was Jackson Hoard's decision to buy Bobbi a car. Real winter was yet to come, he said, and he didn't want her to have to walk home from school in the frigid temperatures of December and January. Neither he nor her mother would be able to leave work to pick her up.

The obvious solution was, in his words, to get her a "set of wheels" of her own.

Victor's father offered an eight-year-old Jeep, the open model with a removable canvas top, at what Mr. Hoard said was a reasonable price. He said he'd always wanted a Jeep and knew one would be both great fun and reliable transportation for Bobbi. His only qualification was to make sure the heater worked well. Bobbi was driving it before the end of the week.

There probably is no way I could exaggerate the miles I rode in that vehicle, even if I wanted to. Bobbi insisted on picking up Sammy and me in the morning on school days and bringing us home when school was out. And on many occasions when she drove anywhere else I was with her. We tried to be inseparable and almost were.

In what I might attribute to the law of unintended consequences, in this case a positive one, Father was impressed by Bobbi's new wheels to the extent he finally gave up the old

Dodge. He took it to Victor's father and traded it for a two-year-old Ram 1500 four-door pickup. The irony in this was the whole family could ride inside, but now we rarely would all be going anywhere together. But this one really would last the rest of his life and he managed to take pride in a vehicle which at another age he almost certainly would have rejected as ostentatious.

Life in the old Prather house was harmonious. Mama was content in her kitchen, things at Ficklin's Hardware were going well for Father and he had plenty of uninterrupted time for reading, and I just went through my normal daily routine with an eye toward the end of school and looking for ways to get more time with Bobbi. Sammy kept to himself more, but still found his way to the kitchen frequently to share some new knowledge with Mama.

Victor's moodiness appeared to have waned. He was doing well on his job at The Print Shop and was rewarded with a substantial raise in pay. Lacy said everything was perfect. She spoke of the Billiken, the god of things as they ought to be, more often than her god of everything.

But it was little Violet who had brought a new and brighter light to the old Prather house. She earned her way and then some by being loved by everyone. We hardly moved about without asking from time to time, "Where's Violet?"

Father no longer tromped straight to the kitchen to get coffee when he got home from work, but went looking for his granddaughter. Mama never lasted more than a single hour without prompting Lacy to bring the baby to her in the kitchen. Violet was the only one who could pull Sammy away from his books, and the only one who could lead me to stop thinking about Bobbi and want to walk with her instead. Victor and Lacy cast themselves in the loving role of new parents, proud to acknowledge it was they who had brought this beautiful child into the world.

Markers of the season came and went. The last week of October was wet and blustery, tamping down much of the usual Halloween activity. Mama prepared an enormous Thanksgiving dinner. We all ate greedily, then sought our own quiet place to rest and digest. Bobbi joined us. She and I slipped up to the attic after dinner and lay on the old mattress, side by side, and talked about the future. It didn't matter what the future brought, so long as we were together.

The next day we had a delayed dinner at her house. The Hoards treated me like family now, and this is the way I felt.

For the first time ever, I dreaded the arrival of the Christmas season. I was no longer a child and yet not fully an adult. Christmas was not about me. It was about Jesus for those who believed in the Holy Trinity or offered their annual temporary homage to the deity most accepted in their gentile society. Mostly, though, it was about family and friends—and Bobbi. Who would expect a gift from me? And what could I give Bobbi?

Even if I had an answer I had very little money to make it happen. Father gave me, Lacy, and Sammy allowances, having commenced on our sixth birthdays, to teach us how to handle money. I had saved what I could over the last two or three years but my fortune was not impressive. There was no way I would have done this had it not involved Bobbi, but in an act of desperation I went to Sarah Jennings and asked for help. She was the only one I could think of I might turn to.

I found Miss Jennings in a crowded hallway. She invited me to come with her to the teachers' lounge just across from the cafeteria. Once inside, she got cups of coffee for us and directed me to a pair of comfortable chairs in a back corner.

"So I believe you'll be graduating this year," she said. "Everything going well?"

I told her it was.

"Are you going to college?"

"No."

"Other plans? Know what you want to do in life?"

I told her I'd been thinking about all this but hadn't made any firm decisions. It took a few minutes more of small talk before she asked if there was anything she could do for me and I told her why I needed her advice. Straight off, she told me I was still in school and had no income so I need not worry about gifts for others in the family. They knew I couldn't afford it and wouldn't expect anything.

"I've seen you and Bobbi Hoard together from time to time around here," she said. "She's a very nice young woman."

"Yes. I'd like to get her something special, but I don't know what. I've never bought a present for a girl before. I mean—"

"I understand. Let me tell you what I think. Your gift need not be something expensive, but it should be special. It should be something that brings immediate pleasure and also has lasting appeal."

I was hoping she would be more specific.

"Do you have any suggestions?" I asked.

"Yes, as a matter of fact I do. And they wouldn't need to cost a lot. For immediate pleasure, how about a box of chocolates? Easy to find and you know she'd like it. And, I don't know, maybe a book for something permanent. Maybe a book of poetry."

I had relaxed quite a bit at this point. Miss Jennings had a way of making you feel like your problems weren't so great, and even had given me ideas about what to get Bobbi. I said I thought her suggestions were very good ones. I wasn't too sure about finding a book, though.

"Erinville doesn't have a real bookstore," I said. "Unless I could get to Paducah or Evansville, I don't know where I could get it. And I don't know much about poetry, I mean, what she might like."

Miss Jennings took her time answering and I was afraid she didn't have any ideas about that. But she did.

"So, I like Tennyson a lot, and Walt Whitman. And, of course T.S. Eliot. But their works are so massive. I'd think someone like Emily Dickinson, or maybe Elizabeth Barrett Browning. And we do have a bookstore, though they only sell used books. It's on Twelfth Street."

"I'd forgot about that. I've walked past it."

"Could you wait here a minute? I'll be right back."

She put her coffee cup on the small table between our chairs and stood, then walked briskly across the room and into an adjacent office. I could see her on a phone. True to her word, she was back in a couple of minutes. She handed me a sheet of paper with handwritten notes.

"I talked to the store manager and she said they have a nice selection of poetry books," she said. "Here's her name and phone number. She's going to get together a few books for you to look at."

The bell was ringing and I knew Miss Jennings had to get to class. And so did I. But I was little short of euphoric as I hurried to my classroom. Sarah Jennings had been of far more help than she ever could know. Not only was I grateful for her advice, but she had been so gracious I wasn't embarrassed for having asked. Now I could congratulate myself for having the courage to go to someone for help.

On Saturday a week later, Victor gave me a ride into Erinville and dropped me off in front of the Books Galore bookstore on Twelfth Street. He said he had just a couple of things to take care of at The Print Shop. I should come there when I finished and he probably would be ready to go home. He'd wait if I wasn't there yet.

Once inside the bookstore, I asked for Mrs. Dodson, whose name Miss Jennings had given me. She was a tiny woman, pretty old but sprightly, who came forward with a pleasant smile. She had been expecting me, she said, and took me to a table in the back of the store where she had laid out several books of poetry.

"Your Miss Jennings suggested some things you might be interested in," she said. "She must be a wonderful teacher to take such pains to help a student in need."

"Yes, she is. She's my favorite teacher."

My eyes went straight to a small book with a stern-looking woman pictured on the cover. It was a collection of poems by Emily Dickinson, and I remembered this was one of the poets

Miss Jennings mentioned. That was my Christmas gift to Bobbi. I'm sure it's still in a drawer of the nightstand beside her bed, all these years later.

12

Our nearest neighbors on the bluff side of Singleton's Branch were the Bromwells. They claimed family roots in Kentucky going back to pioneer days. Father said they exaggerated, but he and Amos Bromwell got on well and enjoyed one another's company during occasional visits.

Like father, Amos was an avid reader and thus one of the few acquaintances with whom he could talk books. Father had told us more than once about a time both men, without knowing it, had been reading the same book on the great geologists and when they got together began telling each other stories about John Wesley Powell.

Amos made the third generation of Bromwells to farm the family's substantial land holdings. The land was mostly wooded and hilly and not overly productive of good income crops after the area tobacco market folded. Amos said he was getting too old to do the work, anyway. He sold timber rights to a large tract of hardwood forest to an Owensboro lumber mill for what Father said was a cash windfall and the aging couple lived comfortably.

Amos was not particularly outgoing but Blanche was. They had two sons a good deal older than I, both of whom had moved away and had families of their own. Blanche complained the boys had forgotten them.

"I have a grandbaby almost a year old that I've never even seen," she told Mama, sitting in the kitchen in the Prather house drinking coffee and eating fruitcake the Saturday morning before Christmas.

Lacy had been there with Violet, but had just taken her to the nursery upstairs and put her to bed. She said the baby had been cross and kept her and Victor awake much of the night. This surprised me. I had slept soundly and not heard any of it. Maybe I simply was getting accustomed to the sounds. Blanche Bromwell asked Lacy to come back down once the baby was settled.

Mama got up to make a new pot of coffee, leaving me sitting alone at the table with our visitor. I liked Blanche a lot and always found her easy to talk to and lots of fun. She looked at me with a glint of mischief in her eyes. She was about to pretend to give me a hard time.

"So, what's with you these days, handsome?" she said. She had called me that since I became a teenager, and in the beginning I suspected it was because she couldn't remember my name.

I put on my best sad face.

"Just tryin' to survive this brutal dog-eat-dog world," I answered.

"My, goodness! Is it that bad?"

"Nobody knows the trouble I've seen."

Mama laughed at me, and so did Blanche Bromwell. I assumed this meant I'd put on a pretty good act. I probably couldn't have kept it going, but Lacy returned to the kitchen just then and saved me the effort.

"Well, now," Blanche said to her, "sounds like your big brother is carrying the load of the world on his shoulders. You know anything we can do for him?"

Lacy had a great sense of humor and enjoyed this kind of foolish carrying on. But she didn't know we were being facetious and evidently thought I really did have problems. She leaned toward me with a frown and concern in her eyes.

"Why didn't you tell me?" she demanded. "What's going on?"

Blanche looked embarrassed. I knew she hated to tell Lacy it was a joke, but didn't want her to worry. My reaction was the same and Mama didn't say anything, either. There was an uncomfortable moment of silence, which only served to heighten Lacy's anxiety. Blanche had to let her know.

She said, "Oh, honey, I'm sorry. We were just being silly. There's nothing wrong with your brother."

Lacy flew into a rage. It was as if all her pent-up emotion from the stress of motherhood and her insecurities about Victor boiled to the surface and burst forth in a way I'd never seen before. She slammed her hand on the table and, seeing she'd splashed some of my coffee out of the cup, swept the cup off the table onto the floor. It shattered on impact and spilled coffee over half the kitchen.

"Damn you!" she screamed. She looked at me. "And you, too. And you, Mama. I hope you all get your jollies making fun of dumb little Lacy! You all can go straight to hell."

She ran out, slamming the kitchen door behind her.

"Oh, god, Evelyn," Blanch Bromwell said, putting her hands up to the sides of her face. "I'm sorry, dear. I didn't mean to upset her. Me and my stupid big old mouth!"

"No, you didn't do anything wrong," Mama told her, looking like she was about to cry. "I've never seen her act that way. She's always the last one to get upset about anything."

I didn't know what to say. On nothing more than impulse, I ran from the kitchen after Lacy. Just as I got out the door I saw her beside the big white oak at the crest of the bluff and then she disappeared, running down the path toward the shoal. It was cold and I knew she had no coat.

When I caught up with her at the river bank, she turned her back and told me to go away. I pleaded with her to listen to what I had to say.

"I don't care what you say," she said. "I don't want to hear it. You're no better than the rest."

Nothing I could say would persuade her. She accepted no apology. She put her hands over her ears and yelled that she never wanted to see me again and threatened to jump in the water if I didn't go away and leave her alone. I was afraid she might do it. I told her I would leave, but asked her to please come in out of the cold.

"Violet needs you. Nobody else can take care of her as well as you." I paused an instant to see if this last best argument had any effect. She didn't respond.

Back at the top of the bluff, I waited again. After a few minutes I saw her start up the path and, with a mild sense of relief, hurried back to the house so I wouldn't risk discouraging her return. She bypassed the kitchen and went to the front door but we heard her going up the stairs and hoped a crisis had been averted.

Blanche Bromwell expressed her regrets to Mama again. The mood in the kitchen was somber. Blanche said she needed to go; Amos would be getting hungry and she needed to be there to fix his lunch.

"We'd love to have you and Amos join us for Christmas dinner," Mama told her.

Blanche said she'd call and let her know.

I slipped out of the kitchen as Blanche readied to leave. Sammy was coming that way as I walked out and I felt better not to be leaving Mama alone. I found Oscar curled up on the floor in a corner of the small parlor and took a chair beside him. As soon as he was aware of my presence he moved closer and went to sleep.

Distress over Lacy's unusual behavior gnawed at my brain.

"I kind of know how you feel, buddy," I said to Oscar, reaching down and scratching his head. "It kind of seems like Lacy's washed her hands of both of us."

Bobbi was going to pick me up early in the afternoon, so I went upstairs to get ready. I slipped quietly toward my door. Lacy's door was closed and so was the door to the nursery. There was no sound coming from either room.

Bobbi showed up early. Her Jeep had a peculiar squeak that helped me distinguish it from other vehicles when it stopped in the driveway. I had barely got downstairs in time to meet her at the door. After the miserable morning, she was an even more welcome sight than usual.

She was in a light-hearted mood as she drove the county blacktop to Erinville. There were a lot of small potholes and each one caused a jarring bounce in the hard-suspensioned Jeep. I complained after an especially rough one and she laughed.

"Next thing I hear is going to be criticism of my driving," she said. "I want you to know, it takes real talent to hit every hole in the road."

I played along and before we got into town she pulled over and asked me to drive. At first I thought this was part of the joke, but soon recognized she was serious. She didn't wait for my response. She was out and walking around the front of the Jeep to switch places before I had time to react.

"What brought this on?" I asked as I clicked the seatbelt and started the engine.

"Nothing. I just realized you've never driven my Jeep and thought you might like to. Didn't want to wait till we got downtown. You want to go to the afternoon movie?"

I did, and told her so. A good movie in a darkened theater might be a good antidote for my mood. I was still thinking about Lacy. Her behavior had been so different from any I'd seen before that it scared me. Was it possible there could be some underlying mental disorder?

I don't remember what kind of movie we saw. I do recall a near-empty theater. I felt good that I had money left after buying Bobbi's presents, enough to buy tickets and treats. We always shared a large box of popcorn and got large sodas.

Bobbi squirmed down in her seat and leaned her head on my shoulder. I balanced the popcorn on my knees and slipped my hand over hers. These small signals of affection, thrilling in the beginning, had become routine. But they still added to the feeling of belonging together and this was as much as I dared ask.

I had a terrible headache by the time the movie ended. I told Bobbi, and said I was afraid I might have something she could catch and I probably should go straight home and get to bed. She agreed. Except she said she was worried about me and not concerned about catching something.

Back in the driveway in front of the old Prather house we skipped the usual passionate kisses. I squeezed her hand and said good night. She said she hoped I would be well in the morning and drove away as I was opening the door. I watched and listened to the Jeep's funny squeak as she drove down the slope toward the county blacktop, standing at the open door until I couldn't hear or see her anymore.

Given the stress I felt, I didn't expect to sleep well. I lay awake and tried to remember the counting and word games Mama taught me when I was little, her way of helping me trick my mind into dozing off. My favorite was counting backwards from one thousand. It worked then but I didn't expect it to work now and I was right.

Still awake a good hour after I lay down, I heard the sound of the door opening and saw light from the hallway. I barely knew what was happening when Lacy slipped into bed beside me.

"Lacy ...?"

"Yes, it's me."

She slid close against me and put an arm across my chest.

"Are you all right, honey? I mean, all that stuff this morning—"

"I'm sorry about that. I don't know what got into me. Forget it, okay?"

I wasn't sure how to respond. Hearing her speak as the Lacy we all knew and loved was encouraging, yet I had an urge to push things a little more and hope to get some clue about what might have caused her explosion in the kitchen early in the day. When I didn't answer right away she started talking again.

"Do you ever pray?"

"Yeah, sometimes I do," I said.

"So are your prayers ever answered?"

"Well, I guess so. But I think a lot of people, including me, often pray for the wrong things."

She whispered, "I don't want to wake Victor. He gets mad if he wakes up and I'm not there. Even when I'm in the nursery. I pray, too. But I think I've been praying to the wrong god. The god of everything. I'm going to pray to the Billiken."

"The god of things as they ought to be?"

"Yes. I'd better get back."

She rolled over toward the edge of the bed. Her breast, soft under her night shirt, brushed against me.

"Oh, oh," I said. "Sorry about that."

"No problem, brother." She giggled. "Makes me wonder, though. You got to Bobbi's beautiful tits yet?"

She slipped out the door and closed it softly behind her. I heard Victor. His voice was angry, but I couldn't understand his words. Violet began to cry. Her loud wail escaped through the open nursery door and echoed up and down the high-ceilinged hallway. The tranquility of the old Prather house on the bluff above Singleton's Branch had been broken.

13

Father always said the world would run much more smoothly if humans were even half as dependable as the seasons. No matter how vicious the winter, and just when you think it never will end, spring always is close at hand. The azaleas on the slope in front of the old Prather house and the dogwood and redbud trees on the bluff were in full bloom by mid–April, surrounding us with a beautiful display of nature in its most welcoming time of the year.

I never really considered how Sammy's view of spring differed from Lacy's and mine until now. Looking back to our younger days, I recognize consistent patterns, different, that emerged over the years. An outsider knowing the details might have guessed we had no common background.

While Lacy and I always had relished spring for its beauty and warm sunshine, Sammy looked for ways to quantify its events. How long after the last killing frost before the first flowers bloomed? Was the passage of migrating waterfowl an accurate predictor of changing weather? What combination of temperature and humidity was most likely to lead to an outbreak of spring tornadoes? He wanted to apply science to nature and looked for ways to do so.

Sammy had been watching a pair of eagles nesting during the winter and was sure their eggs should have hatched by now.

He told Father he was worried. Last year they had hatched before the middle of March. Could there be something wrong?

Father told him no, the essence of biology is variation. There were any number of factors that might account for the delay. He had read something about this recently and offered a substantial list of possible causes. Sammy asked a few questions then went away happy, in quest of other mysteries of the season to investigate.

Victor arranged a play area for Violet beneath the large white oak, digging a shallow pit and filling it with sand and adding toys he thought should fit her tiny hands. He carried flat rocks up from the river bank to make a bench and leveled space for an inflatable kiddie pool to be added later. Lacy brought Violet down from the nursery to watch him work.

Oscar had taken to searching for me. He no longer got the attention he coveted from Lacy and I guess he felt her focus on the little one no longer left room for him. I could sympathize; I felt this, myself, to some extent. There were times it seemed my little sister and I were almost strangers. I realize now this was as much my fault as it was hers.

Added to my great interest in Bobbi was a new focus on the end of school. In a few weeks I would march across a stage and be handed a high school diploma and I would never look back! It wasn't that I'd had bad experiences in school, because I hadn't. Hemingway Terrace was a benign place of learning. I felt somewhat guilty I wasn't more grateful.

But I was tired of school. I was tired of the routine. I was tired of always looking to the future because today seemed to offer so little. I couldn't wait to get out, to get a stable job, and to marry Bobbi and start a family. I probably had heard the adult life I was eager for was no picnic and I might find these had been the best days of my life, but this was nothing I wanted to hear and if I'd heard it I hadn't listened. I was ready to move ahead and experience the future for myself.

It should not have come as a surprise that my impatience showed, but it did. In the kitchen at breakfast one Tuesday morning I saw Mama looking at me with a hint of worry marking her face. She went straight to the point.

"You haven't seemed quite yourself lately. Is everything all right?"

I wasn't expecting her question. But I knew any concern Mama had for me or for Lacy or Sammy was genuine mother's love and there was some basis for it. And now, of course, Violet could be added to this list. Mama had a heavy enough load; I didn't want her to worry about me.

"Everything's fine," I told her. "I didn't know I was acting funny."

"No, I shouldn't say you were acting funny. It's more that you were, I don't know, distracted maybe. You don't have much school left and I wanted to make sure everything is on track for you to graduate."

I told her things were going well at school. She was relieved.

"It could be that I'm only interested in that right now—graduation, I mean—and can't take time for anything else. I guess you could call that distraction. I'm so close. I think maybe I'm just doing everything kind of in a daze, waiting for my last day of school."

Sammy called down the hallway that our ride was there. Bobbi was in the driveway waiting. Mama leaned down and kissed me on the cheek before I could get up, and sent me off with her blessing and best wishes for another good day. We gave her so little in return for the love and care she gave us.

Sammy already had Bobbi tied into a conversation about the differences between wolves and coyotes when I got there and slid into the passenger's side front seat of the Jeep. He was still lecturing on the subject when we pulled onto the county blacktop and turned toward Hemingway Terrace School. Then there was a new topic.

"Bobbi, do you know the difference between rock and roll and boogie woogie?"

"No, Sammy. What's the difference between rock and roll and boogie woogie?"

"No, I'm not making a joke," Sammy said. "It was a question I really wanted to know."

I told him we didn't know anything about boogie woogie. And I asked how he even knew there was such a thing, to begin with. He said he'd seen it on television and didn't see that it was all that different from what he thought was rock and roll.

"I wish I was half as smart as your little brother," Bobbi said, speaking over his voice from the back seat.

He heard her and responded. "Knowing things isn't the same as being smart. I know lots of stuff but I don't know yet whether I'm smart."

She laughed and I turned to face Sammy. "Explain what you just said," I told him, trying not to sound as if I were giving an order.

"It's simple," Sammy said. "Anybody can know things without being smart. You can read it or somebody can tell you or you can see it, yourself. Like, if you remember one tenth of all your teachers have told you, you know a lot of things. If you're smart you understand it and want to find out more about it, maybe know what it has to do with you, or what you can do with it. Does that make sense?"

"I guess. So when will you know if you're smart?"

"If I'm smart I can use the things I know and go to college or something to learn more and find out how I can use what I know to make something better or how to make a living off it or whatever."

Bobbi had been listening. She glanced at me and winked.

"Well, I still think you're smart, Sammy," she said. "I'm guessing you will make good use of all the things you know."

For a fleeting instant I almost used Lacy's masterful rhetoric, "I'm so smart I can tie my shoes in the dark." I quickly thought better of it. I didn't want to muddle things with Bobbi and Sammy, and Lacy's clever saying was somewhat special. It represented two of the things I so loved about her—her determination and fierce independence.

I turned and looked back at Sammy again. His smile would have lit up a morning without sunrise. As I already knew, Bobbi's opinion meant a lot to him. Probably more than that of anyone else besides Father.

When I thought more about what my little brother said later in the day, it made sense. And I was in the exact situation he had offered as a measure of being smart. I would be finished with school in a matter of days. Now what was I going to do? What "things" had I learned that would affect me the rest of my life? It had taken the wisdom of a kid to wake me up to my own dilemma. For the first time in my life I had no idea where I would be and what I would be doing six months from now.

I was certain of only one thing. I wanted Bobbi to be in my life forever.

I wished I could talk to someone about all this. Sara Jennings probably could help, but after going to her when I needed advice on Christmas buying I didn't want to bother her again. Mama simply would brush off my questions and say not to worry about it. She'd say these things take care of themselves if you just go on about your business and let life come as it may. Father might have good advice, but he could be very cross with me if I caught him in a bad mood. I couldn't think of anyone else.

When we all piled into Bobbi's Jeep again in the afternoon, Sammy was somewhat subdued. Bobbi and I exchanged our usual questions and answers about our day in school. Sammy was quiet in the back seat. He still hadn't said anything when we pulled up in front of the old Prather house and it was time for him and me to get out.

"Everything all right with you, Sammy?" Bobbi asked.

"Yeah."

"You've been very quiet."

"I know. I was thinking while you guys were talking."

I folded down the seatback so he could climb out. Bobbi gave me a "let's talk" look. I let Sammy know I would be a while and got back in beside her.

"He puzzles me sometimes," she said.

I laughed as I answered. "Don't even try to figure out Sammy. Right when you think you've done it, he goes off into some new world of his own and leaves you behind."

But we really didn't want to talk about Sammy. We wanted to talk about us, Bobbi and me, and how we could be together tonight and every other night for the rest of the week. Our classes were over for all practical purposes and there was nothing to study for and no more end-of-semester papers to write. It was free time if we could handle it.

"Come home with me," she said. "I'll bring you back later."

I did, after running in to tell Mama.

In recent months I'd often had dinner with Bobbi and her parents, sat and watched television in their living room, and mixed into family conversations like I was one of them. My presence in the Hoard home had become the ordinary. And on this night I might have paid homage to Lacy's Billiken, the god of things as they ought to be. Jackson Hoard virtually made me part of the family.

Bobbi helped her mother clean up the kitchen and her father and I went into his home office because he wanted to show me something. He asked me to sit in a chair facing his desk. He opened a filing cabinet drawer and took out a thick file folder, put it on the desk, and sat down.

"I never had a son," he said, "so I don't really know how to talk to one." He watched, as if waiting for my reaction, then went on. "Bobbi's mother and I have come to see that you and her are serious about being together, and we're all right with that. I just wanted to talk with you about your future."

He obviously expected me to answer. I was tongue-tied.

"Well, then, I'll just cut to the chase. Bobbi says you don't know what you're going to do after you graduate. I wanted to show you a bit about my company. And what I'm leading up to is, I'm offering you a job."

He opened the file folder on his desk and began to pull things out. I was numb from the shock of what I'd just heard.

"Here," he said, apparently no longer expecting me to respond, "this graphic details the organization and how you'd fit in. If you want to pull your chair over here where you can see, I'll go over it with you."

The rest of the evening might as well have been a dream. I couldn't believe this really was happening. Surely I'd wake up and find I had been sleeping. I didn't have a logical reaction to anything he showed me from the folder on his desk. Philadelphia headquarters, divisions, regional offices, national distribution ... matter on paper and words spoken that blew past me like tissue paper in the wind.

I hadn't proved myself smart by Sammy's definition. What I knew and how I might apply it played no role. This had come about Mama's way—*don't worry about it,* these things take care of themselves if you just go on about your business and let life come as it may.

But no matter how it all happened, I no longer had to concern myself over what I would do after I finished school. Jackson Hoard had signed and sealed the direction my life would take. In the beginning, anyway. I was confident now my future was intertwined with the Hoard family. I considered the ties to be binding; my boss would be my father-in-law. All I had to do was let it happen.

14

Two years after we finished high school and after both of us turned twenty, Bobbi and I were married. We had a simple yet elegant ceremony in the back yard at the Hoards' house, planned and directed by Jen Hoard. Her sister, a Lutheran minister who pastured a small church in South Dakota, guided us through our vows.

The weather was mildly threatening, but all the people were beautiful. Sammy was my best man. Bobbi's sister, Carly, and Lacy were bridesmaids. Violet walked hand-in-hand with her mother and carried flowers. There was no aisle to walk down, but there was recorded music and Jackson Hoard escorted his daughter from the kitchen to the yard and Father and Victor stood by as if waiting for guests to usher. Seth Ficklin was the only guest. The whole thing was over in twenty minutes. Mama and Jen Hoard both cried.

Weddings are supposed to be for brides, but Bobbi was calm and collected and I was nervous as a baby rabbit just out of the nest. There could not have been a happier person on the planet. I was in a state of complete euphoria. It was a magnificent day and I chose to ignore the ominous clouds in the distance.

Surely being joined as man and wife was the final link in the chain of perfection that bound our lives. Bobbi's father had managed to get me a good salary, well above the normal starting pay, and in my two years at Graffenried Distributors I had earned enough to have money in the bank, a lease on a nice two-bedroom condo, and a good car. Father said I was better off than any twenty-year-old he'd ever known before.

My own view was dominated by a lifelong tendency to oversimplify. I saw life as perfect at that place and in that time and thought it would be this way forever. I should have known better. Life is not a static existence. It is a moving, objective reality bound to its own unique setting and ever subject to change. What lies over the horizon at sunset, invisible, very well may be the first thing you see in the morning.

But maybe Earth-bound mortals should not be expected to place themselves in time yet to come. Maybe images of the future belong to whatever Supreme Being mortals choose to worship. Maybe Lacy's god of everything could see into all the nooks and crannies of all the days of my life. But I couldn't, and probably wouldn't have wanted to if I could.

Was it unfair of me to want no more than I had? I wished only to embrace the wondrous world by which I was surrounded. I had my Bobbi and nothing else mattered.

We thrived on our new study of the arts of love-making. I was happy now that we had waited. I claimed no credit for this, of course. Bobbi had been unyielding in her insistence of no sex until after marriage and I loved and respected her too much to make such demands, no matter the rage of my own desires.

She had taken a job at the library, which was only two blocks from the offices of Graffenried Distributors. Carly worked for her father, too, just down the hall from me, and the three of us regularly got together for lunch.

I liked Carly very much. She and Bobbi bore little physical resemblance, but they were much alike in personality. She had Bobbi's intensity and, best of all, her marvelous sense of humor. And both set high standards for themselves and those around them.

Moving out of the old Prather house on the bluff was little short of traumatic. This had been my home for the first two decades of my life. How could I duplicate the warmth of Mama's kitchen, the sweet odors of Violet's nursery? There would be no Sammy alerting me to things I otherwise might miss, nor Oscar, hungry for attention, nudging me as I sat in the small parlor trying to find answers to questions I didn't understand. No listening for Victor's anger and no more emotional support to offer my delicate Lacy.

Most of all—and I admitted this to myself for the first time—I would miss the reassuring presence of Father. Whether he sat at night in his wingback chair reading a fresh book from the Erinville Public Library or at the table in Mama's kitchen in the morning drinking his first coffee of the new day, merely knowing he was there was a rock on which we all stood. Oh, that I ever could be as strong!

There was not much for me to move. My clothes, a few personal items. Bobbi said this was good. She didn't have much, either, and our whole relocating experience was deceptively quick and easy.

We bought a few things at Walmart and our new household—our *very own* new household—was established. We congratulated ourselves on being nearly perfect interior decorators. Who else could have created surroundings so exactly matching our combined, if compromised, tastes in decor? We wanted to invite everyone we'd ever known into our home.

Mama would tell us later, "You'd have thought you two were the only ones ever to set up housekeeping, you were so proud."

They all came, over time. Family and friends, co-workers, classmates from Hemingway Terrace School. Father stopped by after work now and then and Sara Jennings came after talking with Bobbi at work in the library. If there had been such a thing as society in Erinville we surely would have been high on its list of emerging members.

But eventually we came to look upon our condo as more of a place to live than a place to show. We both worked hard and some days came home exhausted. We wanted privacy and comfort. We shouldn't need to set boundaries, but if we had to we would. Bobbi hand-lettered a poster warning that intruders were likely to be "hanged in the public square" and asked my opinion. I told her I liked the philosophy, but Erinville didn't have a public square.

"So what if I change it to say 'shot at sunrise'?"

"Oh, yes," I said. "I like that. Where do you plan to post it?"

We spent the rest of the evening trying to think of more funny warning signs, each new idea being more outrageous than the last. Being together whenever we could had been fun for as long as we'd known each other; we were eager now to take advantage of our new privilege, being together for life.

Sammy missed me at home—something he'd never admit, but which he gave away by frequent visits with me at work "just to see how things are going." His own graduation from high school was rapidly approaching.

Bobbi gave Sammy her Jeep. She and I would almost always be on the same path, she said, and one car was enough. I think Sammy's joy was about equally the result of having his first vehicle and knowing Bobbi thought highly enough of him to give it.

Like me, Sammy had learned to drive in the old Dodge pickup under Mama's tolerant teaching. Father said he didn't have the time or the patience. Mama said she welcomed the chance to get out of the kitchen, and a few hours up and down the lane and back and forth on the county blacktop gave us a good head start on driver's training in school. Lacy had the same opportunity, but declined. She said she was not interested in learning to drive. The explanation, in typical Lacy logic, was that she had no reason to drive because she had no place to go. Some years later, though, it turned out she could drive and I could only assume Victor taught her.

We still gathered at the shoal on hot summer afternoons. Lacy and Victor always were there first, making the most of Violet's excitement as she played in the water. Carly sometimes came with Bobbi and me. Sammy joined us often, mostly because Violet was there.

We all took turns watching Violet so her parents could swim in the deeper water from time to time. "Watching" meant joining in the creative ways she found to play in the sand and gravel bottom of the shoal and float things on the lazily flowing surface of the river. Lacy's pride blossomed on these occasions. She seemed to look on Violet not only with love, but also with something approaching satisfaction that this child was her own achievement. The mother of this little flower should never lack in self-esteem. I took some pleasure in observing Lacy's new glow. She had earned it and it had been a long time coming.

It brought tears to my eyes one scorching summer afternoon to hear her singing to Violet the children's nonsense song, "I know an old lady." I still could see some of the small child who used to lead me to her favorite spot beneath the great white oak at the crest of the bluff and hope I would stay and play. She loved word games and challenged me many times to do parodies of that song.

Mama, a great fan of Burl Ives, the folk singer who recorded it, had taught her this popular children's rhyme when she was a toddler.

The test for me was to cleverly finish what she began:

"I know a rich banker who swallowed some *money*. I don't know why he swallowed the money ..."

And I sang, "He thought it was *funny*."

And another:

"I know an old possum who climbed up a *tree*. I don't know why he climbed up a tree ..."

"The farther to *see!*"

So much of my own childhood had been spent here on the shoal or on the bluff above, and so many of my childhood memories revolved around Lacy. No matter what had changed, so much still was the same. I still had a sense of belonging in this place on the river.

And there were no more floods. It could be that the "once in a hundred years" tag was more accurate than we'd believed. Yet, as Father observed, there was no rush to rebuild homes on the east bank of Singleton's Branch.

This continued connection with the shoal, the bluff, and the old Prather house helped soften my transition into the new life I enjoyed. And change came quickly. Bobbi was pregnant. The realization that I was to be a father was truly staggering in its impact. My notice came in the form of a baby rattle, tied with both pink and blue ribbons, placed on the table just before I sat down to dinner.

Bobbi, usually able to conceal her emotions, was bursting to tell me. I picked up the rattle and, before I even could comment, she said, "Just a little something for Daddy." I grabbed her in a smothering hug and we danced around the kitchen.

I think we forgot all about eating, reveling in the happy moment and embracing the never-ending thrill of one another's presence. It was a long while before I finally collected my wits and asked the most pressing question.

"When can we expect it?"

Bobbi hadn't figured this out yet. She'd only become aware of her condition a day earlier. She'd been dying to tell me but wanted to make sure.

"We can count it out," she said.

We did. Our baby would come in the spring, about the first of April.

"Have you told anyone else?" I asked.

"Of course not. You had to be the first to know."

We decided to wait a while before letting the word get out. Grandparents on both sides should be the next to be informed. Carly would be delighted. We couldn't decide how Sammy and Lacy and Victor would receive the news. Seth Ficklin would want to know, but Father would be eager to pass the word to him. Ranelle Bishop and others Bobbi worked with at the library should not be left out, either.

Bobbi said there were some social circles in which expecting parents mailed out notices to those they wanted to inform. We laughed over this, wondering how big the mailing list should be to make it worthwhile.

"But Mama or somebody will want to give you a baby shower," I said, and "invitations will be mailed for that."

"I'd rather not have one. But how could I say no to your mother?"

We didn't get to bed until the middle of the night. And even then, it was not because we expected to sleep. We were too excited. We went to bed to make love, our passions inflamed instinctively by our awareness that we could make babies.

Exciting things happening to others over the next several months went unnoticed by Bobbi and me. Sammy applied for and was admitted to engineering studies at Southern Illinois University. Victor was promoted to a minor management-level position at The Print Shop. Jen Hoard was given an award for her dedication and service to an Erinville women's club. Thanksgiving and Christmas came and went.

We went through the motions of being sociable, staying involved. But none of these things was important. Our child would come soon. We knew now it would be a little girl.

15

Our baby made her appearance right on schedule. We named her Sarah, after Miss Jennings. It was an easy delivery, and Bobbi looked as fresh after it was all over as she had when labor began. She lay cuddling our daughter, pleased and smiling, and I was the one who felt I was ready to collapse. Nothing I'd ever experienced before had brought the level of nervous tension that gripped me as I watched the birth.

One of the delivery room nurses had been watching me. Now she laughed.

"I wonder sometimes if it was a good change to let daddies be in here," she said. "Gets kinda tense, doesn't it?"

"It was beautiful."

"Well, I've seen men faint. But I promise you're going to come through it with no pain, unlike your lovely wife here."

Bobbi laughed and I squeezed her hand. I wanted to sweep both mother and baby up in my arms and take them home, hide them away from other eyes, and keep them all to myself. I could relish them like a miserly rich man relishes his gold.

I was able to do that even sooner than we expected. We had readied the second bedroom of the condo to be the nursery, though the lease didn't allow us to do some things we would have liked. Mama and Jen Hoard had rushed out as soon as they heard

Bobbi was expecting and brought us most of what we needed. The library put Bobbi on paid maternity leave.

As I think probably is true of almost all new parents, our principal concern was that our baby be healthy. She was. She had the lungs to prove it. When she cried I worried somebody a block away might come checking on her. I've no doubt the thin walls of our building allowed her opera-strength voice to be heard by any number of other residents, but we got no complaints.

I was disappointed that our child did not have Bobbi's green eyes, but Carly said baby eye color isn't set until at least three or four months of age and may go through subtle changes for a long time after that. What she told me brought me some comfort. I need not have worried. Before she was a year old, Sarah's eyes were as green as emeralds, just like her mother's.

So, all these years later I probably still sound like a proud first-time father. I am. Sarah, and the two children who followed, are the best traces of me I could hope to leave behind. If I proved in the end not to be much of a father, they still are blessed to have half their genes from Bobbi Hoard.

If there is such a thing as natural mothering, Bobbi had it. Mama said she might have thought Sarah was a third or fourth child. Bobbi knew what to do and had no problems getting it done. I never found her exhausted from the struggle. She might be up two or three times during the night with the baby and I would never know. There were mornings, when something had made the little one restless, I'd find Bobbi asleep in a chair beside the baby in her bed. She'd say I had to get up and go to work in the morning and she didn't want me to lose sleep over what she could take care of, anyway.

Violet was fascinated by our little girl. She wanted to hold her, which she wasn't allowed to do. Given this limitation she would stand over the baby and talk to her as if the two actually were engaged in two-way conversation. Sarah responded by smiling and making noises, which seemed to vary from one visit to the next.

Bobbi, Lacy, and I sometimes listened secretly to her talk. She already professed love for her cousin and impatience for a time they could run about the old Prather house and play in the shoal.

"It gets real hot but the water's always cool," Violet was saying. She knew not to expect an answer, but kept on talking like she assumed Sarah understood. "It's the funnest when the sand washes between your toes. But I don't know if you'd feel it with your little bitty toes. My mother says you'll grow real fast and we can play together. Won't that be fun?"

Lacy said they had to go. Victor would be waiting for them and would be irritated if they were late. Violet made clear she didn't want to leave, but caused no trouble.

"She's so sweet," Bobbi said. "They're near enough in ages they may be really close. Don't you think?"

"Yes. We'll have two little girls in the family for a long time to come."

Father was cast in the role of proud grandfather again. He said he hadn't recovered yet from Violet's arrival. He hinted that he was sorry Sarah wouldn't be living in the old Prather house, too. Nothing would please him more than to be "surrounded" by pretty little girls.

"I expect you to come see your grandfather often," he said, leaning over our baby until their noses almost touched. "Got to be sure your daddy and mama don't forget the way. Got a deal?"

He took her tiny hand between his thumb and fingers and shook. Sarah smiled and made sweet expressions with her mouth.

Sarah's early months came during a busy time for me. My work load increased as the company went through further expansion. Bobbi's father reached a point at one time where he said he was about ready to throw up his hands and tell higher management we couldn't handle it without more help. He talked about it with Carly and me and said he still might call and suggest more staff, but without the panic. We never knew whether he did, but we didn't get any more people.

His first reaction to a new granddaughter was much different from Father's. He pretended it wasn't anything unusual. I think Bobbi was a little hurt, but she told me that years back he had started trying to show less emotion after causing a scene at his father's funeral.

"I'm pretty sure nobody had a problem with him crying over the loss of his dad," she said. "But he was embarrassed and worried he had embarrassed the rest of us, too. I guess it had to do with his manliness or something."

Whatever his level of emotion in the beginning, after a week or so Jackson Hoard simply melted when Sarah was around. He urged Bobbi to bring her by his office every day or so. She did, so I got to see the precious little one too. And Bobbi. With her not working in the library we weren't close enough to get together for lunch.

Being a father did not change my life, or even my daily routine, as much as I had expected it would. When Bobbi went back to work, we found a wonderful woman, Mandy Fouts, to take care of the baby during the day and couldn't wait to get home to our little one after work. Mandy also was available, at a modest hourly rate, for occasional work on evenings and weekends. Our social activities were far too limited for us to need her often.

Our lives weren't perfect, but probably as good as we could have hoped for. Nothing changed much and one day was pretty much like another over the next two years. Sarah began walking early. We took her to play in the shoal with Violet when summer heat arrived and watching the two of them interact was a treat in itself. Lacy said she'd be glad to pick up Sarah on week days when Bobbi and I were working and keep her for two or three hours so the little ones could play.

We didn't give Lacy a definitive answer. Neither of us wanted to make a commitment until we'd talked about it. We both had reservations and in the end decided not to do it.

"I don't like the thought of Lacy watching both of them in the shoal all by herself," Bobbi said. "I trust Lacy, but that could be a challenge."

I felt the same way. We hated to tell Lacy, but she never mentioned it again so we didn't have to.

Although our little one was only a toddler, we began to feel crowded in our small condo and decided it was time to consider buying a house. Bobbi's father encouraged us to do it, and offered to help any way he could. He did business regularly with a couple of real estate companies and said he'd been told now was a good time to buy.

We hadn't expected to move so quickly, but once he knew of our interest he kept the topic alive. Hardly a day went by that he didn't ask if we'd made a decision yet.

"It's great that he's that interested, but he's driving me crazy," I complained to Bobbi. "I'm about ready to just do it."

"But can we afford it?"

We went over our finances and figured we could manage the down payment on a modest priced house. As long as both of us were working, we should be able to make mortgage payments. Bobbi said although she would hate to ask, her father always would be happy to help us out if we ran into problems.

Jackson Hoard was way ahead of us. He already had talked to a couple of realtors and told them we'd be looking for a home soon. Each of them had marked a few houses among their listings they thought would be of interest. All we had to do was go look.

One agent, a driven young woman named Alexandra Keyes, expressed open surprise that we were potential clients. "I have to tell you, I don't think I've ever sold a house to a buyer under thirty," she said.

We knew she meant this as a compliment, but it seemed somewhat sarcastic and we didn't like it. I wanted to mark her off and go with the other realtor, Louie Denny, and Bobbi said she had no problem with that. In any case, he had more listings in our price range. We made a weekend appointment to look at three houses and loved one of them so much we bought it on the spot. The fact its owners already had moved out was an important advantage.

Bobbi's father assured us he had no intention of getting into our affairs, but then did exactly that. He called his banker and made an appointment for us to discuss a mortgage and said he would like to be there, too. We were grateful. We hadn't expected to be buying our own home and applying for a mortgage for several years. Both of us were a bit nervous.

Everything went very smoothly. We were moved and settled into our new home in three weeks.

Mama wanted to have a house warming for us. She said a new home merited a celebration the same as a new child. She wanted to send out invitations and host the event in the Prather house. We couldn't think of any reason not to let her do it. She did, and it was a very pleasant get-together that drew a good many more people than we expected.

Long-time friends and neighbors of hers and Father's filled the two parlors and spilled out onto the porch. Blanche and Amos Bromwell were the first to arrive and were so cheerful they got the celebration off to a great start. Except for them, the Shields and Seth Ficklin and his wife, Alma, were the extent of those on Mama's list Bobbi and I even knew. It didn't matter. Everyone treated us like family. Mama's and Father's community roots were deeper than I realized.

If the gathering needed entertainment, it was provided by the little ones—Violet and Sarah. They held hands and ran from room to room and around the porch, attracting the attention of their elders wherever they went. Lacy tried to keep up but they soon left her behind. Just watching them and the joy they found in each other would have made the gathering a pleasure for me even if other things had not gone well.

But they did. Mama's efforts brought a rich collection of useful and needed things for the new house, and also led indirectly to one of the greatest happenings of our young lives. Blanche

Bromwell asked if we ever were going to have a honeymoon. We went home thinking it was time we did.

We talked about wanting to get away, many miles from Erinville, and Bobbi said she'd always wanted me to see the ocean. Maybe we could go to Philadelphia, where she still had friends and relatives? There might even be someone we could stay with and save some of the cost.

I said it didn't matter. I had stubbornly refused to touch the money Grandpa Childs left me and it would pay our way. We began making plans.

Beyond the Hoard family's move, no one we knew had done any traveling to speak of. We had not heard stories of places we just "had to see." Sammy was the only one who offered actual advice, and his was merely that wherever we went we must fly. His own love of flying made him somewhat less than objective but what he told us was reasonable.

"If you don't fly," he said, "you'll spend all your time on the road and be too tired when you get somewhere to enjoy it."

Father suggested we go to the library and look at a few travel magazines. We did, and decided on an easy and relatively inexpensive two weeks at Myrtle Beach. There were ads for the "Grand Strand" in all the magazines and one had a good article on South Carolina beaches in general. Bobbi found these more attractive than the Jersey Shore, where she'd been a few times as a child, and they obviously were exotic and inviting to me. And she thought this would be a great place for me to get my first sight of an ocean.

Busy work schedules suddenly didn't matter. We had friendly and accommodating management who said they'd survive without us. Bobbi's mother and Mandy Fouts would take care of Sarah. Almost before we knew it our travel plans were made.

16

Our landing in Charlotte was rough. I knew Bobbi was nervous. This was our first plane ride. The flight from Paducah had been smooth enough, but she was sitting at a window seat and once our plane was over the runway it did look as if the ground was coming up to meet us awfully fast.

"I don't know why Sammy loves flying so much," she had said earlier, soon after we were in the air. "I'd rather be down there on a road on solid earth, on four wheels."

The Charlotte airport was buzzing with activity. Bobbi said she might be content to just sit and people watch for an hour or so. We only had thirty minutes between flights, though, and in no time were landing at Myrtle Beach. There was easy transportation to the resort where we had reservations.

I had promised myself not to make too big a deal over all this. I might as well have promised I would fly on my own wings.

"It's beautiful," Bobbi said, as we stepped onto the balcony of our fifth-floor room. "I'd forgotten how blue the ocean is—how far you can see."

I was almost speechless. I had tried to think how I might react when I saw an ocean for the first time, but I wasn't prepared for what lay before me. I actually could see the curvature of the earth. I remembered Father trying to explain to us how sailors used to communicate between ships with signal flags and how if they got too far apart they couldn't see each other. It didn't interest me then, but suddenly I was fascinated by this simple fact. Sammy, of course, had asked questions, but Lacy and I had grabbed the first chance to escape and go down to the river and play in the water of our shoal.

Bobbi sensed my excitement. She put an arm around my waist and pulled me close. "I was hoping you would like it," she whispered. "Everyone should see an ocean at least once in their life."

I could tell she felt free of the stresses of everyday life back in Erinville. We had agreed this would be the honeymoon we never got when we married, although the time had flown by so fast the wait didn't seem all that long. I had promised myself I would do everything in my power to make this the most wonderful two weeks of her life.

As she leaned on the balcony rail, she looked even more radiant than usual. How pretty she was! The ocean breeze blew a wisp of auburn hair across her face. It caught a flash of sunlight as she brushed it away. I looked into those beautiful green eyes and suddenly I was 15 and falling for this girl all over again.

We went inside and made love.

After a day of travel and our prolonged act of passion, we should have been exhausted. But Bobbi hurried to get dressed for the beach and I was eager to follow. We held hands and walked leisurely away from our home away from home, oblivious to people around us, the crying sea gulls, the compact formations of pelicans swooping low over the water and diving for fish, the dolphins swimming parallel to the land, a hundred yards out. We would see all these tomorrow, sitting over coffee on our balcony, but today we could have been the last two humans inhabiting the earth. I was with Bobbi and Bobbi was with me.

The beach, for me, proved truly captivating. To some extent it was the ordinary and expected—the power of the ocean, the incessant coming in and going out of the tides, the delicate pull of sand washing from under my feet, the competition between merciless sun and cooling waves. But there was more.

I soon found myself lost in reverie. Here, it was as if there were primitive echoes of people immaculately in tune with nature. We all were innocent children again, with no inhibitions. We didn't care if we revealed imperfect bodies or dressed in something less than the most stylish swim wear. Lacy would have pronounced us all equal in the eyes of the god of everything, and this is the way I felt.

Bobbi laughed when I described my fanciful musings to her.

"You obviously haven't seen the college girls showing off their tanned bodies in high-priced Neiman Marcus bikinis," she said.

"I don't know. But it doesn't make any difference. What does it matter whether that old man walking alone down there along the water's edge is a rich banker or a homeless vagrant? Or whether that young woman walking toward us is a doctor or a poor, overworked single mother?"

She laughed again, but it was a sweet laugh.

"Okay," she said. "I understand what you mean. The beach does kind of level everything out. Someday we need to check out a nude beach."

"I'm all for it. There's nothing about a naked body that gives it any unearned stature. But the only naked body I'm interested in right now is—"

"Whoa!" She held up a hand as if signaling a stop. "I'm not a teenager anymore. You want an old woman like me to let you see me naked? Now why would I do that?"

"Because this old man is going to be naked too, and I'm going to do more than just look at your naked old body, lady!"

It was one of Bobbi's great qualities that she always was open to suggestion. Some might even say she was a pushover. An even greater quality was her tendency to make frequent suggestions, herself. And I was a pushover, too.

We stayed up late at night and watched the moon as it rose over the water, its silver reflection shimmering in the waves. Some nights we walked on the beach and some nights we found our balcony the place we most wanted to be. We let the moist winds cool us and listened to the slap-slapping of waves on the hard sand, as rhythmic as the music of a symphony.

No two days were the same. Some mornings we slept late and other mornings we were awake and on the balcony to watch the sun rise over the Atlantic. Some days we spent hours in the water. We didn't swim, but waded out and met the surf head-on. We played like teenagers, struggling to stay on our feet while the waves rolled over us, me holding Bobbi and pulling her tight against me so she wouldn't go down.

Some days we never went in the water, but sat and played in the sand. We built sand castles with kids at play and created small lakes and watched them capture tiny fish as the waves washed over their sand levees. Bobbi said some looked like baby sharks but I didn't think sharks came that small, even as babies.

"When we get home," I told her, "we'll go to the library and find out."

But just now, getting home was at the top of our list of things in which we had no interest.

We walked miles of beach, going in alternate directions each time, trying to see everything. Our pattern proved similar to that of other walkers and some became familiar. We began to greet them after a few meetings, just as if we were greeting friends on the street in Erinville. We walked Ocean Boulevard looking for restaurants and found many more than we had time to try.

"One of the housekeeping women told me no one leaves Myrtle Beach hungry," Bobbi said. "Now I can see why."

Like the days of any given season in whole, these days tend to meld into a single span in my memory now. I say this with all due respect to Rachel McNary. It is to her credit I can tell you in detail about things we did and, in some cases, when we did them. We lived our lives at Myrtle Beach day by day. Yet my memories are of a *time*—a time when Bobbi and I were happy, and so much in love. It is a time which still can replay in my dreams and a time such as every human deserves at least once in life. It is a time which brings me pain today, because I could not have believed then I would so fail Bobbi in the end.

If there is irony in this time, it is that the future was laid bare for me had I chosen to accept it. We hear many voices. Which ones merit our hearing? Perhaps this is not ours to know, lest we deny the lesser ones and in doing so discourage voices critical to others. Father said voices are only sound waves until they enter an ear and only noise until deciphered by a brain.

But the voice I heard was not one from which I might have expected any particular outpouring of wisdom. On a night when I couldn't sleep I slipped out of our room quietly so as not to waken Bobbi and went to walk the beach in the moonlight. I didn't walk alone, as there always are night-walkers when the moon is brightest. Non-sleepers like me, I suppose, along with many who want to be up and on the beach at night.

I planned to walk to near exhaustion. Surely this would bring sleep.

I had no way to measure distance, but I walked for an hour, past the tall beach-front hotels and the lesser establishments and, finally, a few small homes set back from the Atlantic tides. Then there was a narrow river flowing into the ocean, a sudden barrier to further advance. I walked close to its edge in hopes it might prove only a shallow stream.

"You don't want to try to cross it unless you're a pretty good swimmer."

The speaker was somewhere behind me. I turned toward the sound of his voice.

"I'm over here," he said, and I saw him.

He sat on the sandy embankment above the high tide mark, nearly hidden among the sea oats. He waved just as I saw him, and stood.

"Come and sit a while."

I climbed up through the dry, loose sand toward him and he took a few steps toward me. It was too dark for me to make out his features. He extended a hand in greeting, as if welcoming someone he expected.

"I'm Jonathon," he said.

I told him my name and stood facing him, trying for a clearer image of what kind of man this was. He turned so that more moonlight struck his face and I saw he was old and bearded, innocent looking, surely safe for me to be close to. I followed his motion and we both sat down in the sand. Being used to the crowded beach, I was acutely aware that this place at this time of night was completely deserted except for the two of us.

"You a night walker?" he asked, his voice low-key to the extent I thought it could be monotonous in extended conversation.

"No, not usually. Tonight I just couldn't sleep. I didn't want to toss and turn all night and keep my wife awake, so I decided to take a walk."

"Can't beat a walk on the beach in the moonlight."

"So what about you?" I said. "You usually out here this time of night?"

"Yeah. Most nights I am."

"So ... You just sit here in the weeds all by yourself?"

"Can't call sea oats weeds. If it wasn't for them, a lot of this beach would have washed away."

I could tell he was somewhat put out with me, apparently because of my ignorance when it came to the importance of sea oats. My first inclination was to simply get up and walk away. But I was curious about him. What was his story? What kind of man sat alone on the beach at night in a place where he was unlikely to encounter others?

"I didn't know that," I said, trying to sound friendly. "This is my first time on a beach."

"First time you saw an ocean?"

"Yes."

"Sorta gives you a thrill, don't it?"

I agreed. He asked where I was from, did I have family with me? I told him about Bobbi and our baby.

"A man couldn't be more blessed than to have a good wife," he declared. "I had one, too, but I lost her."

"I'm sorry."

"I don't mean she died. I mean she left me. And it was all my fault. I made a foolish decision without thinking. See, when you have a good wife you have to realize that marriage is more than just loving one another. Like I think it says in the Bible, the two of you are one. Know what I mean?"

"I think so."

"You got to remember that she hurts when you hurt. If you get cut she bleeds. Problem most men has is they think they're good husbands just because they provide good for their wives and families. That's not a real partnership."

His voice began to tremble. Even in the dimming light of a fading moon I could see there were tears streaming down his cheeks. The old man clearly was reliving painful memories and there was nothing I could offer that would be of any help. I was tired and wanted to go back to our room, but I didn't want to leave him sitting here alone just yet.

I asked him personal questions, about his life, his profession, where did he call home? How long did he plan to be here? Where would he go when he left this place? Everything I could think of that would force him to talk about himself. Maybe this would help him forget.

The sky in the east, over the ocean, began to lighten. It was almost dawn. I had spent the whole night talking to this stranger—except he didn't seem a stranger anymore. I knew his life. I knew him. He had come to matter to me.

Bobbi had begun to worry when I got back to our room. I knew she would, and I had walked as fast as I could. I was completely exhausted.

"What in the world got you up and out so early?" she asked.

"Actually, I was up and out *late*."

"You mean ...?"

I laughed, and felt foolish. But I knew Bobbi would understand. I told her about the old man, and how I'd stayed and talked the night away and how I believed I may have helped him feel better.

She hugged me.

"I'm going to hit the shower," she said. "You lie down and get some sleep."

This was the good wife the old man and I had talked about. Bobbi and I were one. When I was cut, she bled. How could I ever have forgotten this?

We spent the afternoon in the surf. Bobbi looked more beautiful than ever. I wanted to hold her to me until our bodies meshed and wrap my head in her auburn hair. We were knocked down time and again by the waves, coming up coughing and spitting even as we relished the salty taste of the Atlantic Ocean. Then we'd turn and face the next wave and cling together to meet it with all our strength.

We were half way through the second week of our honeymoon. We already were starting to dread the coming end of our escape. And we already were beginning to talk of coming here again.

We went back to our room completely worn out from our exertion in the surf. The evening hours still were ours to capture and to do with as we chose. Bobbi said she'd race me to the elevators and started to run. I waved her off in resignation.

"Hey, girl," I called after her, "I couldn't run two steps if a grizzly bear was chasing me. But you get on up there and hope I make it before sundown."

She laughed, and waited

The phone was ringing when we opened the door. Bobbi ran to pick it up, answering with her soft, "Hello. This is Bobbi." She slipped her palm over the receiver and whispered to me, "It's your father." I started to reach for the phone but she held up a hand to signal no. I could hear my father talking.

I knew this was not good news.

Bobbi paled, and slumped forward to brace herself with a hand on the desk. "Oh, no!" she said. "Oh, my god, no!"

17

Because I was not there, I can never be totally confident I know exactly what happened. Accounts I heard varied in detail. But the outcome was the same and it would be hard to imagine a tragedy that had more effect on a family. It was as if each of us lost a part of our self, and life in the old Prather house on the bluff above the river would never be the same.

Father had given us only the briefest report on the phone. I had taken the receiver from Bobbi when it looked as if she might faint. Father was in the middle of a sentence and didn't seem to notice the change on the other end of the line, or maybe I didn't speak. He knew at the end of the conversation he was talking to me but he was in such a state of despair the switch would not have mattered.

Bobbi leaned into me even before I'd hung up the phone, bursting into sobs. I drew her to me, needing the closeness of her body. We stood and held each other for a long while, drawing strength from one another, before either of us spoke. I had only one thought. *How could the god of everything be so cruel?*

Getting home is only a blur in my memory now. I remember calling the airport and scheduling the first flight we could catch, then throwing things together and checking out of our room. We moved mechanically, hurrying without feeling we were getting anywhere. Fortunately we made good connections. Someone met us at the airport in Paducah and then we were home.

The new home we'd been so proud of when we left held no charm. We unpacked and picked up Sarah, doing what had to be done with a great deal of uncertainty about what came next. We were eager and yet reluctant to get to the Prather house—eager because we should be there to join arms and grieve with the family, and reluctant because for the first time it would not be a place of comfort.

Little Violet was gone, and our whole world was in mourning.

Not that it mattered, but it was several days before I was able to piece together the tragic chain of events that took Violet's life. She was playing in the shallow water of the shoal, near the bank, with Lacy and Victor close by. Oscar was there, too, the center of her attention as usual. It was a typical Kentucky summer morning with thunderstorms possible in the afternoon. Lacy and Victor were distracted by the peculiar behavior of a flock of crows in the trees on the east bank of the river.

They believe Oscar brought Violet a stick or something and it floated away before she seized it in her hands. She would have tried to catch it. Her parents were oblivious to her movement until they heard her cries and saw her slip under the deeper water some distance from the bank. Victor ran to her rescue, but she had disappeared.

Mama said their frantic search left both Lacy and Victor nearly drowned, themselves. They dived under the water repeatedly and refused to give up, swimming along the shore downstream and in the deep water in the middle of the river, fighting their own growing panic until in the end they knew their efforts were useless. The little girl's body was recovered the next day, a half-mile down the river.

Singleton's Branch had stolen our little sweetheart from us. Life in the Prather family would center on an unbearable empty space that never could be refilled.

A death in the family usually is a difficult time, even if the one who passed away was old and the end of life was not unexpected. The sudden death of a child is devastating. Those who are religious may try to rationalize it as God's will and seek comfort in believing there was a reason. Some abandon their faith; if God is all-powerful, how can he allow this to happen?

The Prather family was not particularly religious. Mama went to church when she could and professed to believe in God. Father never talked about it. I'd guess he was an agnostic, neither denying nor professing God but unable to accept by faith something for which he could see no physical evidence. He often criticized ministers and claimed they were more concerned about the offering plate than they were about peoples' souls.

My closest brush with a church had been through Vacation Bible School when I was little. They told us stories about Jesus and had us sing songs about God, but we accepted these as adult things and took much greater interest in the games and physical activities—playing together as a group and learning to make things with our hands.

Victor probably never had been to church. None of the Kentons attended any type of religious services, as far as I know.

Lacy was the one among us who truly was religious. Her god of everything was her inspiration. It was through him that she worshipped the natural world around her. He created the trees and flowers and birds and all the other plants and animals that to her were the most vital living things. All these were the visible evidence of his handiwork, framed by the green earth below and blue sky above.

She once said to me, "How can you not hold in reverence the god of everything, who gave us the beautiful world we live in?"

For an instant, I wanted to ask why he allowed the punishing floods on Singleton's Branch. Then I saw how her eyes lit up when she talked about her god and couldn't bring myself to cancel this sweet emotion with a negative thought. If she had faith in her god, what right did I have to be critical?

Father—this strong man we always expected to be stoic and reasonable in any situation and take charge—was awash in grief. Mama sat stoically at the kitchen table, an untouched cup of black coffee and a yellow writing pad before her. There would be events to let people know about. She must keep a list.

Owen Chenoweth, director of Erinville's most prominent funeral home, called Seth Ficklin for advice after receiving little Violet's remains and not being able to reach anyone in our family. He had tried several calls but no one answered the phone.

Seth came to the house and talked to Father, and after that spent a moment with Lacy and Victor. None had come to grips with the need to make arrangements. Seth asked and received permission to do what he could.

Between them, Seth and Mr. Chenoweth arranged a service of such magnitude I suspect it still is talked about among the locals. In lieu of a church, and with only a small chapel at the funeral home, they reserved the Erinville Civic Center's large auditorium. It was a given that, in the sense of community, even those who knew no one in our family would want to pay their respects and grieve with us over the loss of a child.

Mr. Chenoweth arranged for the small city symphony orchestra and a combined choir from the Methodist and Lutheran churches to provide music. Seth reminded him that John Meriwether, the school board president, was a lay preacher. He'd heard the old farmer was an inspiring speaker.

Mr. Chenoweth told us later that when he asked, John Meriwether not only agreed to conduct the service but also insisted on paying all the costs of the funeral. No one in the Prather family ever received a bill.

A single question remained. Where would little Violet be buried? There was a well-kept public county cemetery that would have been a logical choice. But Lacy said no, her baby would be laid to rest atop the bluff, beneath the great white oak where she never would be far away. No one objected.

The funeral was held on a scorching Sunday afternoon. Thunder rumbled in dark skies to the southwest. It was a day most of the good citizens of Erinville normally would not have cared to venture out. It didn't matter. The Civic Center auditorium was packed with mourners.

Several minutes before it was time for the service to begin, the Erinville fire chief—I don't remember his name, now—decreed that no one else could be admitted. The auditorium had reached its safe capacity. The forty or so people waiting outside simply stood in place. None complained, and none left.

When the orchestra began playing, every other human sound instantly quieted. The combined church choir sang "Rock of Ages" and "Abide with Me."

Then John Meriwether emerged from a side door and walked to the podium. The aging farmer and meticulous school board president was a striking figure. I had only seen him seated before. Now he stood, tall and straight, immaculately dressed in a black suit over white shirt with a garnet tie. There still was much black in his salt-and-pepper hair.

The audience stilled.

Mr. Meriwether looked out over those gathered before him, as if taking count, and smiled. There was a soft roll of thunder in the distance. He tilted his head and cupped a hand to his ear.

"Did you hear that? It means God is alive, in heaven. It is the sound, not of stormy weather, but of celebration. The bells are ringing in heaven, too. It is a time of jubilee. Heaven has just welcomed a new angel!"

A soft murmur spread across the auditorium.

John Meriwether made death seem insignificant. Instead of loss, he spoke of resurrection. He painted an enchanting picture of little Violet, with the wings of a butterfly, soaring above us. She looked down from paradise, he said, and laughed the innocent laugh of a child as she saw us all together, mourning her passing.

"'Why do you mourn?' she asks. 'Rejoice!'" He still spoke in a low, soft voice, comfortable yet caring. "And she is right. There is no pain or suffering in heaven, no misery, no fear of tomorrow. It's where we all would like to be. It's where years fly by like minutes. It's where little Violet, the newest angel, will hardly know we've been apart. And it's where she will be waiting to rejoice when you are together again."

He spoke for twenty minutes, leaving the Civic Center auditorium awash in smiles and tears. No prayer was said. The symphony orchestra and combined church choir closed with sacred music. I and other members of the family stood and accepted the condolences of a large number of Erinville residents. I could tell that Mama and Father knew most of them. To me, they merely were a sea of strange faces.

Victor responded the way he was expected to, in virtual robot fashion. There was an occasional person he knew. When they came through the line he embraced them and said he was honored by their presence.

Lacy stood only for a few minutes, then dropped back into her chair and bowed her head. Her pain was there for all to see. Soft sobs racked her body. Only a few of those passing in line spoke to her, most choosing instead to put a gentle hand on her shoulder and let their faces show their feeling.

John Meriwether was at the end of the line, along with Seth Ficklin and Owen Chenoweth. Each in turn offered condolences and asked if there was anything else he could do. We all expressed our gratitude, though Father was the only one who made an effort to let them know how much we truly valued what they had done.

He voiced special praise to Mr. Meriwether. This man who had addressed us with such eloquence appeared to be humbled by his kind words—perhaps embarrassed, even—and promised to see him soon at the hardware store.

With everything said that needed to be said, we got into the long sedans from the funeral home and rode in silence back to the old Prather house on the bluff. There had been no viewing of the little body. The child had been in the water too long before they found her, so that the mortician felt it unlikely he could allow an open casket.

The hearse was at the big house when we arrived. There were two trucks behind the house, one of them having hauled the backhoe Mr. Chenoweth knew would be necessary to dig a grave through the roots of the large white oak tree. Four workmen with shovels and axes stood by. They had done all they could do until the little casket was lowered into the ground.

Having no pallbearers, Mr. Chenoweth and his assistant put the casket on a rolling cart and wheeled it to the gravesite. We all were gathered around, except for Lacy. She had left us, with no word of explanation, and gone to her room. There was an awkward silence. Mr. Chenoweth waited, uncertain whether to lower the casket into the grave or wait for there to be words spoken.

Father stepped forward. For the first time since the tragedy happened, he looked to be almost his old self. But words did not come easily.

He put his hands on what amounted to a box for little Violet's mortal remains. He started to speak, and then had to pause and draw a handkerchief from his pocket and wipe away the tears and blow his nose. When he looked up, he managed a smile.

"We're not saying goodbye to our precious Violet," he said. "She will always be with us. Even though we may not be aware of her presence, her spirit will never desert this place."

He stepped away and indicated we all should join him. We went inside through the back door. Father closed the door behind us, then went around and systematically closed all the blinds on the back side of the house. We did not see or hear our precious little Violet being lowered into the dark hole under the big oak tree and covered with the very earth her little feet had trod.

Bobbi and I would stay over at the big house for the night and possibly longer. There always was extra room. We didn't want to disturb Mama to ask about bedding. Bobbi said she remembered her way around pretty well and was confident we could find what we needed.

We sat in the small parlor and talked about the day's events. I thought Bobbi was taking the loss of our little niece even harder than I was.

We finally reached the point of almost complete exhaustion and were ready for bed. We would sleep in the tiny downstairs guest room, which Mama kept ready for company which never came. The bed already was made up so that all we needed was towels. I waited while Bobbi went to get those.

I thought I heard her coming back, and stood and turned to meet her. It was not Bobbi. Lacy was walking toward me but not really looking my way. Her eyes were nearly swollen shut from crying. She barely seemed to notice me, and walked on by without speaking.

Bobbi came with the towels and soon we were in bed, desperate for rest and hoping for sleep that would not come easily. I had not seen Lacy again.

18

The big house was eerily quiet when we woke the next morning. I reached over to the nightstand and picked up my watch. It was ten o'clock. Both Father's and Victor's employers had given them the week off to be with family and Lacy and Sammy and Mama would be here, so where was everyone?

I was trying not to wake Bobbi, but when I turned back toward her she was looking at me and smiling. I wanted to lay my head back down on my pillow and look at her, too, and lose myself in the depths of those beautiful emerald green eyes.

"We need to get up," she said, her voice barely above a hoarse whisper.

"I guess so. But I'm in no hurry."

"You'll want breakfast."

"You know Mama. Her kitchen's always open."

She laughed, and reached and tousled my hair. I moved over and kissed her.

"Don't get me stirred up," she said. "We need to get everything taken care of today and get home. We'll both be way behind at work, probably."

I turned away from her and sat on the side of the bed. I knew she was right. We were at the end of the planned time at Myrtle Beach and had commitments that must be met. Violet's death had sapped my spirit, though, and I was going to have a hard time digging up any incentive to go about business as usual.

"It just doesn't seem like anything matters much," I told Bobbi.

"Honey, we're all going to have a hard time. We're going to feel this for a long, long time. Forever, I suppose. Just remember that we're all in it together. We need to lean on each other as we go through the ups and downs, otherwise somebody may fall by the wayside."

"Are you talking about the whole family?"

"Yes," she said, "the whole family. And we probably need to get up and get to breakfast before we get kicked out of the regiment."

We hurried to get dressed. There still had been no sound of others in the house, but I recalled how sound-deadening the thick walls of the structure were and assumed there was nothing unusual going on. We probably would find everyone in the kitchen.

"Are you hungry?" I asked.

"Not very. But I'm ready for a gallon or two of strong coffee."

I said this was another something we shared. Except I was hungry, also. She reminded me it almost was time for lunch. If Mama didn't have anything ready for breakfast couldn't I just wait? I accepted this and we headed for the kitchen.

I hoped Lacy would be there. She had looked and acted like she was virtually out of touch with reality last night. We hadn't talked, though, so I might be exaggerating her worn out appearance. This wouldn't be unusual; for her entire life I had regularly underestimated my little sister.

We were half way to the kitchen when we heard someone at the front door. I cut through the formal sitting room to the entrance hallway and called, "Coming," in the loudest voice I could muster without actually shouting. I opened the door and looked into the weathered, smiling face of Vincent Shield. He had changed little in the years since I had seen him last.

"Mr. Shield!"

"Yes, sir, it's me," he said, his smile broadening. "Been a good while since I saw you last."

"Sure has. How's life been treating you?"

"I've got no complaints." He paused, shifted his weight to the other foot, and said, "I was needing to see your daddy if he's around. I heard about that little girl and was wondering if there's something I can do."

I pushed the door open wider and asked him to come in. Bobbi had come up behind me and I introduced her to Vincent Shield. He took off his cap and shook her hand when she offered it, said he was always happy to meet another member of the Prather family.

"I've been doing business with Mr. Prather for a long time," he said. He turned back to me. "Like I was saying, if I could see your daddy I'd be much obliged."

I had to admit we didn't know where Father was. Bobbi suggested we all go on to the kitchen, where we'd either find him or find out where he was. She invited Mr. Shield to join us for coffee, which he politely declined.

Mama and Sammy were in the kitchen. She was standing over the stove tending pancakes cooking on the griddle and Sammy sat at the table, reading a book and drinking a glass of milk. He looked up when we entered, but Mama apparently didn't hear us and didn't react. Sammy slid out of his chair and stepped over to her and tugged on the back of her dress.

"You're too quiet," she greeted us. "I didn't hear you come in. How are you, Vin?"

"I'm doing good. I heard about that little girl and was wondering if there's something I can do."

Mama pulled a chair out from the table and motioned for him to sit. So far, she had ignored us. He responded as if he had just been given an order from high command. She quickly had a cup and saucer on the table in front of him and was pouring coffee. Bobbi looked at me and winked.

Mama finally turned to us.

"Didn't mean to leave you guys out," she said, directing her comment mostly to Bobbi. "Sleep well?"

Bobbi assured her we did, and stepped to the cabinet and pulled out coffee cups for herself and me. Mama was still holding the pot.

"Everybody else is out there on the bluff," she told us, pouring coffee after we held out our empty cups. "Lacy went out to the grave right after the sun come up and was right back in here crying her eyes out. She said something had been digging at the grave. Your father went back out there with her and then Victor got up and went out there too."

Someone had opened the blinds Father had closed the night before. I saw Lacy and the two men standing over the fresh grave of little Violet. Father's head was bowed and Lacy's distress was evident even from the distance. Victor put his arm around her shoulders, but there was no other movement.

Vin Shield finished his coffee and stood. "That sure was good," he said to Mama. "I thank you for it."

"You are most welcome, Vin. It's good to see you. You and your folks all doing all right?"

"Yes, ma'am. I guess we're doing about as well as old folks can expect." He stood awkwardly and looked somewhat uncomfortable. He picked up his cap from the table and held it against his stomach. "Would it be all right if I go out there and pay my respects?"

Mama said of course, and walked over and opened the back door. I told Bobbi I would go, too, and she said she would stay in with Mama and Sammy. Vin Shield and I walked across the back yard to the gravesite and he quickly paid his respects and expressed his sorrow. He paid particular attention to Lacy. She had managed a slight smile when she saw him coming, and I could see his visit had brightened her day.

I greeted Victor and hugged Lacy. Father and Vin Shield went off to the side and talked.

I wanted to get a better read on Lacy. She had been distraught almost more than I could bear to see when I'd last seen her. Was she able to cope with the heartbreaking loss of her child? Did she need help? What could I do? Victor had walked off a ways as if he wanted to be alone. I put my hands on Lacy's shoulders and looked her directly in the eyes.

"Did you sleep last night? I saw you up, but you disappeared before I could talk to you."

"There was something I had to do."

Whatever she'd been about, it sounded as though there was a sense of urgency. It also was clear she didn't want to talk about it.

"You going to make it, girl?"

She collapsed against me and began to sob. I said nothing else, and we stood like this until she spoke.

"It's so hard," she said, her voice quaking with emotion. "It's my fault. How could I have let her be in the river and not pay attention? This has to be my punishment for something, but I don't know what."

She began to cry again and I tightened my arms around her shoulders.

"It's not your fault, Lacy. These kinds of accidents happen all the time. You would never have been careless with Violet. I know that."

She straightened up and pushed back from me. I could see the pain, the hopelessness, in her eyes. I wanted so very much to help. This was Lacy, the little sister I had tried to protect from the world. I had failed. I would do anything to be able to roll back time and have little Violet here with us again. But this was not within my power, and I knew my words were useless. I wanted to change the conversation, to not talk about her loss, to have us standing here, atop the bluff over Singleton's Branch, back at an earlier point in our lives. There would be no Victor, no baby Violet—only us, the old Prather house behind us and the bluff in front and the shoal below, with its clear, cool water to wash away her cares.

"Lacy, honey!" Father was calling.

He and Vin Shield walked toward us.

"Vin has a wonderful offering for us, sweetheart," Father said. "We need to know what you think."

Father stepped aside and let the other man come closer.

Vin Shield took off his cap and stood directly in front of Lacy with an expression somewhere between pity and admiration. He had a gift, and it was almost like he was pleading for it to be wanted and accepted. And there was self-doubt. Had he done the right thing?

"I found out about your little baby girl," he said. "I'm so awful sorry. I was hoping I could do something—give something you'd want that would be fitting for this beautiful spot you've chosen to lay her to rest."

Lacy's emotions burst forth, driving her to run to him and throw her arms around his waist and laugh through her tears.

"You're such a darling," she said. "You've always been so good! Of course I want whatever you offer."

Father took charge then. The worry on his face gave way to a subtle smile. He told Vin Shield to bring his truck around back of the house and here to where we stood. I saw tears in Vin's eyes as he hurried away. Lacy called Victor. The three of us stood together beneath the ancient white oak tree, next to the child's grave, and waited.

Vin Shield's gift was a rock. It was a large, nearly square, block of sandstone, the kind that could be found easily in small sizes almost anywhere on the slope of the bluff above the river. But I'd never seen one this big before.

And there was something else.

In letters hand-carved deeply into the stone was a single word: Violet.

Victor had to catch Lacy when she saw the monument. She collapsed against him, quaking in violent sobs. Vin Shield looked on in something akin to horror. Was his gift not appropriate? He didn't have to wait long for an answer.

Lacy pulled herself away from Victor and turned to him. "It's beautiful."

No more words were needed. Father, Victor, Vin Shield, and I rolled the heavy stone, which sat on a wheeled pallet, down the ramp Vin always carried in the truck and wrestled it the few feet to the head of the freshly created grave. We turned it and positioned it perfectly, so that it would be here forever to mark the resting place of our departed angel.

Lacy went to the kitchen and got Mama and Bobbi to come see the new monument. She said Sammy was absorbed in his book and said he'd see it later. I could see she was irritated by this, but we all had come to accept that Sammy rarely saw the same value the rest of us did in any given action. But he always was true to his word. He would be eager to see the stone later.

Vin Shield's monument was a perfect addition to the site. It fit the setting in a way no other gravestone could have, marking little Violet's resting place for all time while giving the appearance of being as natural to the bluff above the river as the great oak tree under which it sat. Bobbi and Mama were thrilled with what they saw.

"The Good Lord in heaven couldn't have done it better," Mama said. "It's almost like a religious shrine or something."

Bobbi agreed. She wondered aloud where Mr. Shield found the rock, and how he came up with the idea to begin with.

While the two women went on to discuss the surprising morning events, I walked away. At most points along the bluff the river below was visible through the trees and undergrowth. I was struck by a rush of memories. Here, I still found peace.

Ignoring the others, I made my way down the sloped path to the shoal. The water in Singleton's Branch was unusually low, the river's edge barely reaching into the shallow space where Lacy and I so often had played when we were little. I sat on the rocky edge without removing my shoes, my feet resting on dry gravel, and gazed upon the calm waters.

There was little wind. Branches on the trees on the east side of the river barely moved. Crows called in the distance, but there was no response. It was, for this moment, as if I were back in time and the intervening years had not happened. How good life was!

But had this been so, there would not be Bobbi and our own little Sarah. "A man couldn't be more blessed than to have a good wife," Jonathon had said. The lonely old man on the beach had spoken words of wisdom. It was time for me to put childhood and early memories aside and tend to the needs of today. My mind flashed back to our honeymoon at Myrtle Beach and Bobbi and me playing in the surf like newlyweds. Suddenly it seemed urgent that I get back to the top of the bluff and rejoin the one who mattered most.

I did not think of the rest of Jonathon's story, a narrative that might have been scripted especially for me: "I made a foolish decision without thinking." A time would come when the old man's words would come back to haunt me.

Bobbi was watching for me. She and Mama still stood near the grave.

"I thought we'd lost you," she said as I came near.

"Just checking on the river. It's pretty low right now."

"I think I'll skip it. We have to get ready to go pretty soon."

I paused to admire the stone Vin Shield had carved for Violet's grave one more time, then Bobbi, Mama, and I walked slowly back to the house. Vin was gone and Father and Victor were somewhere inside. Bobbi was right; we needed to try to refocus on the normal day-to-day routine.

Lacy was in the kitchen. She sat at the table, with nothing before her, and looked up when we came in but didn't speak. Mama, almost as if by instinct, poured a cup of coffee and set it before her.

"Have you had anything to eat today, honey?" she asked.

"No. I don't want anything."

Mama looked toward me with an expression that said she wanted help. I pulled out a chair and sat at the table, next to Lacy. Bobbi then sat down close to me. Mama brought more coffee and, almost as if by magic, produced a plate of blueberry muffins. If the end of days were crashing around her, I thought, Mama still would carry out her perceived duties as kitchen-keeper for the old Prather house on the bluff.

I wanted to say the right thing to Lacy, but couldn't find the words. Bobbi filled the silence.

"Please let us know if you need anything," she said to Lacy. "I know we can never fill the void left by your terrible loss, but there will be ways we can help as you move on. You can't see it now but you still have a life to live, to take care of Victor and be a companion here for Mama. There'll be times you don't have things you need or just need a helping hand, and we're here for you."

Lacy managed a slight smile.

"You've always been so sweet to me, Bobbi. Thank you for that. But you have your own precious little one now. Take care of Sarah. Victor and I will make it. Yeah, we may lean on Mama and Father sometimes, but that's kind of how it works around here."

I felt obligated to join the conversation. The communication between the two of them had been both touching and effective, simple words that somehow sliced through the sadness and pointed us all toward the future. And I knew why.

"We're family," I said.

We had not found a gate to close on the emptiness left by our loss, but life would go on. I once again felt the closeness of the house where Lacy and I had bonded in our childhood years, where there always was the warmth of Mama's kitchen, where Sammy had accepted the appeal of learning, and where Father always stood proud and strong against all outside forces.

I was ready now to take Bobbi home. We would pick up Sarah on the way. We would once more enjoy the comfort of our new house. In another day or so we both would be back at work, doing what we knew to do as if we'd never been away. There would be something good about routine.

But first there was a question to which I wanted to find an answer.

As Bobbi packed up our things back in the first floor guest room, I told her I'd be gone only for a few minutes and slipped out quietly. It took little time to climb up into the attic and cross to what Lacy and I had fancied to be our own secret passage.

The opening behind the panel was much smaller than I remembered. Lacy and I had crawled through it many times when we were children, but I had never been back as an adult. I had to hunch my shoulders inward to squeeze through. I didn't need a light. Plenty of sunlight filtered down through the opening in the floor of the tower.

The climb up the ladder, daunting when we were little, was nothing now. A few steps up and my head was above the level of the tower floor. What I had come to look for was here. I'm not sure what I expected, but I was astonished by what lay before me.

There was no longer a little Billiken, the god of the way things ought to be. Instead, there were fragments of the statue scattered all over the tower floor. Its stand had been knocked over and lay in a corner. The figurine of the fat little god had been smashed into small pieces. A hammer that belonged in the garage lay on the floor close to the ladder opening.

We never would know who put the Billiken figurine in the tower to begin with. But I knew who killed it.

The urgency Lacy had felt in accomplishing her mission the night before was clear now. The god of things as they ought to be was a phony imposter and must be destroyed. No child ought to drown in Singleton's Branch.

19

It seems strange to me that I never told Sammy about the Billiken, or even how to get up into the tower. As I tell you all this now, I'm not sure I can offer any particular reason. He would have been quicker than anyone else to learn about the god of things as they ought to be. He probably knew about the Billiken, but not that there was one in the tower of the old Prather house.

Sammy may have taken the loss of little Violet as hard as anyone in the family. He tried to conceal his grief, but it was obvious. His spirit was crushed. In typical fashion, he compensated by burying himself in the search for new knowledge. His early interest in the ancient Mayan civilization already had morphed into a fascination with concepts of time.

I had come to look forward to his frequent visits to my office at Graffenried Distributors to try and catch a few minutes when I could take a break and have coffee. I always had a coffee pot ready, but he brought his own preferred can of Pepsi. I sat quietly most of the time and listened to his enthusiastic reports on some new theory or complex bits of knowledge he'd just gained.

Today, he insisted humankind's common view that the passing of time is nothing more than a repetitive cycle is wrong.

"It's easy enough to just see it as sunset and sunrise, every day the same as the one before," he told me. "Like, you know, days simply stacked up like falling leaves or something."

"And you don't see it that way?" I said.

Sammy took a drink of his soda and leaned forward, intent on what he had to tell me.

"No. Time is linear. Just like a truck moving down a highway. Every day adds another mark to the cipher, but you can't undo what's already happened any more than you could eliminate a bridge you'd just crossed ten miles back when you're driving. Think of it as time moving forward."

Even if I couldn't grasp the total meaning of what Sammy was telling me, I was impressed by his enthusiasm for his subject. He actually was excited to tell me his view and I knew he would have been proud to continue our discussion with scientific evidence to support it. Unfortunately, we both had other things to do and would have to continue at another time.

That night I told Bobbi about his visit. She asked what we talked about.

"Concepts of time," I said. "And don't ask me to go any further. I think it's a bit over my head."

"Sammy's a wonder. He may accomplish great things once he finds his groove."

I asked about her day. She said Ranelle Bishop had talked some about Father, and inquired about his general wellbeing.

"I told her we haven't seen him in a while," Bobbi said. "Do you think we should get out there one of these days and visit him and your mama?"

I said yes, we probably should. I'd like to see him, and Mama and Lacy, too.

The truth was, I'd virtually lost track of time. How long had it been since Violet's funeral and burial under the great white oak? Had Father been by my office within the last couple of weeks? How old was our precious Sarah? Our honeymoon at Myrtle Beach was only a distant memory.

I was too busy, working too hard.

That night I lay awake contemplating my own mortality. I thought about Rachel McNary's confident lectures about living life one day at a time. Her view had seemed unassailable. And yet, like Sammy had said, you can't go back and uncross a bridge you've already crossed. Violet's death was as much a part of the Prather family story now as my marriage to Bobbi.

No one is immune to the quirks of fate, be they blessings or tragedies. I might never have had Lacy as a sister, never have known the bluff overlooking Singleton's Branch or the shoal at its foundation. I might never have met Bobbie and there might be no Sarah.

So why did I matter? I was no more than happenstance. What would the world have missed if it never had been inhabited by me? Did Lacy's god of everything know or care I existed? I wished there really were a Billiken, a god of things as they ought to be. And if there were, I wished he would take control so insignificant mortals like me couldn't find so many ways to spoil the days of our own lives and mangle the world around us.

My fitful sleep, when it finally came, woke Bobbi three times during the night. She never complained, but she worried I might be sick. She pressed me in the morning until I told her it was only my baseless concerns over things I couldn't control that had caused my stress.

"So give it to me straight," she implored. "Are you all right now?"

I said yes, I was all right now.

"But will you still be all right tonight, or will those nasty little concerns come back?"

I assured her I'd be okay. I agreed to her plea to be honest and candid with her, and to seek help if I needed it. Her concern was genuine and I was grateful for it. Whether the rest of the world cared or not, Bobbi did. And that mattered.

I remembered Mama telling me she went through a bout of depression right after I was born. She said it was a terrible time, and if I ever felt depressed to ask for help right away. Then she laughed and said hers was postpartum depression, which meant I'd caused it. I cried in bed that night because I'm made Mama sick. She never mentioned it again but I still worried about it until about the time I started high school. I saw a magazine article or something and found out what it was.

Bobbi's father stopped by my office soon after I got to work and asked me how things were going. He invited me to come to his office and visit for a while.

"We don't get our heads together as often as we should," he said. "We ought to share ideas, and talk about how things are working and all that. I'm going to ask Carly to come by, too. It won't even have to be business. It can be family, you know?"

There was no doubt in my mind Bobbi had called him and told him about my bad night. There was a time when this might have irritated me, but no more. Now I was part of the Hoard family, and needed to be open with them. Marriage was supposed to be a full partnership; I should think of Bobbi's father much as if he were my father, too.

What had he said the night he offered me a job? "I never had a son, so I don't know how to talk to one." It couldn't be more clear. He wanted to treat me like a son.

We had a good session in his office, whether from a business or family point of view. We ended up with some new ideas for the routine things company staff had to do and caught up on a few family things. Jackson Hoard interrupted Carly in mid-sentence to report a thought that had just occurred.

"I'd forgotten this, but it might be worth running by you two to see what you think," he said. "Back in Iowa, almost every business worth its salt had an annual company picnic. Think we might give that a try?"

We both said yes. Before we broke up, we had a modest outline of what needed to be done to pull off the first annual Graffenried Distributors Family Fun Day.

Carly and I walked together back to our offices. We both felt good about the session we'd just had, and agreed it should take place more often.

"By the way," she said, "Father's very happy with your work. He says you've done some things that have made this place better. That's high praise, in my book."

Her words had powerful impact. Not because they were flattering and good for my ego, but because the instant she spoke them I was hit by a mental vision of Grandpa Childs, sitting on the shaded porch of his and Grandma's house in Golconda talking about my future. It was almost as if I could hear his words: "I got good at my job, too. They hated to lose me when I retired."

What more did I need as a guide to carrying my share of the load? I made a silent vow that I wouldn't worry about things I couldn't control, but do my best to make the things I could control come out better. The world might not notice, but surely in some small ways I could make a contribution to Graffenried Distributors that would make my father-in-law proud.

It seems likely to me now that my more positive attitude alone made life better for Bobbi. I couldn't have asked for more.

It was another week before we got to the Prather house again. On a perfect Sunday evening, shortly before sunset, we parked in front and, through those familiar, barricade-strong entrance doors, joined Father and Mama in the large sitting room. It was remarkable to me that I felt like company.

Mama had prepared a small feast of sandwiches and desserts. She had them carefully arranged on large platters, ready to serve without us going to the kitchen. Bobbi said aloud what I was thinking.

"You shouldn't have gone to all this work," she told Mama. "We're not company."

Mama was slightly flustered. She looked to be searching for an answer. I knew at that moment she *had* thought of us as company, probably without realizing it. We'd been away too long.

Father was talkative. He had been reading Steinbeck's *Grapes of Wrath* for the third time, and said he found things in it he'd overlooked before or maybe had merely forgotten.

"It's true what they say about the memory being the first thing to go," he said. "There are times I worry I might forget my way home."

I told him he wasn't old enough to get away with using age as an excuse. He might be like an automobile, though: wearing out from hard use and high miles even though not all that old.

"I couldn't believe how fast the sales staff cars run up a hundred thousand miles," I said. "But I guess they cover a big area."

"Don't you get tired of sitting in an office all day sometimes and think it might be good to get out on the road like that?" Father asked. "When I was younger I was kinda interested in getting a job as a traveling salesman."

Mama laughed. "You just heard too many traveling salesman jokes."

"Well, you know, all those farmers' daughters."

Bobbi held up her hands.

"No more!" she said, with what for her was a big laugh. "I've always thought farmers' daughters got a bad rap. Just sittin' out there in the cornfield waiting for the first traveling salesman that happened by."

We had been there for close to thirty minutes, but Lacy and Victor had yet to show. Mama hadn't mentioned them so I assumed they would be there. Wanting to visit with Lacy had been my most compelling reason to come. I asked Mama if she expected them to join us. She said she did, and was wondering what might be holding them up.

Father offered to go upstairs and check on them.

"Let me go," I said. "I need to stretch my legs, anyway. I think I still know the way."

All was quiet as I walked down the second floor hallway. How could this ever be unfamiliar? The time I'd been away was like nothing compared to the time I had spent in this old Prather house and every inch of it should be as fresh in my mind as any place on earth. But I couldn't escape a curious sense of not belonging.

The door to Lacy's and Victor's room was closed. On the opposite side of the hall, the door to the nursery stood open. I glanced inside and saw that nothing had changed; Violet might be sleeping in her little bed alongside the wall, underneath the guardian angel plaques.

I knocked softly on Lacy's door. There was no answer. I knocked again, and heard stirring inside. The door opened slightly and Lacy looked out. She had been crying and there was swelling under one eye. I knew at once she had been struck in the face.

20

Our little Sarah was four years old when our son was born. We named him Jackson Graden Prather after his two grandfathers. He was a husky baby, with Bobbi's coloring and the same loud voice his big sister had come with. I suppose it was fortunate for him he was a boy; this was his claim to being special, since the first child already was there.

The nursery in our house—no longer new—was modest, still reflecting the firstborn with its pink curtains. Bobbi said there was no reason to change anything. Jackson was not likely to notice.

It was shortly after his arrival that we received good news from Sammy. He had been offered an internship with NASA, where there was a contingent of engineers with Southern Illinois degrees, and was going to accept it. And equally important, he had a girlfriend. Her name was Melinda and they met at an off-campus party in Carbondale and it sounded as if he were stricken. Her specifications were, one, she was very pretty; two, she was an English major and would-be poet; and, three, it was love at first sight.

Bobbi wanted to write and ask if the third element was true of both, or only him. I encouraged her to but she never got around to it.

I still thought of Sammy's view of time once in a while. It was easy to see in my passing days a parallel to travel in a fast-moving vehicle, making various stops to interact with others and accepting whatever fate let me remember of each stop. And, as I'd often been told by elders, the more time passed the faster it flew by.

Father was beginning to look somewhat frail. I couldn't remember how old he was. Bobbi said we needed to ask Mama the next time we saw her but neither of us remembered to do so.

On my front, my father-in-law had hinted to Carly he was grooming me to be his replacement as district manager at Graffenried Distributors. She told Bobbi, and Bobbi of course told me. I wondered if he had come to this decision before or after Carly announced she was going to leave Erinville and join her other sister in New York.

I don't think she would have been interested in the job, regardless. Her life was made whole by pursing her creative talents more so than her ability to manage a business. She was a very good painter and skilled photographer and I have no doubt there were a great many other things she did well. If I haven't said it before, Bobbi was extremely creative, too, at the very least equal to her sister.

Mandy Fouts had moved away, so we had to find someone new to sit with Sarah and Jackson. We went through a parade of teenaged girls and a few older women without finding one we liked who was available on the schedule we needed. When Jessica Buford finally came along, it made our lives much easier.

Jessica was neither a teenager nor an older woman. She was somewhere in her early thirties, married with no children. The frosting on her credentials was that her husband was in the Marine Corps and currently on an extended overseas assignment. She had moved from San Diego back to Erinville, her home town, to be around family. She would be available virtually any time we needed her and we liked her very much.

Victor hadn't been seen around the old Prather house for two weeks and Lacy was deathly concerned. Mama called me at work and asked if I could possibly come by and talk to her. She said Lacy had admitted they had quarreled the night before he disappeared. It was only a small argument, she said, and nothing that would have driven him away. She was sure he hadn't been drinking again.

"You have a lot more influence with her than either your father or I do," Mama said. "You probably are just like us, and don't know what to say to her, but I think just hearing you say you still care about her would help a lot."

I agreed to come by right after work and called Bobbi and told her I'd be late. She was in easy walking distance of home and seldom waited for me to give her a ride. She also had been greatly worried about Lacy, herself, and was glad to know I was going.

"Take as much time as you need," she told me. "You don't have to worry about coming in late."

That was an opening I couldn't let slip by.

"So let me get this straight," I said. "Is that an everyday release from guilt or only for tonight?"

Bobbi's never-failing sense of humor let her down.

"Damn it! This is serious business. Lacy needs you. How do you think I'd feel if you'd been gone for two weeks and I didn't know where you were or if or when you'd be back?"

I backtracked and said I understood. I told her Lacy and I had been down some bumpy roads before and I always was concerned about her, even under normal circumstances. And Victor's disappearance was anything but normal.

I was grateful Lacy had been able to keep her physical abuse secret. If she had admitted to a minor quarrel, as Mama just told me, I had no reason to think it had happened again. But I knew nothing was certain.

When I got to the old Prather house, I went straight to the kitchen. Lacy was there with Mama. Lacy's face lit with at least a half-smile when I walked in.

"You're just in time," Mama said. "Supper's just about ready."

"We're having roast beef," Lacy said. "I know you always liked roast beef."

I pretended excitement. Yes, it had been a long time since I'd had roast beef. And when I did, it wasn't like Mama's. I couldn't wait. Just knowing it was coming made my mouth water. Was there anything I could do to help?

Bobbi had suggested I downplay Victor's absence, pretending I didn't think it was anything serious. She said Lacy put a great deal of stock in my opinion. If she believed I didn't think it was a serious problem, it might relieve her worry some.

Mama rejected my offer to help. She said Lacy was all the help she ever could need.

"She flits around like a little fairy, and before I know it everything's done," Mama said.

"So what happens then? You both go sit on the porch and gossip about the neighbors?"

Mama laughed and I could see Lacy was loosening up. I said I was happy she was such good help, especially if it got roast beef on the table. I asked if it would be ready by the time Father got home. And how long would that be?

Lacy pulled a chair out from the table and motioned for me to sit.

"It's ready now," she said, "and we won't wait for Father. Anyway, he'll be here any minute. Sit down and I'll bring you a generous serving."

"Anything new on Victor?"

I tried to make my question sound casual, hoping Bobbi's idea would work. And I thought Lacy might pick up on the fact I wouldn't have brought up Victor's name right before dinner was served if I was afraid it was a sensitive topic. Whether all this had any effect I don't know, but Lacy didn't show any sign of being upset by my question.

"Nope," she answered, "haven't heard from him. Big lug's still missing."

Father came and we all sat down to eat. Conversation centered on the usual topics of health and the weather and had I heard about such and such. Mama was true to her life-long habit of asking if I knew what happened to someone I'd never heard of.

"I don't know who that is, Mama."

"Oh, you know her. She used to live over east of the river a mile or so, before they got flooded out. The big flood. Surely you remember that."

I had to laugh, and Lacy joined in. Even Father had a big smile.

"I remember the flood, Mama. I just don't remember her."

I enjoyed the dinner very much. Mama's roast beef was as good as ever, Lacy smiled most of the time, Mama was pleased with everything, and Father seemed relaxed and in a good mood. Lacy started to clear the table and Mama shooed her away.

"I can take care of this," she told Lacy. "You go visit with your brother."

Lacy, Father, and I walked back to the large parlor. I suggested Lacy and I go sit on the porch so Father could get to his reading. I said the night air should be cool and comfortable, with just enough breeze, and anyway I hadn't sat outdoors in the evening for ages and thought it would be nice. They both agreed.

"Could you even guess at how many hours we've sat here like this?" I asked Lacy, who was next to me on our favorite bench. "You'd have to start by counting the years first, I suppose."

"There were a lot of happy years," she said.

"I hope you're still happy, Lacy."

She started to cry. I put my arm around her shoulders and pulled her close.

"I know, honey, I know," I whispered. "It's Victor."

"Yes. I miss him so much. I don't think he's ever coming back."

I wanted to tell her he would, to say I was confident he'd be home soon. I wanted to make her believe his absence was a temporary thing, that he probably never intended to be gone even this long. I wanted her to feel safe and secure. I wanted words to make this so. But such words escaped me.

"Sometimes I think you'd be better off without him, Lacy," I said.

"No!" She pulled away from me, and slid to the far end of the bench. "Victor's my life. I need him. Nobody else cares about me the way he does."

"I care about you, Lacy. We all do."

We sat without further words for what seemed like an eternity. It was Lacy who finally broke the silence.

"You'll think I'm crazy, but I want another baby."

I slid to her end of the bench and put my arm around her again and pulled us close together. Now I was the one with tears.

21

Carly and I spent much more time than we could spare getting ready for the Graffenried Distributors Family Fun Day. She was not too happy having to do this, especially since her move to New York was imminent. She still was fun to work with, though, and the more I was with her the more she reminded me of Bobbi.

Much of what we had to do simply was because this was the first time around. As we planned and got commitments, we tried to make these continue into next year. No need to have to do it all over again next time, Carly said. I readily agreed. What I was thinking but didn't say was next time around I would not have her good help.

One of my ideas—I still think it may have been my best—didn't fly. I thought we might have some sort of music, maybe a group sing-along. I cited the performances of the city symphony orchestra and combined church choir at Violet's memorial service. Carly liked the idea in general, but said we wouldn't have a budget for anything that added an expense and this probably ruled out the orchestra and choirs.

We talked about other ways to do it. At one point I said we could mimic the Kentucky Derby and have a group sing of "My Old Kentucky Home." Carly said her father wouldn't go for that because the song was racist. She reminded me they changed the original Stephen Foster lyrics from "'Tis summer, the *darkies* are gay" to "the *people* are gay." I think I knew this, but had forgotten. We ended up skipping the music.

When it came, Fun Day was a giant community picnic, exhibition baseball game, and a carnival, all rolled into one. The weather was good and the turnout far better than we had expected. We tried to estimate the attendance but couldn't figure out a logical basis for even a wild guess. Some way to count how many people came was added to next year's "to do" list.

Carly said her mother was especially impressed by the number of children who were there.

"She said she didn't know there were that many kids in Erinville."

Bobbi and I got to the park early, hoping there still would be plenty of parking space, and drove up right behind Jackson and Jen Hoard. He was as excited as a school boy on the last day of school.

"Why didn't we think of this a long time ago?" he shouted over the noise of other cars coming into the parking area. "I don't even care about the public relations effects, I just want everybody to have fun."

Bobbi already had warned me not to feel like I was there as an inspector or something job-related. She wanted it to be a care-free day and if I worried about all the things that might go wrong this wouldn't happen. But she had no more than told me her concern than she laughed and admitted this was unlikely.

"I know you better than that," she said.

And she was right. I found the day immensely stressful. By the time twilight fell and the grounds were vacant of all but those who had things to pack up and load, I was worn out. I felt good, though, because by any measure the day had been a great success.

My good feeling came crashing down when I saw Lacy, sitting alone on a park bench staring vacantly into space. She didn't hear me coming and was startled when I spoke.

"Lacy! Surprised to see you here. Are you all right?"

She looked away, as if watching something across the park.

"I can't work tonight and I don't want to go home," she said.

"You can come home with us. Bobbi and I would be glad to have you overnight."

"It's not just tonight. It's forever."

I knew this was about Victor. His behavior had not improved with time. When he came home after his long absence, Mama said it clearly was because he'd run out of anyplace else to go. He tried to make amends, and I think genuinely wanted to, but it just wasn't in him. Losing Violet still ate away at him and alcohol had become his crutch.

After a few months, Father laid down the law. He told Victor he no longer was welcome in the old Prather house. Victor found a decrepit mobile home for rent and he and Lacy moved out. Lacy took a job washing dishes at Miss Wilken's Diner. She worked mostly at night, so I made it a point to go by occasionally during the late hours and see her. It had been a couple of weeks, or maybe longer, since I'd been there.

I knew I might as well confront the issue directly.

"Is Victor at home?"

"I don't know. He's supposed to be."

"Have you been here all day?" I asked.

"Yes."

"Lacy, honey, I'm really sorry for your problems with Victor. I know you still love him, but if he's mistreating you it can't go on. You just have to move out."

"I didn't say he mistreated me!" She stiffened, and turned and looked me directly in the eyes. Her own flashed with anger. "Victor wouldn't hurt me. Okay, he did a couple of times. But he'd been drinking and didn't know what he was doing."

"I'm sorry. I just thought—"

"I told you. I want another baby. He won't have sex unless he's been drinking, and then he demands I take pills or something so I won't get pregnant."

"Maybe he only needs more time."

We talked a while longer, but I knew I was making no progress toward cheering her up. Bobbi was waiting in the parking lot and Lacy finally agreed to let us drive her home. She promised she would call if there was any problem there, tonight or any other time, but claimed she was certain there wouldn't be.

When I told Bobbi later what had gone on, she was upset enough she had difficulty sleeping. She was sure Lacy was in danger.

"I don't know what we can do about it," she said. "But we need to keep an eye on things over there and if there's ever a sign of physical abuse get her out of there."

Lacy's situation added a new worry for Bobbi and me, but we still had to get on with our own lives. With our two little ones, I was enjoying fatherhood even more than I'd expected to. Sarah was getting tall and looked more like Bobbi every day. Jack favored Sammy more than me.

It didn't surprise anyone when Ranelle Bishop retired and Bobbi was promoted into the library director position. She quickly proved superb in that role, as I knew she would. One of her first projects was a community-wide photographers' exhibition which drew far more interest than anyone expected. It was such a success the library board decided it should be permanent, and I think it continues to thrive even now.

Sammy got his engineering degree and took a position with NASA. He credited the delegation of Southern Illinois University engineers already there for his good fortune, but I suspect the quality of his work during his internship had more to do with it. He's still modest about his own accomplishments.

He and Melinda were married soon after she finished her degree. They visited briefly in Erinville on the way to their brave new world and were of course subjected to an informal "get acquainted" gathering at the old Prather house. We found Melinda to be a very pretty girl and a lovely person. Sammy mostly just sat to the side and beamed with pride.

He hadn't told us his new wife was of mixed ethnic background—her mother, from Cuba, was Hispanic—so we were surprised when we saw her. None of us cared, of course. Except Lacy. Lacy pronounced herself thrilled to have "beautiful new variety" in the family and said she'd give her left little finger for Melinda's gorgeous skin tone.

Mama told Melinda her new responsibilities included keeping her husband out of the poison ivy. She said Sammy got into the vine somewhere on the bluff when he was little and suffered mightily.

"He wouldn't go down there for a long time after that," she said. "If I tried to get him to go down to the shoal and play in the water with his sister and big brother he'd say 'It's poison down there.'"

It was the first time I'd ever heard this. I marveled at not knowing all these years. Father had eliminated such little poison ivy as there was on the bluff many years ago. Sammy laughed and said there were many secrets he'd kept from me. Melinda looked somewhat confused, as if she was unsure how much of what she heard was serious and how much of it was nothing more than Prather family fun.

I made sure to get by Miss Wilken's Diner often and waited as long as necessary for Lacy to finish in the kitchen and come out so I could see and talk with her. Some nights this meant closing time, which was half an hour before midnight. She always emerged tired and dirty and apologized for looking so "ratty."

When I tried to dismiss her appearance as coming with the job, she said I probably never had seen Bobbi looking the way she did. This was true, but then Bobbi never had worked as a dishwasher in a diner. Lacy dismissed this argument out of hand. Nothing changed for a few months, then one night there was a ray of hope.

Lacy was all smiles when I saw her. And she looked different. Her hair was trimmed more neatly and it was apparent she had started to use makeup. This was new, as she always had refused to use it because she thought it was "phony." Given her pretty face, makeup wasn't necessary to make her attractive.

"Do I look good?" she asked.

"Sure you do. What's different?"

"I'm making myself pretty for Victor."

I told her she already was pretty. Surely Victor was happy with her, without any changes. I knew she liked hearing this, but she still shook her head.

"Victor didn't say anything," she said. "I didn't do it because he wanted me to. I did it because I wanted to look good for him. You know why."

I tried to stay positive, but in my mind I was thinking Victor or any other man would be a fool not to find this woman standing before me very attractive and want to make love to her. It was painful to hear she thought she had to do more to make herself appealing to him.

"I'm sure Victor has always found you very pretty," I said.

"Not pretty enough. But I'm going to change that. You just watch."

My spirits hit bottom as I drove home. My little sister had just told me she didn't think she was pretty enough for a man who, in my candid opinion, wasn't good enough to exist under the same sun. I wanted to confront him, tell him he never had been and never would be good enough for Lacy. I wanted to order him to get out of Lacy's life and never darken a Prather door again. If I had confronted him then, I very well might have said those things.

Fortunately it was several days before I saw him.

Lacy, meanwhile, kept up her new front. I stopped at the diner to see her more often, and on alternate nights Bobbi sometimes did the same. Each time I expected to find her broken and dispirited, having recognized the hard truth. But she still was confident she was doing the right thing. She had made herself prettier and Victor was sure to find her more desirable. And Lacy had the last laugh.

A few weeks later, Bobbi stopped at the diner on her way home from the library. She expected Lacy to be busy back in the kitchen and was prepared simply to look in and go on home. Lacy saw her the minute she stepped in the door.

As Bobbi told me afterward, Lacy ran from behind the counter and threw her arms around her, obviously excited about something. Bobbi asked her what had her in such a happy mood. Lacy's answer made Bobbi happy, too, and belatedly, me.

"I'm overdue," she whispered. "I think I'm expecting again."

Despite our uncertainties about Victor, we accepted this as good news. Lacy had made clear she wanted another baby. Another child was undoubtedly the best thing to help both of them get past the loss of Violet. We waited in eager anticipation over the next several days until Lacy called Bobbi and announced that, yes, there indeed was going to be a new little one in the family.

Father's reaction surprised me. He said if there was going to be another baby the ramshackle old mobile home was not a fit place for Lacy and Victor to live and insisted they move back to the old Prather house. He said Lacy should give up her job at Miss Wilken's Diner immediately, noting she would have to quit eventually anyway. And if the loss of her salary posed a hardship, he would hire her, himself. She would be assistant kitchen manager to Mama.

I knew Victor would resist. Somehow, though, Father said all these things in such a positive and almost lighthearted way he soon came around. Lacy couldn't wait.

All this affected me in a way that is hard to describe, but it was good. No, we couldn't go back and destroy bridges already crossed, but the road ahead had become a lot more inviting. There would be a baby again in the old Prather house and in no time at all Sarah and Jackson would have a new cousin big enough to play with them on the shoal, in the calming waters of Singleton's Branch.

22

Father once declared the goal of every living thing is to reproduce. He said this drive is abetted by nature through its endless cycling of the seasons. Autumn's seeds are spring's seedlings and plants emerge from winter's sleep as the earth is warmed by longer hours of sunlight. Animals also take a cue from the sun, and begin to pair off for a new mating season.

The old Prather house on the bluff was once again home to the expectant parents and Father was impatient for the coming of his newest grandchild. Mama found him a couple of times going through the children's books he had bought for Violet.

Lacy's only complaint was that her advanced pregnancy kept her from running up and down the bluff to the shoal. She said even though it still was winter, she would have liked to stand at the water's edge once every few days just for the sake of old times.

I understood this. Had I been in her position I most likely would have had the same wish. Being at home on the bluff again should mean reconnecting with Singleton's Branch.

Victor took the move in stride. He was not one to show much enthusiasm for mundane things like moving their meager household out of the old mobile home back into the confines of the Prather house. This was daily living to him, no more or no less than sitting down to supper. Father had once told me he thought

Victor's hard upbringing left him afraid to get excited about good things that might not last.

Lacy spent two days looking for Oscar. Mama told her the old dog hadn't been seen for weeks. She thought he got lonely and went looking for a new family after spending endless days lying around the house waiting for Lacy or someone to show an awareness of his presence. She had fed him regularly, though he seemed to have lost his appetite. He had started with short absences of one or two days but always came back, then one morning didn't come to breakfast and she hadn't seen him since.

This was all over and done with before I heard about it. Lacy had accepted Mama's interpretation of events and was good with everything. She had faith that Oscar had a new home somewhere up or down river and was thriving in the care of people who loved him.

Whether or not the seasons had anything to do with it, Victor Howard Kenton, Jr., was born on the first day of spring. He was a healthy baby and once again Lacy had an easy time. Victor stuck with her and looked to be as excited with the big event as I had been with Sarah's arrival.

Mama had changed a few things in the nursery—replacing pink with blue. It still was a sunny, happy room to be in. When Bobbi and I visited the day after they took little Junior home, Lacy said she counted on the nursery having the same calming effect on him as it did on her. She had slept little the night before and had spent most of it there with the baby so as not to disturb her husband.

"I don't have much choice, anyway," Lacy said. "Victor may be a good daddy but he can't feed the baby."

She had nursed Violet and claimed this provided a connection impossible to achieve any other way. We knew without asking she would nurse little Victor, Jr.

We didn't see Victor. He had made it a point to miss as little work as possible, claiming facetiously he couldn't afford to lose pay now there was another mouth to feed. Lacy said The Print

Shop was unusually busy and he didn't want to get farther behind, but Mama teased he was afraid he'd have to change a diaper.

We left the Prather house after that visit believing things were going well. Father had become a more patient man, Mama still thrived on being kitchen czar, and Lacy and Victor were happy to be back on the bluff with their new baby. I hated to hear about Oscar, but wasn't surprised. His surely had been a lonely life.

If our small circle of life was moving toward normalcy, though, I had stumbled into a new fanaticism that would have been shocking to my former teachers had they known. I had come to love and read poetry.

This began one night when Bobbi brought out the small book of Emily Dickinson poems I had given her for Christmas after seeking advice from Miss Jennings. She read a few aloud and I was intrigued by the beauty of the message yet simplicity of words. Yes, this was in part because they were spoken by Bobbi— I still loved the sound of her voice—but it was more than this. I barely knew poetry existed in my long-gone student days, but now I heard the richness of language I should have heard then:

I hide myself within my flower,

That wearing on your breast,

You, unsuspecting, wear me too—

And angels know the rest.

Over the next several nights, we alternated reading poetry to each other. I hated the sound of my own voice after listening to Bobbi, but she was content to take turns and said it was good to *hear* the poems and not have to read them, herself. She said with mock surprise she was amazed to find poetry the way to my heart.

This was true in a sense. Reading and hearing the poetry together drew me into an ever greater awareness of the bond between us. Jonathon had said it well: "The two of you are one ... when you're cut, she bleeds."

Bobbi brought thick volumes of selections from a variety of poets home from the library. Names like Keats, Tennyson, Whitman, and of course Elizabeth Barrett Browning were modestly familiar to me, but I'd never read their work. And then came Rudyard Kipling! I was entranced by the sheer drama of his verse.

The love poems carried the added reward of making our nights more romantic. If the passion had lessened in our relationship, the poetry brought it roaring back.

We took no cue from the sun, but Bobbi soon turned up pregnant again. We decided to keep this our secret until she began to show, hoping not to steal any of the family attention currently heaped on Lacy and Victor and their little one. Bobbi said circumstances made their's more important. I knew she meant the loss of their precious Violet.

Meanwhile, like Victor, I struggled to keep up at work. Graffenried Distributors continued to expand. We hadn't replaced Carly yet. As time passed I worried more that Jack might not hire anyone to fill her position. He was hurt by her decision to leave, even after he reminded her she would inherit the significant share of the company he had acquired through periodic stock purchases over the years. He reassigned a good many of her duties to others on the staff he felt were most qualified to handle them, but my areas of responsibility also got a bump up.

Bobbi was not happy with the way her father did all this. She wanted to talk with him about it, especially the added work load it left me with. I asked her not to. First of all, this could only create tension between the two of them. But even more important to me was the thought of him thinking I had asked her to do it. I knew Jack well enough to see how this would leave a lasting impression. And certainly not a favorable one.

As far as work was concerned, I was careful to view Jackson Hoard as my boss, not my father-in-law. His view apparently was the opposite; at times he talked as if I were a family member, not an employee. I didn't mention this to Bobbi. She was too protective of me. If she thought it was in my best interest she would fight off a tiger at the door, much less complain to her father.

Father, meanwhile, had gained much improved working hours. Seth Ficklin passed away and when a younger brother from Kansas City took over the hardware store he promptly hired two additional clerks and cut back Father's hours.

Lacy said it was a sure sign Father was getting old and tired when he didn't complain. I agreed. He always had wanted to work every hour he could get in.

"He took a cut in pay," she explained. "Can you believe he wasn't put out about that?"

I agreed this wasn't the Father we'd grown up with.

Seth Ficklin's passing and Lacy's comment brought me face-to-face with the realization that generational change is inevitable and our parents wouldn't live forever. I suppose it's a simple equation: We aged at the same rate as they did, so the gap between us never widened and we never thought of them as getting old.

Father and Mama both still looked to be in good health and neither showed physical signs of aging. But I discounted the laws of nature. A great loss was right around the corner.

23

Jack Hoard called a family meeting. This meant a gathering of him and Jen and Bobbi and me. Both of Bobbi's sisters were long gone and of course our Sarah and little Jack were far from being adults. It turned out they were very much the main topic of his concern, and why he called us together.

"I'm getting old," he said, opening the discussion. "I'm going to retire before the end of the year."

This should not have surprised us, but it did. I wanted to say something appropriate to express my astonishment. I was too slow, and Jen spoke first.

"Oh, I'm glad, Jack!" she said. "You've put in enough years on the job. I didn't know you were thinking about it, though."

Bobbi said she was happy to hear this, too, but—

"I know, I know," her father said. "What's going to happen with the company? That's what I wanted to talk about."

I finally had found my tongue.

"I'm surprised to hear it," I told him. "I know you've earned it and I'm glad for you. But like you just said, I wonder what will happen down town."

"Okay. Here's what I see. Graffenried is pretty good about rewarding loyalty, but we're far removed from top management down here. I'm not real confident they know what's going on."

"So what do you see as best case and worst case scenarios?"

"Best case would be for them to replace me with you. Worst case would be for them to send down some young hot shot from Philadelphia who doesn't have a clue how an outlying division like ours goes about business."

One of many things I liked about Jack Hoard was that when he felt like speaking his mind he did so in plain language. I was flattered by his comment, and told him so. Bobbi put on her best smiling face to show her approval. Her mother nodded in agreement.

My father-in-law went on to say there was no need for us to spend time on the issue of his replacement. We wouldn't know what was going on until top brass made a decision and let us know what it was. His own personal interest in the company would be limited to the value of the considerable amount of stock he owned. Since he and Jen would have ample income in retirement, he had no intention of selling any. If he didn't change his will it would be left to Bobbi and her two sisters.

"I don't even want to hear this kind of talk," Bobbi said. "We'll get what's coming to us. But that's a long ways off."

Her father shook his head.

"We don't know that," he said. "And anyway there's more I want to say about it. I want everybody to know what I'm going to do before I do it so nobody gets all bent out of shape later."

Jen, who had been quiet for most of our get-together, made a sound somewhere between a giggle and a real laugh. And immediately apologized.

"I'm sorry, Jack. It's not funny. It's just that you made it sound kind of sinister. I didn't mean to laugh."

He laughed, too. I'd heard him say self-deprecating things often enough that I wasn't surprised when he said he was the one who should be sorry. He hadn't meant to be overly dramatic. But he did want us to know what he was about to say was important.

"It's about my grandchildren! Here's the point." He turned to Bobbi. "You girls will be okay. And if you aren't we're not talking about enough to fix that. But the same money put in trust for

Sarah and young Jack would grow enough, maybe, to put them through college."

Bobbi looked me square in the eyes. I knew what was on her mind.

"Yes," I told her, "now probably is the time."

She made the first announcement about our coming family addition.

Her news ended business talk for the night. Her mother and father sounded happy for us, and said all the right things. We talked about the different world second and third children enter, and her mother told a couple of stories about Bobbi as a baby. Bobbi was the third child, of course, and Jen Hoard said there were pretty clear displays of jealousy on the part of her two older sisters and signs of insecurity from her.

We finished the discussion by asking them to keep our secret. Bobbi explained how this related to Lacy and Victor and little Junior and they understood.

"Honey, we won't mention it to anyone until your belly sticks out so far you can't see your toes," her mother declared.

I guess it was odd, but Bobbi and I had had very little to say to one another about our expected new child in recent days. This occurred to us after we got home and checked on the two we already had and went to bed.

Bobbi laughed about it.

"I still believe in the miracle of birth or whatever," she said, "but this one seems like nothing special and I've kind of come to take it for granted."

"Maybe there's more to that third-born thing than we realized."

She squeezed closer.

"Don't forget. I'm a third-born. Aren't I still special?"

I tried to show her how special I still found her to be. Third time or three millionth time, I would never get enough of making love to this most beautiful woman. She said we apparently had had enough practice; we almost had reached perfection.

We slept late the next morning. It was Sunday. Sarah and little Jack were up ahead of us, already had finished their breakfast and were sitting in the living room watching television. They made fun of us and called us lazy. We were in no hurry, though we did plan to visit the Prather house in the afternoon. Now I was more conscious of the fact Mama and Father were aging and we should visit more often.

Sarah couldn't wait to get started. She would have been thrilled to see her grandfather Prather every day.

As we drove up the lane, the big house almost gleamed in the afternoon sun. I wondered how many coats of pastel yellow paint covered the ancient cypress planks that combined with the brick and stone to form its façade. And how many of these had Father applied?

Bobbi also was struck by what lay before us.

"That beautiful house will never get old for me," she said. "It looks like it was designed by some master hand for exactly where it sits."

"Yes, it does. And every time I come up this driveway I understand a little better Father's pride in it. Lacy and I used to make fun of that. She said if a tornado came through and carried us all away like in 'The Wizard of Oz' he wouldn't even miss us, but if it ripped one shingle off the house he'd go into mourning."

Bobbi laughed, but had no comeback.

I asked her to remind me to talk with Mama, and see if Father had given up the notion he had to paint the house himself. I knew he had done it the last time around and since this was close to four years ago he'd want it done again soon.

Father met us at the door and complained it'd been too long since he had a big Sarah hug. This was the new, more relaxed Father who looked back now and wished he had taken off more time from work all these years. Bobbi and Sarah went off to the kitchen to find Mama. Father went to the small sitting room and Jack and I followed. He had been watching television, too. I was about to ask if he ever watched at night or if this still was exclusively reading time and he answered before I spoke.

"I saw something terrible last night," he said. "I didn't know they had made a movie of that Iris Chang book, you know, *The Rape of Nanking*. I read it again about a year ago."

"You mentioned that. It's about the Japanese atrocities in World War II, right?"

He said yes, and there were things in the movie he didn't recall reading in the book. More numbers, too. Specific numbers of Chinese residents of Nanking raped, tortured, and killed by Japanese soldiers. And there was more.

"They tied Chinese farmers to trees and used them for bayonet practice." I could see his anger rising. "I wonder if the younger generation even knows there was a World War II, much less things like this. Of course this was in 1938 or '39, before the war even started for us."

I wanted to change the subject. Jack didn't need to hear this. Maybe when he was older, but not now.

"I'm glad people write books," I said. "That's how we learn history. By the way, don't know if I've mentioned it. Bobbi has taught me to like poetry. I've been reading Tennyson all month."

Father was not to be deterred.

"Iris Chang committed suicide, you know. So young. I guess hearing and telling the stories she did was more than she could stand."

Sarah came running, and did what I hadn't been able to. She ran to her grandfather for another hug and he forgot about wars and atrocities and young writers taking their own lives. But I didn't. I made a mental note to ask Bobbi to bring me the Iris Chang book from the library.

Sarah eventually got around to telling us her grandmother had sent her to get us all to the dining room.

We'd skipped lunch, knowing Mama would want to feed us and probably would have gone to a lot of trouble to have a big meal ready. She still thought it ought to be engraved in stone that getting a large Sunday "dinner" on the table at noontime was required of every home kitchen and threatened mayhem if we ever let her forget.

She actually had set a formal table. She hadn't gone so far as to get out the "good" china, but the settings were a step up from every day. A roasted chicken sat on a platter in the middle and the food smelled so good I would have been eager to sit down and eat even if I'd had three breakfasts.

Lacy and Victor were there. Junior was strapped into a cushioned high chair. Mama was higher than a kite. She still found her calling in feeding her masses.

Lacy raced over and hugged Bobbi and then me. Her pretty face was done in heavy makeup, including mascara. I hadn't seen her wear this before. But all the concealing creams and powders in the world couldn't hide completely the large bruise under her right eye.

24

Our third child was another girl. We named her Evelyn Jen, after her two grandmothers. The only thing to change this time around was Bobbi's decision to breast-feed. She said she'd been impressed by Lacy's talk of the added bonding it brought between baby and mom. I pretended to be offended she was taking unfair advantage.

"Yes, indeed," she said. "It's time mamas of the world unite to take every advantage we can get. How else are we going to take over?"

Baby Evelyn proved to be more needy than our first two. She had problems digesting her food. Bobbi feared it was her breast milk but our pediatrician said no, she would have even more trouble on any made up formula. Bobbi took it all in stride. She said I got the last laugh, after all.

She had generous maternity leave from the library. Before that was used up, though, she decided not to go back to work. We could manage without the added income and she wanted to be home with the baby. Sarah and Jack were happy to hear it, too. They would miss Jessica, but there was no substitute for Mom.

I had tried not to worry about Lacy. From our view, things between her and Victor had looked to be going well. But I couldn't forget the bruised face. Bobbi said if there had been another cause Lacy probably would have mentioned it. Or Mama would have known. It would have taken a pretty hard bump, which Lacy would have had no reason to keep secret.

I had kept a tight schedule of visits to the old Prather house on the bluff, watching Lacy closely. There hadn't been any more signs of trouble. Lacy brushed off my questions about her home life, usually with a shrug and snappy, "Nothing new."

Bobbi worried, too. She said I needed to talk with Mama, who surely would know what was going on. I thought so, too, because I knew I'd never hear anything negative from my little sister.

Unfortunately, I never got the chance to talk to Mama.

The call came early in the morning. Lacy tried to tell us, but was too emotional. Father came on the line. Mama had passed away during the night. They had found her in the kitchen, seated at the table. In spite of my shock at the unexpected loss, my first thought was that, like Grandma Childs, she had gone the way she would have wanted to.

Mama always had said she wanted to be buried in Golconda, the place of her childhood memories. We honored her wishes, of course. There was a simple graveside service and it was all over.

I watched Father going from the grave to the funeral home's limousine for the ride home and wondered how he would handle life without her. He walked between Lacy and Victor, leaning heavily on one and then the other. I wasn't close enough to see his face. But at the graveside he had been almost without expression, almost as if he was in a daze and hardly aware of what was going on.

My own grief was not tempered by reason. Mama had reached an age at which her passing should not have been a surprise. She obviously died peacefully, in the one place more important than all others for most of her life. She had watched her children grow up and relished being a grandmother multiple times.

And yet, I could summon no image of my existence without reference to those early years in the old Prather house. The bluff, the shoal, the great white oak under which little Violet lay buried, Lacy and Sammy, Bobbi and Victor, Father and Mama. This chapter still was the thesis around which the story of my life revolved.

Bobbi also took the loss hard. And Sarah. How much our little girl had loved time with Grandmamma Prather in her wonderful kitchen!

But there still was an Evelyn Prather. Our baby never would know the grandmother whose name she carried and would have no memories of her in her kitchen in the big house. But Mama's blood flowed in her veins and we could hope that Mama's wonderful, generous love of others would mark her life. Father was a firm believer that the human spirit is everlasting and I had long since accepted his faith. Mama's spirit would go on.

Unfortunately, though, practical effects of her loss swirled down on us quickly. With Mama gone, things in the old Prather house soon fell into serious disarray. Father seemed to think he needed to exercise more authority. Junior fell sick with some kind of flu. Lacy, busy with him, spent little time in the kitchen. And Victor was drinking again.

For me, all this presented a bizarre paradox. I wanted to be there, and I did not want to be there. I felt an obligation to try and help, yet the thought of facing the turmoil I knew I'd find left me timid. I stayed away until I felt guilty—and until Bobbi insisted I go.

"Surely your father's got more than he can handle," she worried. "You just have to get up there and check on him."

I knew she was right.

My whole world had been reshaped. Mama was gone, we had our little one, Bobbi no longer was working, things weren't going well at the old Prather house, and my workplace had lost its spirit to the extent nobody wanted to show up in the morning. I wouldn't say it was grim, but compared to the way things had been with Jack Hoard in charge it was an unpleasant environment to say the least.

The big brass at Graffenried Distributing in Philadelphia had done exactly what Jack had feared most: They sent down as new head of our division a greenhorn whose only possible qualification could have been that he was a favorite protégé to one of them. We would never know anything more.

His name was Roland Phillips and his greatest fault was that he had no humility. He was confident he was up to the job when things happening all around him said he wasn't. I was careful not to give my father-in-law a hint of the situation. He knew I wasn't a whiner; my report would only upset him.

A visit to check on Father made me feel better, if only for a short time. He was eager to share some news.

"I've made a big decision," he said. "Things at the store just aren't the same. I don't know if they even need me anymore, but I know I really don't need them. This is my last week of work. I'm going to retire for good."

I was surprised but happy. Father had plenty of money and lived frugally. He didn't need to work. And it would be good for him to be home with Lacy and the baby around the clock. I told him I was glad to hear his news. I had noticed he looked extremely tired and run down physically. He said he hadn't been eating well. He was doing his own cooking, since Lacy didn't seem to have time.

"That boy's all she has time for," he said. "I don't know if that is a necessary situation or whether it's just what she wants. We don't talk very much."

The longer I sat and talked with Father, the madder I got at Lacy and Victor. They had no problem accepting his free housing but didn't seem to care enough about his wellbeing to lift a hand. I told him I'd talk to Lacy before I left.

"If you can find her."

"She's not in the kitchen or upstairs?"

He said no, he'd looked for her twice during the afternoon and didn't find her. She wasn't in the kitchen and he'd called upstairs and didn't get an answer.

"When's the last time you saw her?"

"I guess it was yesterday morning at breakfast time. Maybe the day before. I lose track sometimes."

I stood and told him I would go find her. I wanted him to sit tight for now. When I found her I'd be back. He wanted to go with me but I persuaded him to wait. I didn't need him to slow me down, and he didn't need any extra exertion.

The only place Lacy could be was the shoal. The day was cool, but she didn't have to be in the water. If Junior was like the other kids he could be entertained with no more effort than sitting on a rock on the river bank and throwing things in the water. So many days we'd all spent doing this with Violet!

The distance from the kitchen door to the great white oak and beginning of the path down the bluff seemed longer than I remembered. I slowed and then stopped to look at the beautiful carved stone marking Violet's grave, and wondered if Vin Shield still brought fireplace logs.

"Windshield. Old Windshield and his load of wood and he wants us to unload it."

I imagined I could hear Lacy's little girl voice at the table, when she had no cares and nothing more than a name could be a fun thing to play with. It had been a good time, and it hardly could have been all that long ago. Where had the years gone?

The footpath sloping down the bluff to the shoal was somewhat overgrown. One of the large, flat rocks that formed the few steps we'd added over time was washed out. The path obviously wasn't used like it used to be, guiding happy feet to and from the shoal many times a day. I descended slowly and carefully.

There was no sign of Lacy when I reached the bottom.

I called her name.

The only response was a flutter of wings as my voice startled the crows in trees across the river. They raised a loud fuss and circled over the treetops and the edges of farm fields as if carrying out careful surveillance. Who was this intruder? Did he pose a danger? This spectacle, at least, had not changed.

Back on the crown of the bluff, I paused and looked back across the river and to the patches of woods and open fields beyond. It was hard to believe all this ever could have been under water. But at the same time, the old image lying latent in my memory would not be denied. I saw it again. Water as far as the eye could see, drowning the land and all it held close. I still believed Mama's vow to move away from the river grew out of the flood's disastrous impact on those who made their homes on Singleton's Branch.

When I got to the kitchen, there was no sign of Lacy and Junior there, either. I moved quietly up the stairs. I didn't want to see Father yet, especially since I had nothing positive to report. There was no one in the nursery or anywhere else on the second floor.

I went to the housekeeping closet and climbed up to and through the trap door to the attic. Lacy lay on the floor on what probably was the same old mattress, Junior clasped close to her breast, wrapped in a blanket and sound asleep. I walked toward them and then was stopped in my tracks by what I saw. Even from a distance of several feet, I could see the blackened eye and purple bruises on the lower part of her face.

My rage was almost uncontrollable. This was my sweet little sister, who never would hurt any living thing. She had been beaten. And there could be no question: She had been beaten by a man who had vowed to love and honor her for the rest of their lives.

I wanted my hands on Victor.

25

Jack Hoard was a reasonable man and he understood. When Bobbi heard my story she asked if I'd agree to her calling her father. She said he had experienced a similar situation with one of his employees some years ago. He knew a great deal about the legal ramifications at play, and because this was in her family he'd treat it as if in his. I said yes. I trusted him and I needed advice.

My father-in-law sat at a table in our kitchen, across from me. Bobbi poured fresh-brewed coffee and joined us.

"So, just tell me what happened," he said.

I struggled to find the words. It was not a complex story. A man had beaten his wife. But it was a story almost too hard for me. Bobbi put her hand on mine and said it was okay. She would tell her father what he needed to know.

When she finished, Jack Hoard sat silent for a minute, considering what he'd heard.

"The first decision you have to make," he said then, "is whether you want Victor arrested and jailed right up front. If you do, we need to call Landon Cloyd right now. It's out in the country so it is sheriff's business. The Erinville police department likely won't be involved. If we call the sheriff, he probably will go straight to The Print Shop and pick up Victor there. He'll be handcuffed in front of his coworkers and taken away. Like I said, we need to be certain before we make that call."

"I don't care what happens to Victor," I said. "I'd be fine with seeing him hanged in front of City Hall."

Jack got up from the table and took his cup to get more coffee. Bobbi seemed to have nothing to say, but worry was written all over her face. I hated all this for her almost as much as for Lacy. And Father. I had not stopped to speak with him before I left the Prather house after I found Lacy. He would see her sooner or later and no doubt would confront Victor.

"I should have talked to Lacy and Father," I said to Jack, as he returned to the table. "I just ran like a scared rabbit."

"So Lacy doesn't know you know?"

"I didn't wake her."

"Surely your father has some idea what's going on. Don't you think?"

I said I couldn't even guess how he would not know, except I hoped this was the first time and he had not seen Lacy since it happened. Now we knew why he couldn't find her.

"There's no way she can avoid him forever," Bobbi said. "I understand why Lacy doesn't want him to know, but he needs her. She's the woman of the house now and it's getting pretty hard for him to get around and do for himself."

Her father nodded agreement.

"Your father's wellbeing is at stake here, too," he said.

We all fell silent, a clear indication that none of us really knew what to do. There would be too much pain for too many people no matter what direction we chose. But I knew we had to do something. Lacy was in danger. And it was time for me to show the courage of my convictions and confront Victor directly. I said as much to Bobbi and Jack Hoard.

"I wish you'd call the sheriff," Bobbi said. "Victor needs to be in jail."

I felt helpless, and maybe hopeless. Jack pointed out that even if Victor was arrested today he wouldn't be in jail for long.

If he was charged he'd be arraigned and given a trial date, then most likely released on bond. And there was a serious possibility he would come home angry and take it out on Lacy. And Father, if he tried to interfere.

"We have to get Lacy out of there," Bobbi said. "And I guess your father, too."

Jack said he needed to go. He assured me he'd help in any way he could, and asked that we call him right away if he was needed. When he was gone I told Bobbi I would go back to the old Prather house and confront Lacy and Father. We assumed Victor would be working. I should be, too, but I felt this was a crisis. I called my workplace and let them know I'd not be in until tomorrow.

Bobbi wanted to go, but I told her I'd rather we not leave an empty house without the kids knowing we'd be gone. Something could happen at school and one of them might be sent home. This was such an unlikely happening I normally wouldn't have thought about it, but I had become irrationally concerned about such things—anything out of the ordinary. I had come to expect the unexpected.

Though I was eager to get there and confront Lacy, I drove slowly on my way to the old Prather house on the bluff. I tried to think of some convincing argument I could make to persuade Lacy to leave Victor and move out. But what precisely did I want? If she left, Father would be in a difficult situation. No, it was Victor I wanted out. And this could come only if Lacy demanded it.

Should I talk with Father first? I couldn't offer him a positive resolution until Lacy had agreed to one. So far as I knew, he was not aware of Lacy's problem. She had managed to hide it from him. Did I want to be the one to tell him? But why should I even ask this question? He had to know sooner or later, and his welfare and his living place would have to be an important consideration in any possible solution.

By the time I started up the driveway I was virtually without hope of an easy answer. Maybe we should call Sheriff Landon

Cloyd after all, and let the appropriate legal action run its course. Why protect Victor? I soon found myself at the front door, no closer to deciding what I wanted to happen.

The door wasn't locked. I let myself in and walked down the hallway looking for Father, but not calling out. I looked in every room. He was nowhere in sight. On to the kitchen. It was empty. Except for the memories. Mama should be here, standing over the stove or checking on something in the oven, tending to what she considered her true calling—taking care of her family, feeding them well, making the kitchen an enjoyable place to gather.

But Mama wasn't there, and neither were Father or Lacy. This meant they had to be upstairs, and just at that moment I heard the faint sound of a crying baby.

Lacy was in the nursery, standing over the crib in which little Junior squirmed restlessly. And Father was there, too. They looked up as I entered.

"Hey, there," Lacy said, with her usual big smile.

She made no effort to hide the bruises on her face. Father obviously had seen them, and no doubt knew what caused them. Yet he looked to be at peace with his world. Nothing was as I had expected to find it.

"Everything okay?"

"Sure," Father said. "We're doing good. You?"

I said things were good with me, too, and stood awkwardly silent, waiting for one of them to speak. I wanted to demand answers. Would Lacy admit what had happened to her? How would Father explain his acceptance? I felt as if I'd gone to sleep and woke in a strange world among people I didn't know who didn't know me.

"You look kind of puzzled about something," Lacy said. She'd always been able to read me like a book.

"What happened to your face?"

"Oh, no big deal. I slipped and fell on the bluff, going down to the shoal."

So that was it. She had made up this lie and father had accepted it for truth. Had her bruises been different or if she had suffered something like a broken arm, even, her story might have been plausible. One look at her face and it was apparent this was a woman who had been battered by a fist. My anger got the best of me.

"Damn it, Lacy, don't take me for a fool. I'm smart enough to tie my shoes in the dark."

I think if I had vented my anger in normal fashion, demanding the truth, she would have resisted. But her own creative sarcasm thrown back at her struck a chord. We were big brother and little sister again, me wanting to protect her and she wanting my protection. She burst into tears and turned to me. I reached for her and she hugged me to her and cried on my shoulder.

Father was confused, of course, and stood and watched us without speaking. I felt pity for him. The truth alone would be devastating to him, but the truth coupled with Lacy's lie and his acceptance of it would be crushing. I wanted to pull him into our embrace, to have the three of us stand as one while Lacy cried out her regret, her fear and bitterness. But he turned and walked out of the nursery.

Lacy sobbed on my shoulder for what seemed like an hour before she finally spoke. When she did, it was more of a whimper.

"You know what happened," she said, finding her voice between sniffles.

"Yes. It was Victor."

"He doesn't mean to hurt me. I know he loves me, and Junior. It's just that, I don't know, he gets frustrated about things he can't do anything about and has a few drinks and—"

"No, Lacy. You can't make excuses for him. Whatever his problems, he can't take them out on you. We have to put an end to this."

She began to cry again, her slender body convulsing with the violence of her sobs. My own emotions, a mix of anger at Victor and sympathy for her, were boiling over. And little Junior chose this time to burst into loud cries of his own, his powerful eruption echoing around the room like claps of thunder.

Father was there in an instant. He picked up the baby and cuddled him, holding him both gently and powerfully against his breast, and the little one's crying stopped as abruptly as it had begun. Father turned and, swaying slightly from side to side like they were dancing, carried Junior from the room and down the hallway toward the stairs.

Lacy moved with me across the room, until we stood before a window. The familiar landscape visible only through this special view from a place high in the old Prather house spread before us. It seemed to work its magic on her as it did on me.

"I'm sorry," she said softly. "I know you're right. We have to do something about Victor. I just don't know what."

"And Father didn't know?"

"No," Lacy said. "He believed my stupid story."

"You know he won't tolerate Victor living under his roof now that he knows. He only let him come back because of Junior."

"Yes, I know. There's no way around it now."

We had to do what neither of us really wanted: go and talk with Father. We found him with the baby in the small sitting room. He made clear at once he was furious with Victor, and almost as mad at Lacy for trying to mislead him. Lacy's first words to him were an expression of profound regret for her action.

"That doesn't matter now," Father said. "As of this moment Victor Kenton will not sleep under my roof. I will not tolerate a wife-beater, and wouldn't tolerate him even if it wasn't my little girl he was beating. You may as well start throwing out his things."

I tried to protest, suggesting Victor needed a bit of time to find another place to live. Father would have none of it. Victor, he said, was "no longer in this family."

I told Lacy Victor could spend the night with Bobbi and me. He had to have a place to sleep. She said no, he wouldn't accept my offer. He either would sleep in his car or at his workplace. He'd done so before.

In the end it didn't matter. Victor didn't come home that night.

26

Who can measure time? Even if it is linear, as Sammy insists, the days of our lives pass without count, daylight and darkness, season by season. Like bridges crossed and left far behind on our journey, we know the days are gone. We cannot reach into the past and retrieve a single hour, or even a single minute. What has come and gone only matters if it brought change, something new and different. There is only one constant: Life goes on.

I can't tell you in good conscience I know exactly what happened between Lacy and Victor in the months after he left the Prather house. Some of what I knew I don't remember. I suspect I pushed some of it aside deliberately, out of my conscious memory, because it was too painful. Even those moments less critical, whether told to me by Lacy or made visible through a chain of events, painted a canvas of lives hurt and wasted in failure.

Lacy stayed with Father. The principal good to come from all this was his. She took pains to see to his needs. With Mama as her model, she made the kitchen her domain. We soon learned Father was well cared for and had no place in our worn book of worries.

For Lacy, herself, and Junior, the story was not the same. There was almost no contact between them and the outside world. It was almost as if the ancient Prather house on the bluff was their total universe. And it was a universe more limited. Not wanting to leave Father alone, Lacy never left the house except for essential shopping. She drove the Ram into Erinville once or twice a week for food and other supplies, rushing through stores as if she had a critical appointment to keep. Junior usually stayed with Father.

It was several months before Victor summoned the courage to call and check on her and his child. Unlike most wives and mothers in this situation, I would guess, Lacy welcomed his call and told him she'd missed him terribly. Why couldn't they be together again? Victor had no interest in her proposal, but failed to make this clear. Their contact left Lacy confident they would be with each other again one day soon.

She had one photograph of Victor. She presented this to Junior every day, to make sure he recognized his father when he came home.

I've never known whether Father even was aware of Victor's call. I do believe strongly he would not have countenanced any talk of Victor's return. Not during his lifetime. There was only the tiniest fissure in his high wall of trust in his position. He wished Junior could have a father.

Bobbi was alone among us in making even a modest effort to be in contact with Victor. She believed I should do it, but knew this was not likely.

Through her I learned he had moved into a shoddy ground-floor apartment near his workplace. It had been some time since he'd been responsible for rent and utility bills and his salary at The Print Shop still was modest for one who had to pay all of his own cost of living. Bobbi never asked him about supporting Junior, and I never asked Lacy. They lived under Father's roof and we assumed Father paid for their keep.

I visited the Prather house two or three times a week for the first few months. No one there needed me, nor acted as if they cared whether I came. I soon stopped going.

There were other things needing my attention. I wanted more time with Bobbi and the kids. My work load was crushing as Roland Phillips seemed to find a new way every day to mess up operations at Graffenried Distributing and I didn't have Carly's able support. Rather than a blessing, I came to look on growth of the business as a curse. There were times I wanted to call Jack Hoard and beg him to come back to work.

Sarah and little Jack were in school. Evelyn would be in another year. Bobbi was happy not to be working and I was happy for her. And for myself. With her at home, we seldom needed Jessica Buford except on those rare occasions when we went out in the evening. Bobbi said we were not socialites by nature, which was good because there were few social activities in Erinville where "socialites could practice socialiting."

Sarah heard her say this one day and told her there was no such word as "socialiting." Bobbi said creative minds create new ideas and even new words. Sarah wanted to know how far this could be allowed to go.

"Can they break the rules?" she asked. "I mean, what if their new ideas break the law or something?"

Bobbi called for help. I declined to get involved.

Bobbi told Sarah she talked like a lawyer.

"I hope so, Mama. I'm going to be a lawyer someday."

This was the first time either of us had heard of our daughter's interest in the law. We took comfort in knowing there were years to go before she could act on this interest, so there was plenty of time to change her mind or make herself ready for law school if she didn't.

But we had learned that our first-born was a bright girl, inquisitive much like her Uncle Sammy. He had turned out to be a brilliant scholar, Bobbi said, and she would be happy if Sarah did as well. I was left feeling quite proud of both my brother and my little girl.

Whether Victor eventually had a true change of heart or merely found living alone and paying his own way difficult or unpleasant I can only guess. But he let Lacy know the time had come; he wanted to move back into the Prather house right away.

I think she still clung to the hopes built up from the earlier call and probably didn't recognize his position as a new one.

It was a Saturday morning when Lacy called me, almost noon. I had been in the office for a couple of hours but had finished work for the day. From the tone of her voice, I knew at once she was terribly upset about something. But in typical Lacy fashion she started the conversation with questions about our welfare, Bobbi's and mine, and asked about the kids. I responded briefly and quickly. I wanted to know why she called.

She hesitated after the formalities, took a deep breath, and told me.

"Victor wants to come home," she said, "but Father says he can't. Do you think you could talk to him and maybe make him change his mind?"

I told her I'd try, though I was doubtful I could get Father to agree to Victor's return. I would be there in the early afternoon.

I wanted Bobbi to go with me. She had a subtle way of persuading Father when no one else could. But Jessica Buford didn't answer her phone, and Bobbi didn't want to impose on her mother and so would have to stay home with the kids. I would come to wish later we'd taken them, too, but hindsight brings no satisfaction.

I felt almost like I was going into the unknown as I approached the old Prather house. In reality it hadn't been long since I'd been there, but the immediate sense of belonging I usually got when the house came into view was lacking. I was struck, instead, by a certain foreboding—things would be different. This would prove true soon enough.

No one met me at the door. I had hoped Father would. The fact that he didn't probably meant Lacy hadn't told him I was coming. I found no one on the first floor and was ready to go upstairs when I caught a glimpse of activity through a kitchen window. Lacy and Junior were on the bluff, beneath the great white oak.

She saw me coming as soon as I was outside, but made no move to meet me. Rather, she stood stoically and watched me approach, almost like I was a stranger of whom she was wary. I remembered a day when we were little and a state conservation officer showed up to check on something related to Singleton's Branch. He was in uniform and wore an expression so serious we found him threatening. Lacy wanted to run and hide, but I said he'd already seen us and we'd best stand still and wait. He walked past us with a smile and pleasant greeting.

But I was not a conservation officer from Frankfort here about the natural environment. I was Lacy's brother here about a chronic concern I had no notion how to fix. She and Junior were the ones paying the greatest price, although the problem was not of their making. Was I doing the right thing?

Junior reacted to my approach before Lacy did. He smiled and waved as I came close. So my little nephew still knew me. I would have this to feel good about no matter how the rest of the day turned out.

I attached no significance to the fact that Lacy stood beside the engraved stone Vincent Shield had made for Violet's grave. But I was wrong.

"I come out here every day and pray over her," Lacy said as I stopped in front of the stone. "She was a precious angel and we let her die like a baby animal with no one to protect it."

So she still grieved over the loss of her first child. How long had it been? She could not be expected ever to forget, of course, but this was a level of agony that should have passed well before now. Her failure to recover might be related to Victor's absence but I didn't know if this was likely. I did know, though, that Lacy needed help and just now I was her best hope.

I stood beside her and put an arm around her shoulders. She leaned against me without speaking.

"You need Victor," I said, a statement I would not have made earlier.

"Can you help me?"

"I'll do everything I can, Lacy. Your family ought to be together again."

It seemed as if her spirits brightened some as we walked back to the house. She tried to tell me things to bring me up to date but Junior's voice drowned her out. He had important things to tell me, too. With both of them talking at once I missed much of what they said. I understood that Father was upstairs somewhere, though, and she was optimistic he would listen to me and maybe change his mind.

We found him asleep on an antique settee in the second floor hallway, near to the door to the nursery. Junior ran ahead and started to climb on him. Father woke with a big smile for his grandson, but flushed with embarrassment when he saw Lacy and me.

"I didn't intend to go to sleep," he told us. "Sometimes this old age kind of creeps up on me and urges me to rest before I even know I'm tired."

He offered no particular greeting to me, as if my presence was nothing out of the ordinary. Lacy suggested we all go down to the kitchen and have iced tea and cookies and he said that was a good idea. He stepped aside for me to go in front, still showing no awareness that my being there was unusual.

When I took a seat at the kitchen table, I found myself having second thoughts about Lacy's grief over the loss of Violet. This was Mama's kitchen. Mama should be here, brewing fresh tea and serving cookies right from the oven. This was Mama's kingdom but Mama was not here. My sense of loss over Mama's passing still was much stronger than I had realized. And surely my loss would be dwarfed by a mother's loss of a child.

Father sat and smiled while Lacy poured his tea over ice cubes, filling an extra large glass. He looked at me as if waiting for me to say something, and Lacy caught my eye and nodded.

She may as well have told me, "Go ahead and say what you came to say!" And she was right. There was no reason to draw things out.

I said, "Father, Victor wants to come home and Lacy and Junior need him here. You wouldn't mind, would you?"

He didn't respond immediately. I could see Lacy's nervous anticipation, and the longer we waited the more my hopes fell. He had made his position clear. I had been foolish to expect him to capitulate.

"This is a good time to tell you something I've been putting off," he said, when he finally did speak. "I've thought about this a lot. Truth is, I need for Victor to come back. See, I've decided to move into a place in Golconda, where I can visit your mama's grave. It's not exactly assisted living, but I'll have everything I need and be taken care of. I'll have an apartment all on one floor and, to tell the truth, these stairs in this place are getting kind of hard for me sometimes. One fall and I'd be in assisted living, anyway. I'd rather go while I can still walk in."

It is barely adequate to say Father's announcement took us by surprise. I hadn't been around much and there was no reason I should have expected to know his plans, but I'd always believed he would stay in the old Prather house until he died. Lacy, on the other hand, had been close. I think the only reason he hadn't mentioned his plans to her was he hadn't had time. I believe he had just now made the decision, and circumstances made this the perfect time to tell us what he was going to do.

Bobbi and I would speculate later about what he would have done had Victor not wanted to come back. Lacy and Junior surely would not have wanted to continue living in the big house all by themselves and for them to move would have meant no longer living rent-free.

None of this mattered. Father was free to move out and Victor was free to move in. The waters of Singleton's Branch would continue to flow into the great Ohio, the shoal at the foot of the bluff still would be a marvelous place for the little ones to play, and life in the Prather house would go on.

Lacy called two days later and said Victor was home.

27

Father had everything packed and ready to go. We loaded boxes of his personal things into the bed of the Ram pickup and laid his clothes across the back seat. He had been conservative in making his selections; if he didn't think he would need something, he would leave it.

"Golconda's not that far," he said. "If I find out later I left something I need I can always come back and pick it up." And then, to Lacy, "Anything still here after six months you want to get rid of you can throw away."

His words caused Lacy to shed more tears. Now that the time had come, she found Father's leaving difficult. We all did. There never had been a single minute of our lives when he was not there, in the old Prather house, as much a fixture as the tower on the roof and an anchor we thought never could be loosed.

I expected Father to get emotional, too. After all, he had lived here his entire life. He had taken great pride in this old house and worked hard to maintain it at a level at which it attracted the attention of passersby. And it was here he had lived with Mama all their married life and here he had raised his children. Surely it would be a painful departure.

But once again, Father proved unpredictable. If leaving bothered him at all it didn't show. He gave the appearance of being light-hearted and eager to go, almost like he was off on a new adventure he'd been looking forward to.

Lacy, Junior, and I rode with Father in the Ram and Victor followed in his car so we'd have a way home. The trip to Golconda was surprisingly fast. Even the wait for the Cave-in-Rock ferry across the Ohio River was a short one, as it was pulling up on the Kentucky side when we drove up. Loading was simple. The highway went straight off into the river and the ferry lowered a ramp right down onto the concrete so we could drive directly onto the deck.

Father's new apartment was ready and waiting. It was much nicer than I had expected it to be, and even as we unloaded boxes two other residents stopped to introduce themselves. One was an older woman and the other was a man about Father's age. Both were friendly and welcoming. It looked as though he had chosen his new home wisely. Everything was off the truck and inside in less than an hour.

Lacy still was emotional, and reluctant to say goodbye. Junior was confused, not at all certain what was going on with his grandfather but worried. Victor was eager to get on the road. He said he had to get back to The Print Shop by early afternoon and already was behind in his work.

I tried to sort out my own feelings, but they were too ambiguous to classify. I would miss Father's nearby presence terribly. At the same time, though, I was confident this was the right move for him. He would be in a place where all his needs were met and he was well cared for, and it looked quite likely he would find common interests with residents of other apartments in the complex. Surely he had felt isolated and a bit lonely at the Prather house.

And he would have the Ram, reliable transportation for the rest of his life. He could come and see us any time he liked or take interesting day trips around western Kentucky and southern Illinois. When I considered this I was almost envious.

Lacy, Victor, and I tried to view the move from all angles on the ride home. No matter how great the change his absence would bring, we decided that on balance it was a good thing. We would miss him but at the same time be happy for him. The single biggest negative was that Junior would not grow up in his grandfather's company.

When I got home to Erinville early in the afternoon, Bobbi said I seemed to be surprisingly unemotional over what had just taken place. Would not Father's move be a great change for all of us? I told her it would, but in many ways it would be a move for the better.

To the extent the day of Father's move was a turning point in all our lives, it was an important date we would mark on our calendars. But if we thought it would mean noticeable change in how we went about our daily affairs we were to be proved wrong. Except for the indirect result that Victor was now home with Lacy and Junior we hardly noticed the difference.

With apologies anew to Rachel McNary, I have to say that for many months after Father's move our days were hardly worth separating as dates on the calendar. They melded into weeks and months and then a season and I had little sense of time passing. But it did, and I noted somewhere along the way that Sarah and Jack and even Evelyn no longer were little kids. Changes are subtle and may go unnoticed as they happen, but then you look up one day and wonder how you didn't see it. And you feel a sadness that comes with understanding. Once childhood goes it is gone forever.

Bobbi had become the consummate homemaker. She said this was life's highest calling for a woman with children. She told me she had two jobs, though, a day job and a night job. Her day job was to always be there for me and the kids. Her night job was to prove that making love to an older woman still was exciting and could be a special treat to the right man. She issued a call for a volunteer to help with this undertaking and I jumped to the head of the line.

Jen and Jack Hoard took a month-long trip to New York to visit Bobbi's sisters and came back with interesting stories. They were eager to bring her up to date and she was eager to hear. I promised Bobbi we would follow in their footsteps before long, but for a shorter visit. She said she wanted to go but if she was planning a trip right now she'd rather it be for another two weeks at Myrtle Beach. I knew choosing between the beach and New York would be an easy decision for me but kept this news to myself.

Routine visits to the old Prather house on the bluff morphed into family fun once the weather was warm and the kids could play in the shoal. It almost was like old times when we sat on the rocks and watched Junior and our three splash in the cool waters of Singleton's Branch.

Except Lacy wasn't there. She might have been Mama now, master of the kitchen and czar of her domain. She felt compelled to tend to her responsibilities in the house and shun the fun things the rest of us were doing. She came out only occasionally, and then it was to visit little Violet's grave under the great white oak.

We seldom saw Victor. Lacy said he worked long hours. He had been promoted into a newly created management post at The Print Shop, which carried a significant salary increase but also additional responsibilities.

One rainy Sunday afternoon, Bobbi and I sat at the Prather house kitchen table enjoying cups of coffee and cinnamon rolls fresh from Lacy's oven, and she pulled out a chair and joined us. This was unusual; she liked to stand over us the way Mama used to and be ready to serve.

Junior and Jack were playing on the front porch and our girls had not come, choosing instead to visit with friends. No one needed our supervision.

I could tell that Lacy wanted to talk. She asked about Sarah and Evelyn and said she didn't miss Father as much as she had feared. She asked if Bobbi was contented not working outside the home and declared herself grateful she didn't have to, especially now, with Victor's promotion.

"But he's under a lot more stress now," she said, still talking about Victor. "He's a hard worker, though, and I know he can do the job."

Bobbi asked how much his work load increased with the change.

"He says it almost doubled. That doesn't sound likely to me, but Victor's honest. He wouldn't say it if it wasn't true."

I said this surely was too much. I thought Victor already had about all the work he could handle. Advancement with better pay always was good, I told Lacy, but I hoped The Print Shop management realized there was a reasonable limit on what one employee could be expected to do.

"Who makes those decisions, anyway?" Bobbi asked.

"It's Mrs. Gruber. I can't ever remember her first name. They usually just call her 'Old Lady Gruber.' I guess she's the widow of the man who started the place fifty or sixty years ago. They don't think she knows what she's doing sometimes but she handles the money."

"She must be happy with Victor's work," I said.

Lacy got up from the table without responding to my comment. She poured more coffee and brought more cinnamon rolls, then got more napkins from an upper cabinet and refilled the holder on the table. When she was sure we needed no more service she sat down again, picking up the discussion as if she'd never moved.

"Victor's a hard worker," she said. "Nobody's ever questioned that. His only problem is, he just lacks confidence. He almost didn't take the new job, or promotion or whatever you want to call it. He was afraid he couldn't do the job, but there wasn't nothing he wasn't already doing. I had to push him on it."

Bobbi stayed with Lacy in the kitchen to help her clean up. I wandered through the old house looking into nooks and crannies I had nearly forgotten. There were a few things to remind me of

Father and Mama, but mostly there was what now struck me as nothing more than ancient junk. Much of it no doubt had been there since the house's early days, going back even beyond the time it was purchased by Grandfather Prather.

Father's reading chair still sat where it always had. The lamp was still there, too, waiting to offer its brightness to readers who never showed up.

I thought about the attic, the tower on the roof, the little Billiken, smashed into oblivion by Lacy after the loss of her firstborn child. And I remembered the happy spirit that pervaded the house when Violet was among us, long since replaced by a somberness nearly depressing. She had been a shining star. When her light was extinguished a new darkness had descended.

I went on the porch to check on Jack and Junior. The rain had stopped, but any place not under roof was dripping wet. The boys were trying to decide whether to venture down the slope in front of the house for reasons they couldn't specify. But I told Jack we needed to be going home soon and not to stray.

Back inside, I found Bobbi looking for me. She'd done all she could to help Lacy in the kitchen. She was ready to leave, hoping I was, too, and in a hurry to retrieve Jack.

The rain came again as we drove the county blacktop back to Erinville. The three of us got soaking wet just running from the car to the house. Sarah and Evelyn were there, and laughed when they saw us. Evelyn reminded us of the proverbial "sense to get in out of the rain" as a measure of intelligence. She said we'd just failed the test.

Being in our house again, with Bobbi and the kids, hearing the girls' laughter, our good-natured complaints about getting wet—all this struck me as good and proper. This was home. Perhaps I had no added purpose, but there could be little doubt I had new place. And life would go on.

28

Jackson and Jen Hoard were the best in-laws anyone ever could have asked for. They were doting grandparents, too, and Jack took immense pride in having a grandson named for him. He always called our Jackson "little Jack" and frequently reminded him they bore the same name. When school was not in session Bobbi often took the kids to visit the Hoards two or three times a week.

I sometimes wondered how I might have made a living had it not been for my father-in-law. Graffenried Distributing wasn't General Motors, but it grew into a large corporation with branches nationwide and in Canada. It had a great number of employees and developed liberal personnel policies that gave me good benefits and financial security for Bobbi and the kids.

And though it took a couple of years, Roland Phillips actually became a pretty good manager. The Erinville district prospered under his direction—in the early years we would have said *in spite of* his direction—and we came to like him. He eventually gained enough confidence to admit the things he didn't know and ask advice. I believe he called on Jack Hoard several times.

It bruised my ego a bit when I learned that little Jack had gone to his grandfather for advice he should have sought from me, but then I remembered how I had trusted Grandpa Childs and been impressed by his interest. Why should I expect any more of my son?

We didn't hear from Sammy often. Bobbi joked that it might be possible being in the space program kept him busy. Among the kids, it was Evelyn who was most impressed by having an uncle who worked at NASA. She even bragged about it at school, and on a couple of occasions used the relationship as the basis for class projects.

Sammy opened himself to both praise and ridicule by writing an article for some cult journal devoted to the subject of extraterrestrial intelligent life. I don't remember the name of the publication, but his article was titled, "Will We *Let* Them Come in Peace?"

In it, he speculated we are surrounded by intelligent life much farther advanced than we are, and they obviously wish to be friendly. He said they could have obliterated us long before now if they wanted to, but haven't. He wrote about crop circles—which I know nothing about—and claimed it's inevitable that someday a space ship will land on Earth, its occupants having come in peace, only to be met by armed humans bent on their destruction.

I knew the roots of this article went back to that visit to the Illinois Garden of the Gods, all those years ago. The old Dodge pickup, the family together, Sammy's discoveries, these were precious memories.

Although there were some rough spots along the way, I'm proud of the man Sammy became. He will be famous in years to come, in large part because—unlike me—he looks to the future and not the past.

Both age and circumstance have much to do with most peoples' view of life—certainly they do for me. We get older and have less time to count as future. But in my case age was vastly overshadowed by circumstance on a terrible day I merely tried to do the right thing. I did it without thinking. I deserve the price I've paid, but others don't.

I think of the wisdom of Jonathon, beside the ocean at Myrtle Beach. I should have recalled his passionate assertion that a man and wife are as one, that "if you get cut she bleeds." That day I forfeited all claim to such sagacity, but like him I regained it through the painful experience of loss.

But this black day was yet to come. My time with Bobbi was marvelous time. She was a wonderful wife and mother. We had long since reached that point at which we each knew the other's thoughts and feelings, watched for the other's signs of stress, encouraged when we believed the other faltered, and did our best to lift some of the load when the other was burdened. As we had bonded physically in the beginning, over time we had bonded in spirit.

We congratulated one another that our three children fit well into our world. They were bright and well-behaved. I credited Bobbi for that and she credited me. Bobbi's parents credited both of us. They had been good parents to her and her sisters and we were proud to have their approval.

If there was an occasional cloud between us and our sun, it almost always involved Lacy. Bobbi had come to love this gentle wonder-child as I did. She urged frequent visits to the old Prather house on the bluff. It was Lacy's now. She was master and mistress, heir to the roles of both Father and Mama. It was little more than a way station for Victor, a place to eat and sleep, to play his role as husband and father. He demonstrated no respect for its heritage and little recognition of its inherent grandeur.

Lacy sometimes found this hard to accept. She never intended to complain, but sometimes slipped and said things she would try to take back.

Once when she said she was sorry for having criticized Victor, I tried to summon up lines from Emily Dickinson. I may have paraphrased, but I managed the poet's message. "Sorry is as useless as the morning sun where the midnight frost has lain," I told her. She understood.

"I know," she said. "The word is out and the damage is done. And Father always taught us you can't recall words once they are spoken."

"Do you ever read poetry?" I asked.

Lacy said no, she had no books and did not read.

I suggested a visit to the Erinville Public Library.

"Browse," I said. "Find something of interest. You have plenty of time and Father's reading chair sits there like it's just waiting for you."

Lacy shook her head.

"I used to go to the library some when Bobbi was there," she said. "Mostly I just looked at magazines. And I would never use Father's reading chair."

I asked why. She wasn't able to put her reason into words. It had to do with memories and feelings and missing Father and security and images of Father there, a book in his hands and reading glasses down on his nose and sometimes asleep in the old wingback chair. I understood.

But I wanted to know more about Victor. What was she unhappy about? I did not tell her Victor had not regained my trust. I did tell her I hoped he had grown more stable, that she'd never again have to deal with him trying to gentle his anguish with drink.

"I'm sure he knows by now you are his main source of comfort, Lacy."

I hoped for a quick and positive response. It didn't come.

She made clear she had no wish to talk about her husband. An undertone said their problems were none of anyone else's business. Mama would have said she'd made her bed and now she had to sleep in it. Victor was the father of her child—her children. She loved him and she was positive he loved her. I wondered if she really believed everything she said, but this was a question I couldn't ask.

Bobbi and I were driving up to Golconda the next day to see Father. I asked if she wanted to go. At first she brightened and I thought she was about to say she did. She hesitated and all was lost. She was afraid not to be at home if Victor was able not to work. I reminded her it would be Sunday. This didn't matter, she said. Victor often worked on Sunday.

I tried to retrace my conversation with Lacy that night for Bobbi. She wouldn't hear Lacy's actual words, but I would offer an honest reconstruction of my little sister's worries and her reluctance to attempt anything that might displease Victor.

"I'm afraid for her," Bobbi said. "I think Victor still is short on self-confidence, and if it catches up with him at work he's going to start drinking again. Don't you worry about that?"

"I do. I've never stopped worrying since the first time I saw bruises on her face. But I don't know what to do about it."

Bobbi wanted to read poetry. We both were getting too worked up, she said, and we needed something to sooth our spirits so we could sleep. I offered to go to the liquor store and get a bottle of bourbon to accomplish this. She found no humor in my pitiful little joke.

"I'd rather you sing to me," I said. "That way I don't have to do anything."

I have not told you, but singing was one of the few things Bobbi didn't do well. As she would be the first to tell you, she did not have a good singing voice. This always puzzled me. She had a beautiful speaking voice, soft but somewhat husky, lower in range than usual for a woman. She was the first to make fun of herself after any burst of song.

"If I do you will be sorry."

"No, I won't. I really want you to sing."

She played along with my game.

"Okay. Would you like some opera?"

"Really? Do you know any opera?"

She began singing "Summertime," and she sang it beautifully. It was one of relatively few songs I'd heard her sing before.

This always had been one of my favorite songs. I often sang it to myself while alone, especially while driving. I have a terrible singing voice, too, but this never kept me from pretending I could sing when there was no one else to hear. I started to mouth the words with her.

We were wide awake now and Bobbi told me about the Hoard family taking a vacation in Charleston, South Carolina, when she was a girl. They were there for the Spoleto Festival and a highlight for her was a local opera company's performance of "Porgy and Bess."

"I guess Charleston's where it's supposed to be set," she said. "Anyway, I loved it. I've been trying to sing 'Summertime' ever since."

We talked another hour before finally drifting into sleep.

When the kids got up later in the morning, Sarah had a sore throat. Bobbi said she would stay home with her and the other two, so I would be going to Golconda to see Father by myself. I left an hour after that and she asked me to tell Father she loved him and would see him again soon.

I knew this was true. She loved Father almost as much as Lacy, Sammy, and I did. And Father loved her. We were family.

29

Father was waiting when I drove up to his apartment in Golconda, walking up and down in front the complex of some twenty living units. I noticed he was slightly stooped but still robust. He walked at a vigorous pace and did not look his age. He insisted we go inside at once and have coffee.

His small home was neat and functional, well suited to a single man. As he had described it earlier, "Nothing fancy, but everything I need." And he'd been very happy to find he had "good neighbors."

As soon as I walked in I noticed something new. A thickly padded reclining chair sat to one side in the living area and next to it a tall lamp.

"You have a new reading chair!"

He smiled, and motioned me to sit in the chair.

"Couldn't get along without one," he said. "We have a great little public library and I've already found a lot of books I haven't read. I thought I could do my reading there, but I need books here, at night."

I sat in the chair and told him I found it very comfortable and I was happy he had it. I said when I thought of him in the old Prather house my usual vision had him in his reading chair at night. He probably had read more books than anyone else I knew.

He laughed about this. He said maybe he just had fewer other ways to entertain himself than anyone else I knew. But I could tell he was proud to be on the pedestal on which I had just placed him. For my part, this was no exaggeration. For as far back as I could remember there had been few nights that hadn't found him in his reading chair for two hours or more before bedtime.

"So what are you reading?"

"Just read *To Kill a Mockingbird* again, probably the third time. And I read *Uncle Tom's Cabin* and *Robinson Crusoe* at the library."

"You're back into the old stuff, then."

"Not entirely," Father said. "I've found new material, too. This, for example."

He reached to a side table and picked up a book. I was about to stand but he handed it to me before I could make a move. It was *The Prophet*, by Kahlil Gibran. I'd never heard of the book or the writer.

"It's some fascinating reading," Father said. "I can honestly say it's changed my views on some things."

I was intrigued by his statement. I always had thought of him as being as firm in his beliefs as an individual possibly could be. He was, as Mama said, "set in his ways." Surely it would take some powerful writing to change his views on anything. I wanted to know more.

"Check out a few pages," Father said.

I opened the book at random, in the middle of a section on religion. "He who wears his morality but as his garment were better naked," I read. I had no quarrel with this, but couldn't see it as something that would have wrought change in Father's point of view. Then a section on marriage: "Let there be spaces in your togetherness." Same thought.

Father was watching me closely. I wondered what reaction he expected or hoped to see.

"Look at his writing on children," he said.

I took a quick look at the index, and then thumbed hurriedly to the section he cited. It didn't take long to find passages I knew would have given him pause.

"You may give them your love but not your thoughts,
For they have their own thoughts.
You may house their bodies but not their souls,
For their souls dwell in the house of tomorrow, which you cannot visit, not even in your dreams.
You may strive to be like them, but seek not to make them like you,
For life goes not backward nor tarries with yesterday."

The words struck me as profound, if plain and direct. Had I been guilty of these, demanding too great a role in the lives of our children? I thought of Lacy's childish approach to the standards of parenthood. Why couldn't humans be like the birds, who pushed the babies out of their nests and claimed no further relationship? And the words of John Meriwether, who said little Violet looked down on us from heaven and laughed as we mourned her passing. It was true; life goes forward and has no time for yesterday.

Father seemed to know I had found passages from which he had taken great meaning, though I don't know how. It may have been the expression on my face or maybe the near catch in my breath as the words hit home with me, too. He waited as I closed the book and put it aside.

"Do you like him as much as I did?" he asked.

"Really something there to think about, no doubt about that."

Father chuckled. Yes, he said, he had given a great deal of thought to Gibran's message. That's what he called it, a "message."

"You can't go back and undo what's come and gone," he said, his big voice low. "But I wish I could. I was guilty of exactly what he warned against."

"But Father—"

"No, please let me finish. I didn't do right by you and Lacy. I doted on Sammy because I thought I could make him like me. And I had nothing to do with it. He was his own person, just as you and Lacy were. Sammy turned out to have interests like mine but they were his own, just as the two of you had your own interests. You've all turned out well and I love you all equally. I hope you'll forgive me if I haven't always made this clear. Let your kids set their own directions, son. Like he says, they dwell in the house of tomorrow."

I stood and, for the first time in my life, received from this man the strong embrace I felt was a true measure of fatherhood. We both had tears in our eyes, but they were tears of joy.

For the rest of my visit, we were as giddy as kids at play. Father took me to visit Mama's grave, then down inside the levee to watch the strings of barges pass by on the Ohio River. He claimed to be as attached to the Ohio now as he had been to Singleton's Branch for most of his life. I knew this wasn't true and made him admit it. He pretended not to miss the old Prather house, and I made him say this wasn't true, either.

Still, he wanted me to understand he had made his compromises without regret. I remembered how he used to tell us, "Once you turn a corner you go in a different direction." I suppose if I had them all written down I could publish a book of Father's wise sayings.

I was happy to see he was contented and doing well in his new home. He had place. To some extent, even, he had purpose. I think I enjoyed Father's company more that day than at any other time in my life. I hated to leave when it was time for me to go.

I got back to Erinville well after dinnertime. Bobbi said she and the kids had had a good day. In deference to Sarah, Evelyn and Jack had stayed inside and they all had watched television movies. Sarah's sore throat was much better. Bobbi had a toasted ham and cheese sandwich waiting for me.

"I missed my old man," she said. "It didn't seem right not to be spending a day off together."

She asked about Father and was pleased to hear he'd asked about her. It was almost like an afterthought when she got around to telling me her bad news. She had received a call from Carly in New York informing her that Gayle had been diagnosed with breast cancer. I suspected she had been slow to tell me because she found it hard.

I had met Gayle on only a couple of brief occasions and barely knew her. Even Bobbi didn't feel she knew her sister well, given the years they had lived far apart and seldom seen one another. She had happy memories from years with her two big sisters when she was a child, though. She said Carly had told her not to worry; Gayle had good medical care and with early detection was almost certain to come through with flying colors.

It had been a long time since I'd heard that old idiom and it struck me as funny.

"Flying colors? Did Carly say that," I asked, "or was it just you?"

Bobbi wasn't sure, but talking about words offered respite from her worries about Gayle. I tried to persuade her there were so many effective treatments for breast cancer now it probably would be little more than routine. I wasn't confident this was true, but Bobbi needed to hear it.

I was tired from my trip to visit Father—even the short drive to Golconda and back—and ready for bed early. I slept well and never knew if Bobbi did, as well. She seemed rested in the morning as I got ready to go to work and we didn't mention Gayle. Breast cancer is not the type of illness likely to create instant emergencies; we'd hear nothing more for some time to come.

It was two weeks before I made it out to check on Lacy. When I did, the news was not good. She and Victor had been quarreling again. Victor resented what he saw as her dominance, based on nothing more than the fact they lived in the old Prather house. He said the house was hers, but not his, and he felt like a boarder.

"I never make a point of living here," Lacy said. "I try to tell him we're lucky to have free housing but he won't listen. He's going to get a place in town and I'll move there as soon as he gets it."

Stunned as I was by the news, I tried to put up a positive front. I told her I was sure things would work out and she might very well enjoy having close neighbors again. Junior would be closer to school, too. She made no effort to disguise her anger, and made it pretty clear she didn't care what I thought.

"I don't give a rat's hairy hind end where we live," she said. "I just want Victor to be satisfied and be a good husband and father. Junior needs him, and so do I."

Then she softened. She really did value my opinion, and she was eternally grateful for my support. She apologized for any expression that might have sounded otherwise. But she didn't want me to worry about her.

"You have your own family now," she said. "You don't need to spend your time trying to pick me up every time I stumble."

I left the old Prather house wondering if it soon would be empty. There was a quick thought that Bobbi and I might move there, but I knew it would not be a good move to take the kids away from their school and their friends in town and quickly put the notion aside. Bobbi and I did talk about this briefly at a later time and she agreed.

It was hardly a week after my visit that Lacy and Junior moved into Erinville to join Victor in a cramped furnished apartment that was someone's garage converted to rental property. The conversion was well done and the address was a respectable location, so Victor had no reason not to feel proud of getting his family into his own home. There was nothing he would be embarrassed to tell coworkers at The Print Shop.

Lacy claimed to be happy with the new quarters. There was a nice kitchen, she said, and the smaller of two bedrooms was perfect for Junior. Yes, there might be days she would miss the shoal but that was in the past and she looked to the future. Such a good fit, the words of Kahlil Gibran, "life goes not backward." It was good she could put the past behind her.

It was time for me to do the same.

Bobbi and I began to talk about a second honeymoon. She said as far as she was concerned it would be Myrtle Beach again. We had had so much fun there before, until the tragic end. But then she said maybe it deserved a second chance at a happy ending. I told her this sounded like a clever rationalization she needn't bother with. I wanted to go back there, too.

Myrtle Beach. Yes. The beautiful sunrises over the Atlantic, the crashing surf, the pale-shining moon on the wet sand. I wanted us to be there again and things to be like they were. We would be newlyweds once more and innocent children and revel in the primitive echoes of people in tune with nature. This time there would be no Jonathon with his pained life story.

The Hoards went to New York to be with Gayle through surgeries and came home with good reports. Gayle came through it all with positive results and they had a good visit with Carly. I told Bobbi again we'd get up there soon and visit her sisters. We'd been telling ourselves this for two or three years now and probably were no closer to actually doing it. We'd decided the kids were too young to enjoy the trip earlier, but now this was not an excuse.

Bobbi pointed out it would be much easier for them to come to Erinville. If her sisters weren't willing to make the trip, why should they expect us to? I had felt this all along but hadn't said it. Anyway, I guess we unofficially removed the New York trip from our "to do" list with this brief discussion.

We began to look at the calendar. Somewhere ahead we would mark off the dates bracketing two weeks for the honeymoon. Mere discussion of it rekindled a great deal of physical passion as we recalled and talked about the time before. Maybe we shouldn't live in the past, but trying to re-enact certain past behaviors proved to be a lot of fun. We didn't need practice, but we practiced anyway. Just not as often as we used to.

In the meantime, life went on at its usual pace—a pace never fast enough for the young and often too fast for the old. By this measure, Bobbi and I had begun to feel ancient but it was not a contrast we could avoid. She said the best antidote for aging was to be sure there always were young ones around, and for us this was a given.

Lacy brought Junior to play with our Little Jack and Evelyn two or three times during their first month in the city apartment. Bobbi got the feeling the visits were more for Lacy than for Junior. Lacy needed someone to talk to, she told me later, and though she tried to get her to open up she felt my little sister was holding back.

We had mixed feelings about visiting Lacy and Victor at their place. Bobbi wanted to, but I said let's give them time to get settled. A month was more than enough time but we still hadn't gone. Our reluctance was based on one notable fact: In the past we had visited them at Lacy's place, and now we would be visiting them at Victor's.

The weed in the lettuce bed, as Father liked to say, was that we were not sure how Victor would receive us. He had been cordial enough, but at the same time had complained to Lacy about being "hemmed in by Prathers." We thought this was aimed at their housing situation—living in the old Prather house—rather than at us, but given Victor's moodiness you never could be sure.

After another week and two more visits by Lacy, we decided we should get on with making ourselves guests of Mr. and Mrs. Victor Kenton. Bobbi called Lacy and said afterward Lacy seemed to be thrilled we were coming. I reminded her how eager we'd been for everyone to visit us when we had our first place. She said the settings weren't comparable because we were newlyweds then and they had been married a long time.

"Just like you to bring logic into it," I teased. "You should have been a lawyer."

"Lawyers have to serve both the righteous and the unrighteous. You know, defend horse thieves and all."

"Yes, ma'am. And if I was a horse thief I'd want a pretty lawyer like you pleading my case."

Bobbi never missed an opening like this.

"If you were a horse thief," she said, "I'd be prosecuting you and probably seeking a long-term prison sentence. Any judge in the land would go along with me, too!"

It would have been inconceivable to us then that a time would come when this pretence would have struck close to home. It was just as well we couldn't visit the house of tomorrow.

We went to Lacy's on Sunday afternoon. Victor should have been there, but wasn't. Lacy was embarrassed. She said Victor hadn't told her before, but right after lunch said he had to get over to The Print Shop and catch up on some work.

"And he knew we were coming?" I asked, fully aware my question was charged with meaning beyond the words spoken.

"I'm sorry," Lacy said. "I know Victor likes both of you a lot. He can be strange sometimes."

Bobbi did her best to smooth things over. She pretended to believe Victor really did have work to catch up on at The Print Shop. And we wouldn't want to be responsible for getting him even farther behind, especially when he knew he could visit with us at any time.

Lacy wouldn't have it.

"He didn't have any work to catch up on," she declared. "He made that up. Victor's a coward. I guess he was afraid he'd have to talk about something he didn't want to."

Lacy's comment struck both Bobbi and me with a sudden fear there was more to this than she meant to reveal. She was hiding something. Victor was afraid we knew about something he didn't want to talk about, and there were too many possibilities as to what that might be. There was no escaping his ugly record.

"Lacy," I demanded, "is Victor abusing you again?"

My little sister burst into tears. Bobbi reached out to her, hoping to ease her distress, but Lacy pulled away. I waited for her to respond, and she knew I would not wait forever. If Victor was mistreating her again I would not sit quietly by and let it go on. I had always walked behind her, watching out for such demons as her god of everything might allow to draw near.

"Give me a minute," she said, stepping to an end table beside the couch to get a tissue. She blew her nose and composed herself the way I had seen her do it a million times. Victor might be a coward, but his wife was one of the most courageous women I'd ever known.

"No," she said, "he hasn't abused me. But he's drinking again. He just can't seem to stop. I thought moving out of the old house would salve his wounded pride, but I don't think it has. He doesn't have any confidence in himself and I think he's afraid he's going to mess up. Then the tension builds up and drinking's like his safety valve or something."

I believed she had summed up the situation perfectly. One thing Victor did not have to worry about was an understanding wife.

Bobbi answered Lacy before I could think what to say. She put my thoughts into words almost as if they were her own.

"Honey, you know Victor so very well," she said. "Understanding the problem is the first big step to finding an answer. You've got lots of support and we'll all pitch in and help. We'll find a way to deal with this, Lacy. You can count on it."

I would have tried to lighten things up a bit in any case, but Bobbi's assertion truly did make me feel better. I hoped it may have had the same effect on Lacy.

"The word of my wise counselor again," I said. "Bobbi's going to be my lawyer if I ever need one. When she says something is going to happen you can count on it."

Lacy was about to smile.

"Take it to the bank?" she said.

"Yes. Take it to the bank."

Bobbi's promise had been effective medicine for Lacy. She was giggling now like she had no problem at all. To see her less agitated was encouraging to me, too, and Bobbi joined in our little celebration. We all laughed, making fun of ourselves and yet believing we would prevail. The magic in Bobbi's declaration was the expression of our togetherness. Lacy would not be left to face this challenge alone.

What we avoided was the daunting recognition that Victor's drinking would not be easy to deal with. He needed professional help and this would come only if *he* asked for it. No matter how noble our intentions nor how firm our resolve, we stood little chance of changing Victor. We could encourage and support him, but in the end his welfare was pretty much in his own hands.

It did seem to me that Lacy's analysis was right on target. What we Prathers had considered generosity very well might have been humiliation for Victor. I knew his own family had not given him the support he needed. He had done nothing to earn the support he got from us. We had put too much stock in family ties.

None of this excused Victor's abuse of Lacy. I would never forgive him for that. But it was for her sake that I'd do anything I could to help Victor straighten out and get his life back together. Stooping to help him would be leaning down to pick up Lacy from a fall not of her own making.

30

Father always told us there are two kinds of drunks: happy drunks and belligerent drunks. Victor was not the happy kind. I didn't think he was drunk that morning, but he had been drinking. Lacy had had enough of him and left the house before I got there.

"I'm glad you came," he greeted me. "Seems like you've not been here for a while."

"I was here last week, Victor."

"No shit? I thought it'd been longer."

I was on my way to work and didn't have time to waste. Stopping by their apartment to see how Lacy and Victor were getting on had been a sudden impulse. I wouldn't have bothered if I'd known Lacy was gone, but on the other hand I supposed this was Victor in his normal state. I had forgotten he was not working this week. Lacy told us he had too much vacation time accumulated and Old Lady Gruber insisted he use some of it.

Lacy had confided in Bobbi that she dreaded having him around the apartment, afraid he would be drinking. And she was disappointed he would be wasting his time off. She'd always hoped they might take a real vacation and go somewhere they'd never been for a few days. She didn't care where, because she'd never been out of Erinville overnight. She thought Victor was making enough money they should be able to afford it now. And then, as an afterthought, she said Victor refused to tell her how much he made.

I went to the kitchen to get a glass of water. The apartment was a mess, and the kitchen looked like it had been abandoned. There were dirty dishes on the table and in the sink. Dirty silverware soaked in soapy water in a large yellow mixing bowl in the sink. In a corner, a trash can was overflowing, spilling its contents onto the floor.

This wasn't like Lacy. She always kept a neat house, and she took special pride in a spotless kitchen. I'd never seen her kitchen messy before and I was surprised she had left things this way.

Victor followed me. He looked about as if surveying the kitchen for a dedicated purpose, swiveling his head to take in the entire room, then began clearing the table. He was visibly irritated and slammed the plates and cups he'd picked up from the table onto the counter next to the sink with such force I expected something to break.

"Lacy's not been feeling well," he said.

"I didn't know. Is she better now?"

"I don't know. She wouldn't hardly talk to me this morning. I wanted her to go to the doctor if she was still sick, but she left without saying where she was headed."

It was hard to tell whether he felt any sympathy for my sister. I had a feeling he was driven more by anger. Lacy had told me he never helped with housekeeping, and even was impatient when he had to help with Junior.

"You could have cleaned up the kitchen, Victor. It doesn't bother me, but it seems to bother you."

"I put in my day's work at the shop. I bring home plenty of money, too." His speech was becoming a bit slurred. "It's the woman's job to keep up the house and take care of the kids. Everybody knows that."

I didn't answer. Victor was in no condition to carry on a logical discussion and I didn't want to make him angry. I was angry, myself, though, at his cavalier attitude toward the subject—toward Lacy, actually. It seemed he had no concept of marriage as a partnership. Was she there only to serve him?

I found a clean glass in the cupboard, drew water from the tap, and drank slowly while Victor finished clearing the table. If he wanted, I said, I would help him wash dishes. I wouldn't worry about being late for work, and anyway there probably was nothing else we needed to do. He said no.

We went back into the living room, where he turned on the television and sat down on the sofa. The next thing I knew he was sound asleep, snoring loudly. I couldn't help but feel a great dislike for this man. He probably would not have married Lacy had she not been pregnant. I thought about the nights I'd lain in my bed in the old Prather house and listened as they had sex in the next room. Lacy was nothing but his whore, there to provide his sexual gratification. I hated him even more.

I couldn't stand the sight of him any longer. He was drunk now, probably incapable of going about his normal activities. There had been a time I might have had some sympathy, but that time was long gone. I left through the same side door I'd entered and rushed to Graffenried Distributing to attend to my own responsibilities.

Two days later I learned that when Lacy got home Victor went into a rage about something and beat her.

There was no way I could allow this to go on. I remembered what Jackson Hoard said about Sheriff Landon Cloyd arresting Victor immediately and assumed the Erinville police would do the same. I wanted him in jail. I wanted him never to be able to hurt Lacy again. I called the police department and lodged my complaint, then called Bobbi and told her what was going on. She urged me to hurry to Lacy's apartment to be their when police arrived.

And she reminded me, Victor would be there.

The apartment was only about five blocks from Graffenried Distributing. Even so, I drove fast on my way there sensing this was a true emergency. Victor's car was on the street and, with no other parking space, I drove over the curb and into the yard. The front door to the apartment was locked and I ran to the side door, which stood open. I called Lacy's name as I entered.

The apartment was dead quiet. No one was in the living room, though Junior's toys were scattered about as if he had been playing there before I came. I hurried to the kitchen. At first I thought no one was there, either, but as I stepped through the door I heard a whimper and saw Junior sitting in a corner next to an overturned waste container.

And then—a scene that will haunt my nightmares as long as I live. Victor lay under the table in a spreading pool of blood. An open slash was visible on the side of his neck. Lacy was on her knees beside him, motionless and soundless, as if in a trance. In her hand was a large carving knife, dripping with blood.

My knees weakened and I felt like I might faint. I held to the table edge and made my way around to the end where Lacy was, walking in Victor's blood on the floor. I was about to reach for her when she pulled herself up. I took the knife from her and held her arm while she stepped to a chair that stood out from the table and lowered herself cautiously, a concession to her trembling arms and legs. Once she raised her head I could see the dried blood around her nose and mouth and a gap from a missing tooth. One side of her face was swollen until the eye was barely open.

"My god, Lacy..." I couldn't find words to make a sentence.

"I couldn't stand any more," she whispered. "Not any more. He hurt me. And he was turning on Junior."

While my little sister told her story, I heard the sirens of the first two Erinville police cars about to arrive on the scene. Neither of us spoke again as we waited.

31

Off in the distance I can see Singleton's Branch. Its smooth surface glistens in the long rays of the sinking afternoon sun. During the winter months, when the trees are bare, I get glimpses of the stately old Prather house I used to call home and my heart aches knowing it sits there empty now and uncared for.

I'm one of the fortunates whose cell has a window. The Copper Hill Correctional Center—they don't like to call them prisons anymore—sits high above the surrounding countryside, dominating the landscape west of Erinville like some medieval fortress. I'm not overly confident I know exactly how long I've been here. Trying to keep track of time got to seem pretty useless, as I know I'll be here for the rest of my days on earth.

I try not to think about all the ways the river affected my life, but the memories are present and there is no way I can make them go away. There are too many dreams, both peaceful ones and nightmares. In the peaceful ones I am 15 again and back on Singleton's Branch doing things with Lacy, Victor, and Bobbi, inspired by being on the river.

And then, more often, the nightmare. Bobbi, my one great love, is gone. This dream is real. I let Bobbi down in a merciless manner, giving her no thought and leaving her to bleed from a cut I brought upon myself. She was my reason for living and I threw her away like kitchen garbage. It wasn't what I meant to do, but I acted without thinking and before I fully comprehended the trouble I was in there was no way out.

Other than the anguish within my own mind, prison life is not as hard as you might expect. At least not for those of us who don't tend to be unruly. Those few men who consistently cause trouble don't have it so easy, and I'm good with that. The guards are human, too, and can tolerate only so much without responding in kind. I've seen plenty of things that would get guards suspended or kicked off the job if they were reported.

I'm not going to tell anyone, and neither will most of my fellow offenders. This is what they call us, as you probably know. I suppose "prisoners" or "inmates" is not acceptable in these politically correct times, though I don't know who would be upset. Those of us within these walls know what we are.

Father would have called us "convicts" and referred to Copper Hill simply as "the pen." I'm glad he didn't live to see me sent to jail. Events leading up to my trial were more than he could handle. He was furious at me for what I did, but the true hurt broke his heart and left him to die in shame without ever knowing the truth. Jen and Jackson Hoard both are gone, too. Bobbi told me very little about them in their later years.

It may be as much age as circumstance, I don't know, but I spend most of my time these days looking back and wondering how life could have flown by so fast. True, my situation now is not one with prospects for a better life ahead. But it is what it is and there is a daily routine of essential activities that keeps me busy. There are a few men I talk with every day, including one who used to be a minister. I doubt he's ever gone a full week without repeating Martin Luther's statement that "the conscience is eternal and will never die." Though I can't really call them friends, we have things in common. One big thing, for sure. We all are behind bars.

The view from my cell window helps me remember the beauty of the outside world. Lacy would adore the honeysuckle that vines through the lesser trees on a hillside in the near distance and the clumps of pink and purple butterfly bush. There are expanses of wildflowers, too, the prettiest of which are the large patches of daisies and black-eyed Susans. And goldenrod and purple ironweed in the fall.

I often hear the mourning doves cooing down in the woods when we have early yard time. There are whippoorwills at night, though we usually are confined inside after dark. And mocking birds all the time. All these and the constant exchanges among flocks of crows bring their own unique memories.

Bobbi and Lacy visit from time to time. Lacy moved in with Bobbi when they both came to realize how much they needed each other. Sammy said he wanted no part of the old Prather house on the bluff and left them free to dispose of it as they saw fit. They put it up for sale but found no one who was interested. Their agent said the cost of maintaining the aging structure turned buyers away. The kids hardly know me anymore. Their visits have become far less personal, more obligatory, and there are times we find we have very little to say. Whoever said absence makes the heart grow fonder didn't put a time frame on it.

I never had a chance to get to know Sammy's family, Melinda and their two boys. It may be just as well. The boys would not be looking up to their uncle as a hero. I heard that Melinda has had some of her poetry published. I'm happy for her, although hearing about it brought painful recollections of Bobbi and the books of poetry we shared. I tried in vain to remember an Emily Dickinson verse or two but all I could come up with was a few lines from Rudyard Kipling.

I'm grateful Sammy was far away in another part of the country the day Lacy's god of everything looked the other way and let the world collapse around the rest of us. I've seen him only a time or two since, and may not see him again. It's my loss that we never became close the way brothers should.

Copper Hill is a minimum security institution and I'm not surrounded by the kinds of men who populate the max units. My brilliant defense attorney, Angie Worth, got me off on a charge of manslaughter when the prosecutor wanted to go for premeditated murder. I didn't realize at the time how much difference there was in this, but today I'm extremely grateful. If I counted my blessings and listed everything I have to be grateful for, Angie Worth would be near the top of the list.

When they showed the jury those pictures of Victor's bloody corpse, I had a feeling I would be convicted of any charge I might have faced. It was painful, not just because of the effect it clearly had on those sitting in judgment of me, but because it was Victor. I thought about all the times we played together as boys, swimming in the cool waters of Singleton's Branch on tortuous summer afternoons, swinging out over the water on a stout rope tied to a high branch of one of the ancient sycamores growing just above the water's edge. Sometimes we competed for the highest swing and longest drop into the water. Victor almost always won.

Lacy was always around and it wasn't long before her affection for Victor was obvious. And honestly, over time I've come to be less bitter toward Victor. Alcohol was his downfall. He could be inconsiderate even when sober, yes, but on the whole he was good to Lacy then and I know she could be difficult. I really never knew what had gone on between them that day I walked into their apartment and found her standing over him with a blood-dripping carving knife while the last breath softly escaped his body. She was far too distraught to tell me anything and police arrived right after me and all sense of reality was lost in the blink of an eye.

I suppose a lifetime of protective instinct took over. I held out the knife I'd taken from Lacy to the first officer who came through the door and said, "I didn't mean to kill him. I just couldn't let him treat my sister the way he was any longer." By the time they had me in handcuffs and out the door, two or three more police cars had arrived. The first ones had come in answer to my call, which was a matter of record that worked against me. It established that I knew what was going on at Victor's and Lacy's apartment before I got there, and so could have planned an attack on Victor in advance.

Even though I wasn't charged with premeditation, the judge let the prosecutor drive this home to the jury.

Lacy never would have willingly let me take blame for what she had done. I think she was too much in shock at the time even to realize what was taking place. She tried to tell them later, but I'm sure she was not very convincing. Angie Worth wanted to call her as a witness. She believed there was at least a small chance this might lead to dismissal of charges against me and argued that with a self-defense claim no jury would convict Lacy. I wouldn't allow it. Having to recount how she'd slashed Victor's throat with a carving knife might be beyond Lacy's mental and emotional survival.

Angie reminded me I had confessed on the spot. The case was open and shut. When I eventually came to recognize the inevitable consequences of what I'd done, I wanted her to enter a guilty plea and avoid a trial all together. I could see no other way to save Bobbi any more hurt. Angie said Judge Evangeline Tuley had offered no hint of leniency in talks about a possible plea deal, and she hoped she could gain a jury's sympathy by making them see I had acted only to protect my little sister. Maybe she didn't take into account the horrible pictures of Victor lying in a spreading pool of blood on the kitchen floor. No one could have looked at those and found any sympathy for the person who wielded the knife.

It came out in the trial that a nosey old woman who lived next door also had called the police. She told them she heard a big fight and was afraid someone would get hurt. Angie Worth made her admit she'd never heard the couple quarrel before and had no particular reason to think either of them was in danger, but the prosecutor turned this around and said it reinforced the state's contention the quarrel was so violent it led me to interfere. But he said "loudness" was no justification for me attacking Victor with a knife, repeating for about the tenth time that Victor was not armed.

The prosecutor was very effective in his own questioning of the neighbor. He got her to talk about what a sweet couple Victor and Lacy were and how it was obvious they loved each other very much and she couldn't believe a good young man like Victor could be murdered in his own kitchen. Angie produced a medical examiner's report that showed Victor had been drinking but couldn't offer a reason why he deserved to die for this.

Angie told me later the old lady's testimony likely had more effect on the jury than all the physical evidence combined. I couldn't see that it mattered, one way or the other.

The trial lasted only three days. The jury took less than two hours to return a guilty verdict. I guess it doesn't matter whether it was the pictures or the neighbor's testimony that landed hardest on the men and women who convicted me. Judge Tuley obviously believed I was a horrible and dangerous man and imposed the maximum sentence.

My failures as a man are too many even to contemplate. I set no high moral standard to be looked up to. Even so, I can take some satisfaction in believing I lived up to Grandpa Childs' advice to leave the world a better place. I fathered three children who, thanks mostly to Bobbi, have matured into generous and caring adults. They cannot be diminished simply because my blood runs in their veins.

I always encouraged Lacy not to dwell on the past, but to look to the future and know there could be better days ahead. It would be senseless for me to try to take my own advice now. The past is all there is; I have no future.

Still, in many ways I know I have had a good life. My past is rich in happy memories. When I go to the window today and fix my gaze on that empty house by the river, even across the miles, I see a happy family. Lacy, Victor, Bobbi, and I will be somewhere nearby, finding a new interest along the water's edge or at a point on the steep bluff above it. Mama and Sammy are inside, probably in the kitchen, and Father will be home in due time to seat himself in his wingback chair with a book in hand and seek the page where he left off reading. This memory takes me back to a peaceful, contented time. I will try to hold onto it until lights out, and then hope for beautiful dreams of life on Singleton's Branch. This is as it should be. There always will be the river.

--The End--

Other Books by Robert Hays

Fiction
An Inchworm Takes Wing
A Shallow River of Mercy
Blood on the Roses
The Baby River Angel
The Life and Death of Lizzie Morris
Circles in the Water
Equinox and Other Stories
Early Stories from the Land (editor)

Non-Fiction
Patton's Oracle
Editorializing "the Indian Problem"
A Race at Bay
State Science in Illinois
G-2: Intelligence for Patton (with Gen. Oscar Koch)
Country Editor

About the Author

Robert Hays is the author of six previous novels and a book of short stories and has written, edited, or collaborated on a half-dozen works of non-fiction. His short stories have appeared in anthologies and he has published numerous academic journal and popular periodical articles. Selections from three of his novels have gained Pushcart Prize nominations. He is a U.S. Army veteran and, though retired from classroom teaching, holds professor emeritus rank on the faculty of the University of Illinois. He lives in the beautiful southern Illinois wooded hill country about which he often writes.

Made in the USA
Columbia, SC
10 October 2022